ABOUT THE AUTHOR

Claus von Bohlen is the author of *Who is Charlie Conti?*
He spent several years studying psychology in Los
Angeles, and now lives in Gaza, where he works as a
mental health counsellor.

D1421475

BY THE SAME AUTHOR:

Who is Charlie Conti?

TO GREET THE SUN

First published in Great Britain in 2011 by Old Street Publishing Ltd
Trebinshun House, Brecon LD3 7PX
www.oldstreetpublishing.co.uk

ISBN 978-1-905847-63-1

A CIP catalogue record for this title is available from the British Library.

Typeset by Old Street Publishing Ltd.

Printed and bound in Great Britain.

TO GREET THE SUN

CLAUS VON BOHLEN

OLD STREET PUBLISHING

Wille schafft das Neue,
Wille zwingt das Alte,
deutscher heil'ger Wille
immer jung uns halte,
himmlische Gnade
uns den Führer gab,
wir geloben Hitler
Treue bis ins Grab.

Wir Jungen schreiten gläubig,
der Sonne zugewandt,
wir sind ein heil'ger Frühling
ins deutsche Land.

* * *

The will creates the future,
The will overcomes the past,
The holy will of Germany
Will always keep us young.
The grace of heaven
Gave us the Führer,
We pledge allegiance to Hitler
Unto the grave.

We young step out in faith,
To greet the sun,
We are a holy springtime,
In the land of Germany.

HITLER YOUTH MARCHING SONG, HEINRICH SPITTA, 1933

Prologue

THREE FAT crows sit on a branch above the snow-covered earth. Recently they have been feeding well. At times the frozen flesh is cold and hard and does not permit easy picking, but there has been no shortage. And today should be no exception. Wherever the machines go, food follows. These three crows – an efficient and compact murder – are the vanguard of the Allied 7th Armoured Division.

The sun is rising in the east. The sky is clear. The rays of light catch the three crows. The largest of the three spreads his black wings. His feathers are beyond black; they shimmer with violet iridescence. He tips his head this way and that, then pauses, alert. He hears the first rumble, then he leaps from the branch and flaps his great wings once, twice, three times. Now he sees them below him, just cresting the brow of a hill in the far distance. The machines.

All three crows circle high above the Teutoburger woods. Beneath them, the farmland is divided from the forest by the narrow Raesfeld-Brunen road. Other than the occasional bush, there is little vegetation on either side. The dirt road is narrow but the openness of the terrain means that the 7th Armoured Division can use this route. They are advancing into the heart of Germany.

From their vantage point in the sky, the crows watch the progress of the column. One of the machines with the long tubular noses is some distance in front. Behind him come more of the long noses, then smaller machines like bugs, then the big ones with the people inside. At the back, there are clouds of smoke and strange smells and then the trails of debris.

Looking down, the largest of the crows sees that a small patch of earth in the middle of the road is discoloured. The mud and the snow are more thoroughly comingled here. Next to the road, the snow has also been disturbed. There are no footprints but it looks from above as if the snow has been manipulated – smoothed over so as to resemble the surrounding area. But the action of smoothing has damaged the tiny surface crystals which would otherwise sparkle in the morning sun.

The noise grows louder and louder, but the crows are accustomed to it. One of the long-nosed machines is in front of the rest of the column. It is approaching the patch of discoloured earth in the middle of the road. At that moment, a brief flash of bright shiny metal attracts the attention of the largest of the crows. The flash came from inside the bush which is next to the road, more or less level with the patch of discloured earth. The crow wheels in the hope that the flash will catch his eye again – he loves the shiny metal.

As the crow banks, he sees the first machine pass over the discoloured patch of earth. Then he sees two sticks upend themselves in the middle of that patch. A dark rectangular hole opens up in the road. The crow sees a small human hand reach out and place a stick with a bulbous head on the snow. Then more sticks upend themselves and a boy in a green military overcoat climbs out of the hole.

The boy immediately looks over his shoulder. He sees that the rest of the column are still some way behind. He drops to one knee and picks up the stick with the bulbous head. He points this at the machine with the long nose in front of him. The bulbous head travels rapidly between the boy and the machine. The next instant, everything is flame and the crow is knocked sideways and carried aloft on a sudden updraft of burning sulphurous wind.

The three crows have been scattered by the explosion. They are deafened and do not hear each other's caws. A few moments later, the largest of the three regains his equilibrium. The violet iridescence of his wings is tarnished by dark dust but he can still flap them with slow and ominous ease. He peers down once more through the thinning smoke. He does not see the flesh and blood carnage he had hoped for. The machine with the long nose is a burnt-out wreck, but the boy is very much alive. He runs to the bush and wrenches free a bicycle. The shiny handlebars catch the sun and flash brightly but this time the crow is not tempted. He will bide his time.

All around the boy, the earth is being torn up. Splinters of wood are ripped from the trees. One of the larger branches falls. The column is gaining rapidly. Then the boy sees a man, also in a green overcoat, standing at the edge of the woods. The man shouts to the boy. The boy does not respond. The man shouts again, then the boy drops his bicycle, runs across the open area of snow, and follows the man into the woods.

When the firing stops, the three crows settle once more on a branch not far from where the boy entered the woods. The column halts while the blackened machine is pulled off the road. The charred remains of the occupants are removed and carried to one of the larger machines at the back of the column. The crows are unable to feed but they need not worry; they will have plenty to eat over the coming months.

Chapter 1

IT IS quite noteworthy that one brutal event can release such a flood of memories. In the last few weeks, and with Pietro's assiduous questioning, I have recalled a number of episodes which last crossed my mind over half a century ago. I imagine the hateful psychologists would say that I had deliberately forced these memories into the unconscious; well, let them play their little games. What is important is that, since the attack, I have remembered much that was once dear to me. For someone of my age, that is worth gold.

It is one of the greater ironies that I had moved from São Paulo to Sambaqui, on the island of Santa Catarina, precisely in order to escape the vicious crime wave that has that poor beleaguered city in its grip. The newspapers in São Paulo carry daily reports of shootings, stabbings and armed robberies. When I moved there in 1957, crime was confined almost entirely to the *favelas*. Over the years it has crept slowly into the centre, and into the experience of people who wish nothing more than to lead good, tidy lives.

After retiring from my position on the board of the Feldmann brewery, I fully intended to live out my remaining years in São Paulo, the city that had become my home. However, I soon started to feel afraid of leaving my own house. When my neighbour was burgled and his security guard shot in the bottom cheek, I decided that the situation had become insupportable. I thought about returning to Blumenau, the city in the south that had welcomed me when I first arrived in Brazil in 1947 and where I had been fortunate enough to find employment with the Feldmann brewery. Sadly, almost everyone I used to know there had either left or died, in addition to which I knew I would find the hot, humid summers very straining. And so I thought about moving to Santa Catarina, an island where many Blumenauers used to spend their summer holidays, and of whose quiet beaches and fishing villages I had very pleasant memories.

It would be dishonest of me not to admit that Anna-Maria's repeated exhortations did not also play a small role in my decision to move. I am of course not at the mercy of my housekeeper, but after thirty years I feel a duty of care towards her happiness as well as my own. Anna-Maria's daughter Lua and her grandson Pietro – a most amusing boy - still live in Blumenau. She would have preferred me to return there, but she knows my feelings about the place. Nevertheless, Santa Catarina is just a couple of hours from Blumenau, and a move there was still pleasing to her.

It did cross my mind that Anna-Maria would be disappointed if she expected her grandson Pietro to be the same blond cherub who used to come every summer to spend a week with us in São Paulo. Those visits had not taken place for ten years and I thought to myself that Pietro, who would now be almost twenty, would no doubt have other things on his mind than visiting his grandmother in Santa Catarina. However, since Anna-Maria herself had confirmed as much – she had told me that Pietro was an acclaimed and dedicated surfist – I thought it unlikely that she was labouring under any significant misapprehension.

As it turned out, when I visited Santa Catarina with Anna-Maria before I had made my final decision to move, it was Pietro who met us at the airport and drove us to the Hotel Imperial in Florianópolis in his rusty old 'combi'. Of course I expected Pietro to have changed; nevertheless, it still amazed me that the same ten years which had robbed me of a little more hair and a little more mobility had turned him from a cherubic child into a handsome young adult. It was not hard to recognise him, however. He had the same shock of blond hair and still bore a quite surprising resemblance to Siegfried, the dearest friend of my childhood.

Pietro embraced his grandmother affectionately and greeted me respectfully. He shook my hand firmly and looked me in the eye, unlike many other young people I have met. This was a relief to me; the indolence of the young is frequently so enervating. Pietro took control of the wayward luggage trolley whose three-wheeled chassis appeared incapable of linear movement. As we crossed the road into the car park I noticed Pietro's extraordinary trousers, reminiscent of a marooned sailor. They ended just below the knee: neither shorts nor trousers. They seemed to afford neither the ease of movement of the former nor the elegance of the latter - quite peculiar.

The rusty old combi, which had been inexpertly decorated with a floral motif, was standing in the sun. The heat inside the vehicle was infernal. Since it is my custom to wear a suit whenever I leave home I have, over the years, come to see the invention of air-conditioning as one of the most significant technological developments of the modern time – alongside the advances in medicine, of course. But air-conditioning was a feature which the combi did not possess. So, while Anna-Maria fired question after question pertaining to family matters at Pietro, I opened the window and leant back against the headrest and allowed the currents of air to cool my forehead.

The drive to the hotel was mercifully a short one. On the way I resolved to rent a proper car for the next two days, during which I intended to visit the various parts of the island suggested by the real estate agent. Once I had completed my own preliminary investigations, I planned to narrow the search and to have the agent drive me to specific properties in areas that Anna-Maria and I found agreeable. When I had proposed this plan to Anna-Maria back in São Paulo she had suggested that Pietro could drive us around in his vehicle. I was aware that Anna-Maria wanted to spend as much time as possible with her grandson and the offer was a kind one, so I had accepted. At the time I had not been aware of the nature of the transportation. Comfort was one consideration, but it also struck me as inappropriate for the former vice-chairman of Feldmann Breweries to be travelling in a relic from the hippie era. However, so as not to appear ungrateful, I resolved to disguise my true motivations and to suggest the hire of an alternative vehicle as delicately as possible.

We pulled up in front of the Hotel Imperial, opposite the Colombo Machado Salles bridge which connects the island to the mainland. I climbed out of the combi as fast as I could – which, these days, is not very fast – so as not to be associated with the vehicle. After checking in at the reception, I requested an air-conditioned saloon for the next two days. Unfortunately I was not able to do so out of Pietro's earshot; he attempted to break off the negotiation.

'But Seu Otto, did my grandmother not tell you that I will drive you in the combi? I now live here, on the island, so it is really no trouble.'

'Anna-Maria did mention that, and I am very grateful for the offer,' I said. 'Nevertheless, I do not wish to add to the mileage on your combi, nor risk the possibility of a mechanical problem whose repair I would feel obliged to pay for.'

'But she has already done more than 300,000 kilometres! Another 50 or so will make no difference. And if something goes wrong, my father's garage will repair it for free.'

'I intend to hire a saloon and I would be grateful if you would drive us in that. Is that agreed?'

'Yes, Seu Otto,' said Pietro.

Having thus tactfully resolved the transportation problem, Anna-Maria and I were shown to our respective rooms. It may be thought noteworthy that my housekeeper accompanies me when I travel. However, she has been in my employ for thirty years and she is a very competent woman. She knows my needs and is able to live up to the high standards that I have always demanded of my employees. Her husband, Horst Teichmann, had been a worker at Feldmann before the company moved from Blumenau to São Paulo. I had interviewed Horst for his first position at the company. He had impressed me then, and my confidence in him was borne out over the following years. Horst was an excellent employee whose eye for unnecessary expenses helped to keep the company afloat when many others were going under. He was due for a significant promotion when he was diagnosed with leukemia and died very shortly thereafter.

In addition to Horst's eye for detail, I was always impressed by his clear grasp of facts and his level-headed view of every situation. I found this all the more impressive since, as I had learnt from Horst's file upon his initial application to the company, he had not been born under promising circumstances. Horst's mother had got pregnant as a teenager in Germany at the end of the war. Her conservative Catholic family had sent her to Brazil to have the baby. She died here in childbirth. Horst was raised by relatives who had been amongst the first Pomeranian settlers in Blumenau. He continued to live in Blumenau until his own premature death. Fortune did not appear to have smiled on him, but it always seemed to me that he made the most of what he was given.

Horst's sudden death was of course a tragedy for his wife, Anna-Maria. She was left with two children to raise on an insubstantial widow's pension. At the time I was in need of a housekeeper. I did not know Anna-Maria then, but I had thought highly of her husband, and I knew how small a widow's pension was, so I offered her the job on a part-time basis. Later, when her children left home, she became my full-time housekeeper. In all these years, we have never spoken about her deceased husband. I would like her to know that I esteemed him highly, but the opportunity to communicate that sentiment has never arisen. However, I am often reminded of Horst, since it must be from him that Pietro has inherited his fine German looks.

*

The following day we toured the island in the cool and comfortable interior of a naval blue Mercedes, a much more suitable vehicle. First we drove to the north where a number of ugly developments have blotted the landscape. Those wild Atlantic beaches were almost entirely deserted when I first visited back in the early 1950s. Now they are overshadowed by towering white apartment blocks. What is more, the beaches pullulate with Argentinian and Uruguayan holiday-makers, endlessly sipping their tiresome *yerba mate*.

As we followed the coastal road, Pietro indicated to us some of the places where he had competed in surfing competitions over the past few years. Then he pointed out a headland from which, so he said, one could catch the best waves. I saw a number of bodies bobbing up and down in the water without seeming to move.

'Where are their sails?' I asked.

Pietro smiled. I noticed how even his teeth were. 'Only windsurfers have sails,' he said. 'These are surfers.'

'So how do they move?'

'They catch a wave and ride it.'

'But the waves all go in the same direction. What if you want to go elsewhere?' I asked.

'That's impossible. You can swim in order to catch the waves, but then you have to ride it the way it is going.'

'You cannot go anywhere else?'

'No,' he replied, smiling again.

'So what is the point?'

'Well, there are different ways of riding the waves.'

'But you will always end up in the same place,' I reiterated.

'More or less, yes. But it's not really about where you get to, more about how you get there.'

This did not persuade me. The joy of ocean travel is surely that you can go wherever you want, that you are not bound by roads or considerations of topography. Can surfists really be content always to end up in the same place, to ignore the vast expanse of sea in favour of one small stretch beside one little headland?

The over-developed beaches of the north did not appeal to me. However, the following day we visited the fishing village of Sambaqui. It was a place I immediately liked. The empty beach is sheltered from the Atlantic waves since it is on the side of the island that faces the mainland. The sea is very shallow a long way out. Fishermen wading out to tend their mussel beds appear, at a certain distance, to be walking on water. The houses, of which there are few, are set back from the cobbled road and mostly hidden behind palm trees and lush vegetation. A bus bound for Florianópolis passes once every half an hour, otherwise there is little traffic. The overriding impression is one of great tranquility.

Anna-Maria agreed that Sambaqui was an idyllic spot and so I arranged to meet the real estate agent the following morning at the hotel; she was to drive us back to Sambaqui and show us a number of properties for sale in the village. This was, I think, a relief to both Pietro and me. Though he had not complained, I do not think he enjoyed driving the Mercedes as much as the combi. In fact, in the built up areas of the island I had the distinct impression that he shrunk away from the wheel as if he didn't want to be seen. I also noticed that he gazed longingly at the waves whenever we drove along the Atlantic coastal road.

The real estate agent was called Kika. She was a friend of Anna-Maria's daughter, Lua, who still lives in Blumenau. As she drove us back to Sambaqui the following morning, I told her that I had emigrated to Blumenau as soon as I received my papers after the war, and that before the war my father had been closely befriended with Peter Hering of the Hering textile dynasty. I inquired after the Herings - they had been a very prominent family in Blumenau. However, Kika had never heard of the Herings, and thus I left it to her and to Anna-Maria to make small talk about babies and such things.

Kika showed us a number of attractive properties in Sambaqui. There was one in particular that both Anna-Maria and I liked; overlooking the end of the longer of Sambaqui's two beaches, it was a long building painted a Maria-Theresian yellow with dark green slatted shutters, and surrounded by a lawn of extraordinarily fine and soft grass. The previous owner had been a Brazilian tennis star whose finest performances had been on the grass courts at Wimbledon. In celebration of this he had imported grass seed from England and devoted considerable time and energy to tending a lawn which, if not quite equal to a grass tennis court, was nevertheless very impressive. It was a lighter, more luminous green than Brazilian grass and I immediately found it a source of great visual pleasure.

The asking price for the property was not unreasonable, at least not compared to the inflated price of property in São Paulo. And so, a week after we had returned from Santa Catarina, and after a meeting with my bank manager, I made an offer on the house. The offer was accepted and I subsequently put my house in São Paulo on the market; then Anna-Maria and I started to plan the move to Sambaqui.

I found the actual process of moving to be quite straining. The house in São Paulo contained a lifetime's worth of clutter. There were many things I knew I would never use again – old tennis racquets, musical instruments and so on. But I did not have the heart to throw them away. Then there were other objects to which I am very attached, such as my collection of antique snuff boxes. I have assembled the collection over the years, scouring everywhere from the flea markets of Mexico City to the antiques fairs of Buenos Aires. It was hard for me to watch the clumsy hands of the removal men attempt to pack my collection with the care it deserves; in the end I was forced to do it myself. Then, when everything had finally been packed, the boxes were loaded onto a lorry to be driven to Sambaqui while Anna-Maria and I made the journey by aeroplane.

Chapter 2

I've GOT a lot going on right now. There's a lot my mother doesn't know, and it's better that way, but I guess that's why she promised Vovó that I'd be free to drive her and Senhor Eisinger around when they came to visit the island. Actually, they weren't just visiting. Senhor Eisinger was thinking of moving here and they came to look at houses. My mother told me to go and pick them both up from the airport. At first I resented the fact that she'd made that promise – like I said, I've got a lot going on. However, when I thought about it a bit more, I realised there was a chance that I'd get a sizeable tip from Senhor Eisinger. He's pretty rich, I think. Admittedly, nightclub promoters don't usually rely on tips for odd jobs, but I really need the money.

When I was very young, I used to go to São Paulo every summer to spend a few weeks with Vovó and Senhor Eisinger. Vovó would take me to *Sottozero*, the ice cream parlour, and buy me things which I'd never have got back home. That was the first place I ever had *doce de leite* ice cream – the one with swirls of caramel running through it. It was delicious; I used to dream about it for the rest of the year.

I remember the house they lived in. It was large and very quiet – too quiet, really. You could hear your own breathing. And it had a peculiar smell of old wood and moss. But the garden was big and lush and shady. And there was a pool. I remember the old negro with the wrinkled face who tended it. He used to spend hours fishing the leaves out of the water one by one.

I rarely saw Senhor Eisinger. I spent most of the time in Vovó's apartment, which was attached to the main house. But even when I followed her into the main house, I rarely saw him. Of course, this was before he had retired; Vovó told me that he worked very hard. He was a big fish in the Feldmann Brewery business.

I used to play with my toy cars on the terrace, overlooking the garden. The paving stones were irregular and they cut my bare knees, but I liked the way that the sunlight and shade were clearly distinguished on the bright stone. I had one army of cars for the sun and another for the shade and they fought some historic battles.

Vovó tried to make sure that I wasn't playing on the terrace when Senhor Eisinger came out to take his afternoon tea. However, there were occasions when she forgot to chase me away, or sometimes Senhor Eisinger returned early. He would sit and watch me play and if Vovó tried to send me indoors, he would say, 'No, no, Anna-Maria, leave him. There is no need.' He always seemed very serious; certainly he would never have considered taking part in my car wars. But I never felt uncomfortable in his presence. Quite the opposite: I felt he liked me being there.

*

On the morning I was supposed to meet Vovó and Senhor Eisinger at the airport, I woke up in Sara's apartment. That hadn't been my plan, not at all. Marina – my girlfriend –

was due to return from her parents' house in Curitiba later that afternoon. I figured I just had time to rush back to my own apartment, the one we share, before driving to the airport. That way I could cover my tracks.

I raced back home, then I showered and changed. I messed up the sheets and made sure to leave the damp towel on the bed. I knew that would annoy Marina – it is one of her pet peeves - but it would make her think that I had spent the night at home. I didn't know how long Vovó and Senhor Eisinger would want me to drive them around for, so I put all my music equipment in the back of the combi in case I didn't have time to go home before Divino. I'd just launched my own night at Divino and it wasn't going very well so for now I was cutting costs by dj-ing there myself. Anyway, with the surfing and promoting my night and trying to finish my degree, not to mention the sleeping around, I was beginning to think that I had taken on too much.

I drove to the airport just in time to welcome Vovó and Senhor Eisinger as they emerged from the arrivals gate. I'd seen Vovó over Christmas and she looked as healthy and robust as ever. She is always happy to see me and that's a good feeling, though she invariably manages to make me feel like a little boy. She embraced me as soon as she had marched around the barrier separating us. For the first time I can remember, she did not comment on how much I had grown or how closely I resembled my grandfather. Maybe this was in deference to Senhor Eisinger; he was waiting patiently behind her and was rather dwarfed by her bulk. Vovó reintroduced us; after all, Senhor Eisinger last saw me ten years ago. However, he looked identical to the way I remembered him – his fine grey hair was neatly combed back and he wore an elegant black suit. He just seemed a lot smaller, though he shook my hand very firmly while staring me straight in the eye.

'Senhor Eisinger, it is a pleasure to see you again,' I said.

'And it is a pleasure to see you. But please, Pietro, let us not stand on formality. Call me Otto.'

In view of what I was to learn about Seu Otto, this was a strange thing to say. I have never met a man who stands more on formality. Nevertheless, I took control of the luggage trolley, which appeared to be causing Seu Otto some trouble, then I led the way out to the car park. On the way I had the impression that Seu Otto was sizing me up. However, once I had loaded the luggage into the back of the combi and started the engine, Seu Otto leant back and appeared to fall asleep. Vovó began to interview me about the family. I realised that she was also trying, rather sneakily, to pry into my own affairs. Had she asked me directly I don't think I would have minded, but I resented the underhand nature of her questions. I found myself wishing that Seu Otto would open his eyes so that his formality would once again silence my grandmother.

'So Pietro, how is university?'

'It's fine. I'm due to graduate next year.' There's a mountain of work I'll have to do before then and I don't know how I am going to pay for my tuition, I thought to myself.

'Yes...' Vovó paused a moment. 'There must be lots of nice girls at your university.'

'Yes, Vovó, there are,' I replied. I knew she wanted to hear more, but I didn't want to tell her about my current situation. It's strange how people pay lip service to the idea that young men should be allowed to fool around, though when it comes down to the details, no one ever actually approves. 'You're young, you're free... enjoy it,' they say, but when you tell them about the girls you're seeing, they say something like, 'I could never do that', or, 'I'm amazed that you can live like that.' It's confusing.

I didn't think Vovó would approve of my current lifestyle. She is pretty old-fashioned. But she's also insightful. She said, 'You know, Pietro, if there's something you want to talk about, you can always talk to me.' I looked into the rear view mirror and saw that she was studying me. I was surprised to feel a sudden surge of emotion, almost a desire to cry. I am not sure whether it was caused by Vovó herself, or whether there were things I wanted to get off my chest; in any case, it took me unawares. It was as if I had caught a brief glimpse of a wave of sadness which I usually pretend is not there. I wasn't about to spill my guts to her then and there, but just for a moment the thought of having someone to talk to was very appealing. But then I realised how ridiculous it would be to tell my grandmother about Sara and Marina and the club and the surfing sponsorship and my worries about the future. She wouldn't understand any of it. So I just said, '*Obrigado,* Vovó,' and then the front of the Hotel Imperial came into view and I was grateful for it.

Seu Otto opened his eyes and got out of the combi almost immediately. I was impressed by the energy of the old man's movements. I opened the door for Anna-Maria, then I helped the porter unload the luggage. When I entered the hotel, Anna-Maria was sitting in an armchair fanning herself and Seu Otto was leafing through the documents in his leather briefcase which was perched on the reception. I approached him to ask at what time he wanted to be picked up.

Seu Otto suggested meeting at the hotel at half past seven, a time at which I would usually either be surfing or just have gone to bed. The receptionist then reappeared and informed Seu Otto that they could arrange for him to hire a Mercedes for three days. This surprised me; I'd imagined that I would be driving Seu Otto and Anna-Maria in my old combi. I reminded Seu Otto of this, but to my annoyance he abruptly dismissed the idea.

There were a number of reasons why I preferred to drive the combi. For a start, given the fact that I currently owe the owners of Divino a sizeable sum of money, it is certainly not in my interests for them to see me driving around in a shiny new Mercedes. Secondly, although my mother had offered my services as a favour, I nevertheless also hoped to receive some financial reward for three days of driving, and the reward would be greater if the car were my own. And, finally, in the event that the combi broke down, which was quite likely, then Seu Otto would feel obliged to pay for the repairs, or at least to contribute to them, and I could get my hands on some more cash that way. It all sounds very scheming, but I was really in a bit of a fix.

I tried to change Seu Otto's mind but it was pointless. In fact, I saw a brief glimpse of the cast iron inflexibility about which Vovó has often complained to my mother. Seu Otto was very abrupt, almost as if he was doing me a favour by letting me drive him. But then I remembered that for many years he had had an important job in São Paulo; I suppose old habits die hard. And, quite apart from that, maybe it should be the privilege of old age not to have to compromise; it doesn't seem like there are many other advantages.

*

I said goodbye to Seu Otto and Vovó and drove the half hour back to my apartment in Lagoa. There is a steep hill between Florianópolis, on the west of the island, and Lagoa da Conceição, which faces east. The combi battled its way up the hill and even the shrill scooters of local *rapazes* – the derestricted ones with the high-pitched exhausts – overtook me on the slope. I was beginning to feel more positive about Seu Otto's Mercedes when the combi crested the brow of the hill. The view that greeted me is probably the finest on the island. For a few moments I felt grateful for my vehicle's slowness which allowed me to take it all in.

In front of me was the saltwater lagoon called Lagoa da Conceiçao - its shallow margins were a bright emerald green. Just beyond that I could see the dunes and the beaches facing the Atlantic – Barra da Lagoa to the north, then Praia Mole and Joaquina. These were the beaches where I had learnt to surf, where I had made my childhood friends and first smoked pot and first got laid (in the car park, that is). For a moment I remembered what it felt like to be carefree, the way I was back then. The annoying thing is, at the time I never realised how lucky I was. I suppose I didn't have anything to compare it to. But then, perhaps it is only from the perspective of the present that those days seem carefree. When I think about it a little more, I remember worrying about scraping together enough money to buy a board, and how late I could stay out, and whether I'd be able to impress the girls. Maybe the worry is always there, it's just what you worry about that changes.

The combi rolled slowly down the hill. The road was in shadow now; the sun was setting behind the hill. Other, longer shadows stretched east across the island in front of me. Here and there streetlights in the small town of Lagoa were already being switched on. One by one, my worries returned.

My biggest problem right now is money. Two months ago I signed a contract to run Tuesday nights at a popular nightclub called Divino. However, right after I signed the contract, the owners opened another nightclub in Lagoa itself. Now the old crowd goes there on Tuesdays and I'm losing money.

I also get sponsored to surf by Kauai, the surf shop in Joaquina. However, I've surfed so little this year that I don't think they'll renew the deal. I was planning to use the money to pay next semester's tuition for my media studies degree. But the way things are going, I may not even be allowed to register for next semester. I've got a pile of work to get through if I want to pass the courses I'm already taking.

The assignment I'm most worried about is a full-length investigative interview. I don't think anyone reads 3000 word interviews anymore, but we still have to learn how to write one. The problem is, I have no idea who to interview. I guess I could go to a surf contest and interview one of the competitors – I know most of them anyway. Kauai would love that, me interviewing other surfers when I should be getting myself interviewed... No, that's not such a great idea.

I parked the combi and opened the door to the apartment. I had been so lost in my thoughts that I had totally forgotten that Marina would be back from visiting her parents in Curitiba. The faint scent of coconut tanning oil in the apartment gave her away – it is a smell which seems to accompany her everywhere. The apartment was warm and humid; I guessed that Marina was in the shower.

I bent down to pick up the fliers which had been dropped through the post box. I heard a noise and, looking up, I saw Marina's long tanned legs. She was wearing high heels, black underwear and a light blue t-shirt. She was a sexy girl but, even for her, this was unusual.

'*Oi, bem vinda,*' I said, rising to kiss her hello. 'You look like a lingerie model.'

'I had to iron my skirt,' she replied, and I noticed that she was holding the short white skirt in her other hand.

'I'm not complaining,' I said, leaning in to kiss her again. I noticed once again how much softer Marina's lips were than Sara's. I placed my hand on her angular hipbone and allowed the cusp of it to nestle in the centre of my palm. Marina put her arm behind my head and, taking a handful of my hair, she pulled my mouth towards hers again. My thumb drifted towards the elastic of her underwear.

Marina pulled away. 'Not now,' she said. 'I have to go to work, I'm going to be late.'

'So if you're late already...' I whispered in her ear. She didn't respond. 'I've missed you so much.' Again she didn't respond. Up close the smell of her skin and the coconut oil was intoxicating. 'I get so lonely without you,' I breathed.

Third time lucky. She grabbed my belt buckle and tugged at it. I manoeuvred us around until my back was against the wall, then I let her take over.

*

Marina got back around four in the morning. She works at the Jungle Bar in Barra da Lagoa. It's a touristy place but they make great caipirinhas. Four a.m. is about normal, though this time she was pretty drunk when she got back. Knowing that I would have to get up at half past six to meet Senhor Eisinger, I had gone to bed early. However, I'm not used to it, so I just lay in bed with the TV on. I hadn't even been able to concentrate on that. I spent most of the night lying awake and thinking – about Marina, and Sara, and the night at Divino, and the money I owed. Finally I did fall asleep, but not for long. Marina woke me up when she got back. She can be very demanding when she's drunk. When I left the apartment a couple of hours later I was exhausted.

Senhor Eisinger, on the other hand, was very sprightly. He was already in the lobby of the hotel when I arrived ten minutes early. He pressed the keys of the big blue Mercedes into my hand and then ushered Anna-Maria into the back of the car. He opened the door for her and brushed away the attentions of the doorman. Then he walked round to the other side of the vehicle and opened the door for himself. For a moment he seemed childlike in his enthusiasm. He opened and closed the door a second time just to listen to the clunk it made, then he said to me, 'Fine German engineering.'

Senhor Eisinger instructed me to drive north, up towards Praia dos Ingleses. I think he was saddened to see some of the ugly developments that have been built there. I caught glimpses of him shaking his head in the rear view mirror as yet another white apartment complex came into view. As we drove past Rio Vermelho, I remembered the surf contest I had competed in up there some years ago. It had been the first contest in which I had been placed, and one of the last that my father came to watch.

'Do you like it here?' asked Senhor Eisinger.

'Yes, Seu Otto,' I replied. 'I came here with my father once, when I was young.'

'You are not so old now.'

'I suppose not. But it feels like it was a long time ago,' I said.

'Your father, he is not a surfist anymore?' asked Seu Otto.

'No, not any more. He was never much of a surfer really, but he encouraged me.'

'So now?'

'Well, we don't speak much now,' I replied. Seu Otto nodded to himself and was silent.

'Pietro's father Gorka, my son in law, is not an easy man,' chimed in Anna-Maria. 'He left my daughter to bring up Pietro all by herself. I ask you, what kind of a man would do that?'

Seu Otto did not reply. I remained silent too. I think we were both wishing that Vovó were not quite so outspoken.

From Rio Vermelho we headed south to look at the village of Pantano do Sul. The houses there are big but charmless; Seu Otto's expression left me in little doubt that he felt the same way. Instead of stopping there, he told me to drive on to the famous Bar do Arante restaurant. I had been to Bar do Arante once before, on a date with

Marina a year ago. The inside of the restaurant is covered from floor to ceiling with handwritten notes left by diners. There is not an inch of wall visible. The notes are written on serviettes in languages from all over the world. Some notes are more like postcards, others are wishes. My own note must be there somewhere too. I think it said, 'I wish to sleep with Marina tonight.' I think that even happened. If I could make another wish now, I would make a more serious one.

A tradition of the restaurant is to serve each diner a caipirinha before the waiter has even taken your order. Seu Otto didn't know about this. At first he tried to send the drinks back. When the waiter explained that they were complimentary, Seu Otto thanked him and, having waited for the waiter to leave, he told us that he wished to propose a toast to his own future death on the island. I don't know what prompted this thought. Vovó and I were both surprised; neither of us knew how to respond. Perhaps Seu Otto noticed our confusion; he said, 'Well, can you imagine a better place to die?' I shook my head.

I took a sip from my caipirinha which was strong and good, not too sweet. I noticed that Anna-Maria did not touch hers. Seu Otto said, 'What, you do not like caipirinha?'

Anna-Maria shook her head.

'Will you have something else?'

'No, that's okay,' she said.

'Anna-Maria, please. I wish to drink a toast. You must have something.'

Vovó seemed surprised by Seu Otto's insistence. 'Well, maybe a gin and tonic?' she asked, meekly. Seu Otto waved to the waiter and ordered the gin and tonic, then we toasted his future death. I am fairly sure I detected a glint of amusement in his eye.

*

After lunch we headed back to Florianópolis. On the way we had to pass through Lagoa. I sank a little lower in the driver's seat, in the hope that I would not be recognised behind the wheel of a gleaming, brand new Mercedes. If one of the owners of Divino had seen me, I would have had some explaining to do. Although, realistically, I think they would have assumed the car didn't belong to me. Nevertheless, I was grateful that the car windows were tinted almost as dark as a politician's limousine.

I drove Senhor Eisinger and Vovó back to the Hotel Imperial. Seu Otto thanked me and told me that he wouldn't need me for the next two days since Kika, the real estate agent who is a friend of my mother's, had offered to drive him around the island to view a number of properties. Seu Otto shook my hand, once again with surprising firmness. Then he gave me a folded bill which I didn't look at until I was back in the combi; it was extremely generous, more of a gift than a tip. As he handed the bill to me he also invited me to visit him whenever I wished, whether in São Paulo or once he was installed on Santa Catarina.

The truth is that I would like to see Seu Otto again. He certainly cuts a strange figure, always wearing his dark suit on this island of surfers and holidaymakers. I have never met anyone like him before and I have the sense that, underneath all that formality and inflexibility, he possesses some rare and admirable qualities. I can't imagine Seu Otto ever having gotten himself into a situation like the one that

I'm currently in. Of course, things were different when he was young, but maybe they were different precisely because the people were different. Or maybe I just want to see him again because I have always felt that he likes me, and that is an agreeable feeling.

'Won't you hug your grandmother, or don't you love me anymore?' asked Vovó, interrupting my thoughts about Seu Otto. I am fond of her but I find these emotional entreaties quite annoying. Nevertheless, I did hug her goodbye, though I also noticed that Seu Otto had turned around so as not to see. I am not sure whether he did that so that I wouldn't feel embarrassed, or so that *he* wouldn't. In many ways he is still an enigma to me, and that is another reason why I would like our paths to cross again.

Chapter 3

I MOVED into the new house at the beginning of February, shortly before carnival. We spent the first few days unpacking; this was even more straining than the packing had been. Moving house is no occupation for senior citizens, be they of ever so formidable a constitution. There are too many objects whose location needs to be decided upon, and each object triggers too many memories... but I become sentimental.

After three days of unpacking I felt I needed to get out, so I made my first trip to Florianópolis. I also had to go to the bank to withdraw cash to give to Anna-Maria for household expenses. I changed into my suit and proceeded to the bus stop on Sambaqui's cobbled main street. The bus stop itself has a small slanted roof so I was able to wait comfortably in the shade, despite the hot summer sun.

That inaugural trip to Florianópolis coincided with the first day of carnival festivities. I was unable to go to the bank since it was shut. Not only that, I found myself caught up in the procession known as the 'bloco dos sujos': the parade of the dirty ones. It is the custom in Florianópolis for men of all ages and physiques to wear women's clothing for a day. The results are at times quite fear-inducing: I saw a well-rounded gentleman in his later years drunkenly rolling down Rua Felipe Schmidt wearing only a pink tutu. However, it amused me that wives and girlfriends, usually the centre of sartorial admiration, were for once in the shadows whilst husbands and boyfriends paraded like birds of paradise, complimenting each other on their outfits.

Having escaped from the *bloco dos sujos,* I wandered the streets for an hour. I was astounded by the number of clothing shops, the vast majority selling nothing but shorts, t-shirts and sunglasses. Can there really be such enormous demand for these items? I continued past clothing shop after clothing shop until I reached the historic town square. Several restaurants vied for space beneath a tall, honey-coloured portico. I was reminded of the piazzas I had seen during a business trip to Italy many years ago. As in Italy, the red plastic tables in front of the restaurants proudly displayed the ubiquitous Coca-Cola ensign.

Since the main carnival festivities took place in Florianópolis, I thought it was quite possible that Pietro would be there for the day. The chances of bumping into him were of course small, though I was tricked from a distance on a number of occasions – there are many blond Brazilians on the island of Santa Catarina. Most are the descendants of the Germans, Poles and Ukrainians who immigrated at the end of the nineteenth century. Those like me, who came after the war, are a relative minority. Despite the false alarms, I remained vigilant in the hope of spotting Pietro's blond shock of hair.

I wandered underneath the portico to the cobbled square on the other side. Here there was a fountain which had seen better days. The mermaids had been defaced with graffiti moustaches and the water which had been intended to spray in a jet from the dolphin's mouth was just a sad dribble. I sat down on the side of the fountain and observed the *vaivém*. On the other side of the square a large stage was being prepared for the arrival of some musicians. Girls whose ample behinds had been squeezed into tight, shiny trousers began to arrive in large groups. They tottered over to the stage where the technicians were still setting up the equipment. I could tell from the timbre of the girls' voices that they were excited; they must have been expecting musicians of some renown.

One of the technicians was wearing a skier's red hat with a pompom, despite the warmth of the afternoon. He climbed onto the stage and announced that he was going to play the first 'set'. I could still not see the musicians; perhaps there was a hidden orchestra pit which I could not discern. In any case, the technician continued to fiddle around with the equipment. Some of the young people had already, somewhat precipitously, started to dance. Truly, young people today are very impatient – I imagine it is due to the culture which peddles instant gratification. After listening to the discordant notes and circular rhythms for a while, I began to wonder whether the equipment was broken. I did not wish to wait around for the necessary repairs to take place, so I hailed a passing cab and returned home.

*

Once I had settled into the new house, I began to enjoy a pleasing routine. The crescent beach of Sambaqui stretches for two kilometres from a small sandy promontory at the northern end to a similar promontory at the southern end. Before the accident I used to swim from one promontory to the other and back every morning. Now I can no longer swim quite that far. Nevertheless, swimming is a wonderful occupation; I am able to exercise without placing any strain on my hip or my arthritic knee. My knee can be a source of great discomfort, especially on humid days; sometimes I even require the aid of a walking stick.

From the water I can see the tower blocks of Florianópolis to the south and the steeply rising green mass of the mainland to the west. The absence of any waves makes the bay ideal for swimming, unless one of my neighbours decides to shatter the morning calm on a hateful, petroleum-excreting jet-ski. Otherwise flying fish are common, especially before a storm, and on a number of occasions I have seen the horny flipper of a sea turtle rise solemnly above the water like a papal benediction.

After my swim, I take morning coffee on the patio outside my library. A pleasant dappled shade is cast by the vines, which have been trained to grow around the wooden beams overhead. Then I read the *Diario Catarinense,* which is delivered to my door, and the *Folha de São Paulo,* which I buy once a week at exaggerated cost in Florianópolis. When I am done with the newspapers, I attempt to plug the gaps in my knowledge of the literary classics. I recently finished reading the *Nibelungenlied* and I am currently trudging through Dante's *Inferno* with the help of a Portuguese translation. I confess that Dante often sends me to sleep. However, I am usually woken after a short time by the clanking of the garden gate. Valdemar the gardener arrives at midday, and then I too have a job to do. Valdemar is both lazy and of limited understanding, by no means equal to the task of maintaining the perfect lawn that I have inherited. I am obliged to dog his every step.

The previous owner of the house left a file describing how best to care for the grass - a lawn service manual. I was able to purchase extra seed and the necessary fertilisers from the All England Rackets and Tennis Club via an import company in São Paulo. After consulting the file and inspecting the grass, I issue instructions to Valdemar. In the early days of our collaboration, I was not so conscientious and within a couple of weeks the grass was already turning brown and sickly, despite the clockwork regularity of the automated watering system. However, with the aid of a ruler I discovered that Valdemar was mowing too deeply; each blade of grass was losing over fifty percent of its length every time it was cut. The optimum summer percentile, according to the file, is twenty-five.

Since then I have been following the instructions to the letter and I am happy to state that the results have been gratifying. However, I have been surprised by the amount of work required. Great vigilance is also necessary since Valdemar will cut corners (and grass) wherever possible. I have taken to sitting at the back of the garden in a pliable chair with the file on my knees, observing Valdemar whilst he waters or mows or aerates or scatters or scarifies or fertilises. A perfect lawn may mean nothing to him, but I delight in its luminous verdure.

The lawn is certainly the garden's most salient feature. However, around the perimeter of the lawn there are a number of other noteworthy plants. A mat of bright purple bougainvillea festoons the wooden fence at the back of the garden. It is a fine specimen of a hardy plant – even Valdemar's erratic watering does not appear to dull the intensity of the bright, papery flowers. The bougainvillea is named after the French Naval admiral Louis Antoine de Bougainville; he took cuttings in Brazil during his circumnavigation of the globe and brought them back to France. It amuses me to think that this plant, so characteristic of the languorous Mediterranean, is really a native of these shores.

Further along the wooden fence there is one plant which is not a native of this continent – the honeysuckle. It also grows well in this shaded area and it is abundantly adorned with yellow and white blossoms. But for some reason it has no scent. I remember an afternoon a long time ago, a sunny afternoon during my childhood in Germany, during which I was entranced and intoxicated by the sweet fragrance of honeysuckle wafting through an open window. Well, all I can say is that this Brazilian plant, for all its superficial charm, is a very poor cousin of that glorious German relative. How sad, to be a scentless honeysuckle.

Twice a week, following my rounds of the garden with Valdemar, I take the bus to Florianópolis in order to buy the *Folha de São Paulo,* a newspaper which is not sold in Sambaqui. There is a little newsagent on the corner of Córrego Grande which also sells very fine *pastéis,* lightly dusted with icing sugar. It was in this newsagent's that the incident occurred.

I am referring to the fateful Monday morning in March, some weeks after the carnival. I had been swimming that morning, following which I helped Valdemar mix the manganese-boron fertiliser. I watched him begin to spread the fertiliser and, when I had assured myself that he was not going to bungle the job, I went in to change. Large thunderclouds were piling up in the south and from my bedroom window I could see the flying fish flash brightly as they leapt from the water, heralding a storm. My knee was already beginning to ache, so I went to fetch my stick before walking the short distance from my house to the bus stop.

In summer even the Sambaqui bus is crowded; the holiday makers from Argentina and Uruguay are everywhere. I was standing in the aisle holding onto one of the billiard balls attached to leather straps that hang from the roof when a corpulent lady with a downy moustache began to undulate menacingly; then she stood up and offered me her seat. I declined the offer, thinking to myself that she had greater need of the seat than I, though it was a sentiment I tactfully kept to myself. I was momentarily tempted to point out to her that I had already swum over two kilometres that morning and that it was well within my capabilities to stand on my own two feet for a few minutes, but I restrained myself.

The clouds had moved in more quickly than I had anticipated. By the time the bus stopped in Córrego Grande, the wind was picking up too and it had started to spit with rain. I leant into the wind and made my way towards the newsagent's where I selected a pastry. I then picked out the *Folha de São Paulo* from the newspaper rack. As I did so, my eyes were drawn to the black-and-white cover photo of a magazine bearing the title *História*. Why were my eyes drawn to it? I cannot say. Though at the time I could not know it, that moment turned out to be of no small significance.

The black-and-white cover photo depicted a column of

Hitler Youth boys standing to attention in Nuremberg's Adolf Hitler Platz. Despite the graininess of the image, I was able to recognise a number of the buildings from my own visit during the rally in 1938. I looked hard at the column of boys but I did not recognise any of them; that would have been too great a coincidence. Of course I recognised the uniform – the brown shirt, the black neckerchief held in place with a leather knot, black shorts worn good and tight round the waist, black belt, beige knee socks and polished black shoes. And I recognised the salute too, the raised arm with hand outstretched. But maybe I also recognised something else in this photo, in the expression of these boys: the pride that comes from dedicating oneself to something much greater than the individual.

I picked up the magazine and searched for the article about 'a Juventude Hitleriana' in the index. I was about to turn to it when the store suddenly darkened. Looking up, I saw two men burst through the doorway into the shop. Both were burly, both wore flesh coloured stockings on their heads and both were carrying pistols. One of the two men levelled his pistol at the shopkeeper behind the till and screamed at him:

'Mãos na cabeça, rápido!'

The shopkeeper put his hands on his head and took a step back as the second man opened the till and started to empty the contents into a plastic bag. Strangely, neither of the gunmen had seen me enter the shop – I assumed they had staked it out for a while before bursting in. But at that moment one of the two men looked up and saw me for the first time.

'*Merda, tem um velho aqui,*' – there's an old man in here – he said to his accomplice.

The second gunman, who still had his pistol levelled at the shopkeeper, turned round.

'*Está quase mumificado,*' – he's practically a mummy - he said to the first man. Then he shouted at me: '*Oi, velho, no chão, mexa-se!*'

I laid my walking stick down beside me and got to my knees, a very uncomfortable position given my arthritis. The first man had returned to emptying the till; seeing me on my knees, the second man also turned back round. I could see the back of his bull-like neck and his shaved skull, not at all appealing. Through the fine fabric of the flesh-coloured tights I could even make out the outline of a tattoo which ran from his shoulder up the side of his neck to the back of his head, like ivy on a marble statue.

I was not afraid – the gunmen had nothing to gain by shooting me. But I was angry. '*Quase mumificado*'! And they were quite happy to leave me unobserved while they emptied the till. Would they be so confident if they knew that I had been recommended for the Iron Cross Second Class? If they knew that the man they had left unwatched behind them was Hitlerjunge Otto Eisinger who, as a young boy, had single-handedly destroyed the lead tank of the Allied 7th Armoured Division? I think not.

Having emptied the till, the first gunman unhooked a large, jangling key ring from the shopkeeper's trousers. He gave it to the second gunman, then strolled casually out of the door with the plastic bag, removing the stocking from his head as he went. The second gunman used his pistol to indicate the storeroom behind the till to the shopkeeper.

The shopkeeper opened the door to the storeroom; it was little more than a cupboard. '*Entra aí*,' the gunman said, pushing the shopkeeper into the storeroom. Then he closed the storeroom door. While he tried the different keys on the key ring in order to lock the door, I heard a motor start up outside the shop.

The gunman was still fiddling with the keys – there were many on the ring. I picked up my walking stick and stood up. He didn't notice. I took a couple of tentative steps. Still he did not turn around. I took a few more steps until I was within range, then I gripped my walking stick tightly by the end with the rubber foot and swung the pointed handle as hard as I could at the back of the gunman's head. It must have twisted in the air since, when the handle made contact with his skull, it merely glanced off. The man turned round and grinned at me hazily through the stocking. Then he grabbed his pistol by the barrel and swung it lightning-fast at the side of my head.

Chapter 4

In the weeks following Senhor Eisinger and Vovó's visit, my situation didn't improve. Quite the opposite. The night at Divino continued to lose money. I started handing out fliers on campus myself. The term before, I'd employed a number of attractive students to do that for me. That is actually how I first met Sara. I didn't even have money to pay a second dj, so I continued to dj myself. I borrowed João's cds and used the cd mixer in the club. João studied music and he has a huge collection. Obviously most of his stuff is no good for a nightclub like Divino, but he has some dance music too. I also borrowed the red knitted hat which I saw in his room and which he'd bought to go skiing in Argentina the year before. The dj booth was raised above the dancefloor and was pretty dark; with the hat on, it was hard to recognise me. I didn't want people to realise that the dj was the same person who had been handing out fliers. That would not be glamorous. People come to Divino because they like to think it's glamorous.

I'd learnt to mix while I was still at school. I sometimes dj-ed at birthday parties, though I always had to borrow other people's music. I'd even played the opening set at the carnival in Florianópolis, but that was because I was friends with one of the organisers. They had gone over-budget and I was the cheapest they could get, plus they could claim that I was the in-house dj from Divino. Mixing music is not all that hard, at least not the way I do it. You really have to screw up for it to be obvious to anyone apart from yourself, and maybe to a few others who are more interested in the music than in hooking up. In Divino, there's not many like that.

Sara was one of the girls who used to hand out the fliers for me. She also came to the club herself every Tuesday night. Of course she already knew me, and she also knew that I was now handing out the fliers myself, but I think she just liked the fact that I was the dj. I know it's a cliché, but some girls really are like that – or at least Sara was.

The first time I dj-ed, Sara kept coming up to the booth during my set. She'd lean over the low glass partition and whisper something to me and wink. With the noise and the headphones and having to concentrate, I never understood what she said, but I smiled and nodded and that seemed to satisfy her. She'd disappear for a while and then come back again after a bit, a little more drunk each time. After my set we had a drink at the bar and once we went to the backroom where she sucked me off. I didn't enjoy it much the first time; I was thinking about the takings that I had to collect from the doorman and wondering what they would come to. At that time the club was still busy, but nothing like what it had been at the beginning, when there used to be people queuing in the street, and not just students. Back then there were plenty of professional people too, people with large salaries who reserved tables and bought bottles and generally dropped a ton of money.

I didn't have to worry about Marina turning up at Divino. She worked at the Jungle Bar on week nights, so

I was usually home before her anyway. I'd have a shower and then sit on the sofa and watch the late night news on tv until she got back. I always felt like I was covering my tracks pretty well. It's amazing how being clean and watching the news can avert suspicion. Maybe that's why so many married men watch the news.

I was always pretty careful about not being seen to spend too much time with Sara. There were lots of people who knew me at the club and I didn't want rumours getting back to Marina. Sometimes Sara would be with a date, and then nothing would happen. Other times she would come and find me, but I always made sure that we went to the backroom to kiss or whatever. However, there was one night when Marina got back to the apartment pretty angry. I could tell she was angry because she's usually very talkative after her shifts – she likes to get stuff off her chest. But on this occasion she just let herself in and closed the door and didn't say anything.

It was a hot, humid night. The television cast a flickering blue light across the room. I'd had a shower and was sitting on the sofa in my white jiu-jitsu trousers. I haven't trained for years but the trousers are loose and comfortable. Often Marina is in the mood for sex after her shift, especially if she's been drinking, so I was sort of anticipating that too. Sara had sucked me off earlier in the evening but that was a while ago, and anyway, I guess I liked the idea of getting it on with two girls in one night. Isn't that what being young is all about?

'Marina? Are you ok?'

Marina didn't answer. She sat down at the far end of the sofa to take off her shoes.

'Come here,' I said, placing a cushion for her on the sofa next to me. She ignored me.

'Marina?' I repeated. 'What's wrong?'

Silence. The tiny buckle on one of her heals appeared to be stuck. Suddenly, violently, she tore the shoe off. Then she fixed me with her gaze.

'Pietro. Answer me honestly. Are you screwing the girl who used to hand out fliers for you?'

Maybe I should have been expecting this, but I wasn't. 'What?' I asked, buying time. 'What are you talking about?'

'Just answer me honestly: are you or are you not screwing someone at the club?'

Feigning incredulity: 'No, of course not.' Technically true, we had only had sex at her house. Once. At the club she had only sucked me off. 'Why would you ask that?'

Marina's gaze still fixed on me. Her eyes becoming glassy. 'One of the girls from the bar told me. Promise me it's not true.'

'Does she even know me? What makes her think–?'

'Promise me it's not true.' Marina's grey-green eyes are boring into me.

'It's not true. I promise.' I don't feel good about saying that. Though it is technically true, I suppose. Marina is still gazing at me. 'I love you,' I say. That's true, at least it is right now. I reach out to put my arm around her. There is a tiny moment of resistance, then she rocks against me, her head on my naked chest. I feel dampness – is it breath or tears? Hard to tell. She pulls her legs up under her. I stroke her hair. I do love her. But do I only love her because I have hurt her? Again, hard to tell. Either way, I feel pretty shitty.

We sit like that for a while. I continue to stroke her hair. International news is followed by national news, then local news. CCTV footage of a newsagent's in black and white. The image quality is poor but I see two gunmen bursting into the store. The gunmen's features are obscured by stockings pulled over their heads. The small holes for their mouths are menacing, as if they are not men but machines intent on devouring the world. One of the men holds the shopkeeper at gunpoint while the other empties the till. There is movement in the back of the shop; the gunmen appear to be unaware of a customer in the store. One of the gunmen turns round and spots the customer. The customer lies down while the men finish emptying the till. One of the gunmen leaves the shop, removing the stocking from his head as he exits. The other gunman is ordering the shopkeeper into the storeroom; he does not notice that the customer has risen to his feet. The customer shuffles towards the gunman. He has the gait of an old man; he leans on a stick for support. As he comes closer to the hidden camera it becomes possible to distinguish more details. The man is wearing a dark suit. He is indeed old; his silver hair is brushed back over his scalp. He looks very familiar.

'*Meu Deus*! I know that man! That's Seu Otto!' I have rocked forward to the edge of the sofa.

'What? What are you talking about?' asks Marina.

'That man. That's my grandmother's employer. I used to stay in his house in São Paulo when I was a boy.' Marina looks blank. 'That's the old man who moved here – the man I drove around the island in the Mercedes when you were in Curitiba.'

'Oh, *him*,' says Marina.

Now we are both staring intently at the television. Seu Otto has shuffled to within a metre of the gunman who has still not noticed him. He lifts his walking stick and swings it at the gunman's head. Next to me Marina emits a little gasp. The gunman turns round and fells Seu Otto using the butt of his pistol. He picks up the bag with the cash and calmly saunters out of the shop.

The scene cuts to the newsroom where the presenter announces that Senhor Otto Eisinger is the former Vice-President of Feldmann Breweries, now retired. He emigrated to Brazil after the war and recently moved to Santa Catarina from São Paulo. He was taken to the University Hospital Florianópolis, where his condition is stable. The presenter introduces the mayor, also in the studio. The mayor's dark hair glistens in the studio lights. It looks as if it has been dyed – it's too dark for his face. The mayor begins by praising Otto's bravery, then he says that this is exactly the sort of crime that has to be eradicated. What is the world coming to, he asks, when an elderly gentleman cannot leave home to buy a newspaper?

I sit back and Marina leans her head against my chest again. 'What an amazing man,' she says.

'Yes,' I say. And it is true, I am full of admiration for him. In his position, I would never have dared even to look up. In fact, I'd probably be face down at the back of the shop even now. I'm young and fit and I still wouldn't have stood a chance in a fight, not against toughs like that. Seu Otto is an old man; he cannot walk unaided. What was he thinking? Is he suicidal? Delusional? Incredibly brave? Or all three?

'I wonder what made him do that,' I say.

After a short while, Marina says, 'You said you know him quite well.'

'Yes,' I reply.

'Well, you should go and visit him in hospital. Ask him what made him do that. Maybe you can sell his story to a newspaper.'

I think about that idea. It is not bad, not bad at all. After all, when I last saw Seu Otto, he invited me to visit him whenever I wished. What is more, I do genuinely want to know what motivates a man of his age to act the way he did. In fact, I want to know what makes any man act bravely and honourably. Does it come naturally? Is it an effort? These are pressing questions.

I pull Marina closer towards me. She looks up at me with trusting eyes, then touches her lips to my shoulder. Marina's eyes close and her breathing deepens. She is falling asleep. But I am still thinking about Senhor Eisinger. This may well be a stroke of good fortune for me, if not for him. Maybe I can interview him for my investigative assignment? If an interesting story emerges, then I could talk to him about selling it to a newspaper. We could split the proceeds and I could pay my debts and my tuition. And if nothing worth selling comes out of it, well, at least I will have completed the assignment and sated my own interest

Chapter 5

I OPENED my eyes but the world refused to resolve itself into recognisable shapes. Outlines were blurred and the brightness was too intense and hurt my head. I felt something pressing against my right eye. I blinked and heard a soft scraping sound. Then I closed my eyes again and drifted back into the velvety depths of dreams which I now know were morphine-induced.

The next time I woke I was able to open my eyes without the light causing such pain. Almost as soon as I had done so, I heard a familiar voice exclaim:

'*Nossa*! At last! Thank God!'

Turning my head to the right, I saw Anna-Maria perched on the edge of a grey plastic chair in front of a white curtain. There were dark rings under her eyes.

'Anna-Maria, *bom dia*,' I said, or started to say. The movement caused a jolt of pain to shoot through my jaw. Anna-Maria placed her hand on my arm which lay on the bed sheets, palm upwards. I noticed a clear tube emerging from a plaster above my wrist and disappearing out of sight above me.

'You brave, foolish man,' she said, looking at me with that slightly idiotic expression which women usually reserve for very young children.

I closed my eyes and asked, 'What happened?'

'What do you mean, what happened? What do you think happened? I'll tell you: you tried to get yourself killed, that's what happened. You've got a broken hip, a fractured jaw and a black eye, that's also what happened. And now you've woken up I have to call the doctor and they're going to operate on you as soon as they can. My God, at your age!'

I opened my eyes to see Anna-Maria's buxom figure lean over my bed as she reached for a small control panel near my left hand. She pressed the little red button with a picture of a nurse on it. Then she indicated a plastic button half way up the rubber tube that came out of my wrist.

'If you are in a lot of pain the nurse said to press this, right here,' she said. 'It increases the morphine. Do you need anything else? Shall I plump your pillow? It doesn't look very plumped to me.'

My head was beginning to hurt. 'Please, press the morphine button,' I said. Then I closed my eyes and seconds later I felt a wonderful calm flood my body.

'I hit him with my stick,' I said, remembering the bull neck and the shaved head. 'Like ivy on a marble statue.'

'I know you hit him,' said Anna-Maria. 'I saw it on the news. That's when I found out you were here. What were you thinking?'

'On the news?'

'Yes, there's a camera in the shop that films all the time. It saw everything and the shopkeeper sold the tape right after the ambulance took you away.'

As I lay there with my eyes closed, I began to imagine how differently things might have turned out. I pictured myself felling the bull-necked gunman, having my photo taken by the press as I stood over his enormous body like a hunter posing with a stag he has just shot. I am sure that the morphine contributed to this fantasy; it felt as vivid and immediate as a dream and yet I seemed to be able to steer the events in any direction I pleased. I continued to enjoy this fantasy until a man's voice interrupted me:

'*Senhor Eisinger?*'

I opened my eyes to see a thin, neat, grey-haired man in a white coat beside my bed. He was holding a clipboard. His plastic name badge read 'Dr. Antonio da Silva'.

'*Me chamo Antonio*, I am delighted to make your acquaintance. In fact we have already spoken today, though I doubt you remember.'

'No, I'm afraid I don't,' I said.

'How do you feel now?'

'I feel well, very well,' I replied.

'Good.' Dr. da Silva looked at me appraisingly, then he said: 'You were unconscious when the ambulance arrived but the trauma team woke you without intubation. We did a brain scan but everything seems alright there. Well, there is an abnormal amount of activity in the parietal lobe, the part of the brain which we associate with bravery.'

Dr. da Silva waited for a few moments before smiling at his own joke. 'Just a little pleasantry, Senhor Eisinger,' he said, then he continued:

'The head x-ray revealed a hairline fracture in the zygomatic bone, between the eye and the maxilla. That is where the blow landed. It will be sore for a while but will repair itself. Your right eye will remain black for a few weeks. The body scan showed us the hip fracture. It's stable for now, and the internal bleeding is local but we need to operate on it as soon as possible. Considering your age, I'm going to suggest a full hip replacement. It's less likely to produce complications than internal fixation with an intramedullary nail, although in the long term there is likely to be some loss of mobility. We will start you on physiotherapy the day after the operation. You'll be here for no more than a week, assuming everything goes well.'

Most of what Dr. da Silva said passed me by, so I asked: 'But I feel fine right now, won't it heal by itself?'

'No, I'm afraid not. And the only reason you feel fine now is because of the morphine, trust me. I'd like to have a look at your medical records and then book you in for the day after tomorrow. I'm afraid that's the earliest we can do. Of course you will be on a drip until then so the pain will be manageable. Be careful with the morphine, though – it's a very effective painkiller but psychologically it can stir things up a bit.'

Dr. da Silva tucked the clipboard under his arm, then he continued: 'It is an honour for me to operate on you. I watched you on the news today. You are a man of extraordinary bravery, extraordinary.' As he said this he extended his left hand, expecting me to shake it with my left since my right was connected to the drip. In reply I raised my own right hand; the transparent plastic tube bounced up and down as I shook Dr. da Silva's hand. He smiled at me. 'Senhor Eisinger, I remove my hat to you,' he said.

After Dr. da Silva had left, a large nurse with honey coloured skin and an abundance of dark frizzy hair appeared and introduced herself as Fernanda. She had bright eyes and spoke Portuguese with a musical carioca accent.

'So, may I reveal *o famoso Seu Otto* to the world?'

49

'Excuse me?'

'The curtain?' she said, taking hold of the white plastic curtain which separated us from the rest of the ward and giving it a little tug.

'Are you sure that's necessary?'

In reply, Fernanda theatrically pulled the curtain aside. I could tell from Anna-Maria's expression that she resented this display. Then I saw that there were three other beds in the ward, one to my right and two on the other side of the room, separated by a window. Through the window I could see a square of blue sky. All three beds were occupied by men of about my own age. They all appeared to be engrossed in some form of reading material, although I noticed furtive glances in my direction. At that moment another nurse rolled a food trolley into the ward. A table was placed over my legs and a plastic tray with a small pasta dish was put on top. I was not at all hungry.

'Would you like help?' asked Fernanda.

'Yes please,' I replied. 'I would be grateful if you would eat as much of this as you can.'

Fernanda smiled. 'A hero and a joker too,' she said. 'Then I shall have to force feed you.'

'That's quite alright,' said Anna-Maria tersely. 'I'll feed him myself.'

Fernanda raised her eyebrows at me before moving on to the other patients. Anna-Maria lifted a forkful of pasta to my lips but the pain in my jaw was torturous when I tried to chew. I contented myself with a glass of orange juice and another press on the morphine button.

'I spoke to Pietro this afternoon,' said Anna-Maria tentatively. 'He wishes you a speedy recovery.'

'Ah yes, Pietro, a most amusing boy. What is he doing now?' I asked.

'He is studying for his exams, studying very hard.'

'Yes of course, he is a student. Students must study.'

Anna-Maria coughed dryly into her fist, then she said, 'He wanted me to ask you whether he could come to visit you. I think he would like to interview you about the attack.'

'Really? If he wants to visit he is very welcome, though if it was shown on the news, as you said, then I suppose he already knows all about it.'

'I think he'd like to talk to you in person, so long as you don't mind.'

'I would like to see him,' I said, and I wasn't just being polite. I always enjoyed it when Pietro came to visit Anna-Maria in São Paulo when he was a boy, and I had again formed a very favourable impression of him a year ago when he had picked us up from the airport, despite the unfortunate combi.

Again I felt the warm drowsiness of morphine enveloping me.

'Siggi reminds me of an old friend,' I said sleepily.

'*Perdão?* Seu Otto?'

'A most amusing boy... as fast as a greyhound. As fast as *Quex*. Poor *Hitlerjunge Quex*. Poor Siggi. So tragic.

*

When I awoke later that day the electric lights were on in the ward, although I could still see some colour in the square of sky through the window. Anna-Maria was no longer there. The grey plastic chair had been moved a little further away from the bed and was now occupied by the bronzed figure of Pietro. I closed my good eye almost all the way so I could observe him while still appearing to be asleep.

It was astonishing how closely Pietro resembled Siegfried, the dear friend of my youth. Pietro was now of course a few years older than Siggi had been when he died, but nevertheless they had the same regular features, the same intelligent, questioning eyes. Pietro's hair was longer and more disorderly than Siggi's could ever have been, but it reminded me that Siggi himself often used to be reprimanded for not having his cut short enough. Pietro was wearing a white t-shirt with the words *Central Idiocy Agency* across the front, and the same marooned-sailor trousers I had seen when he had picked us up at the airport. On his crossed legs he was balancing a book whose title I could just make out from the spine – *Investigative Journalism, Context and Practice*.

'So, Anna-Maria says you would like to interview me,' I said.

Pietro jumped. 'Seu Otto,' he said. 'I didn't know you were awake.'

'Evidently.'

'How do you feel?'

'I feel well. Morphine is wonderful. The gentle arms of Morpheus.'

'I can come back another time, if you prefer,' said Pietro.

'No, no. I may be a little drowsy today, that's all,' I said. Pietro remained silent so I continued: 'Your grandmother says you want to ask me a few questions?'

'Yes, for my degree. If it's ok with you, that is. I have to write a piece based on an investigative interview. I saw you on the news yesterday – they showed you hitting an armed robber with your stick. I was watching with my girlfriend – she didn't know that Vovó works for you – and she said, 'What an amazing man, I wonder what made him do that?' and so I thought maybe that's something I could investigate.'

'I see.'

'But Vovó told me you were concussed and so you might not remember what happened.'

'I remember it all quite well.'

'Really?' Are you willing to talk about it?' Pietro looked at me so brightly, it would have been hard to refuse him even if I had wanted to.

'Yes,' I said.

A smile flashed across Pietro's face. 'So what made you decide to hit the gunman?' he asked. 'You must have known what could happen.'

'I was angry,' I said.

Pietro leant forward and took a notepad out of the satchel by his feet.

'You were angry because the gunmen were holding up the store?' asked Pietro.

'No, it wasn't so much that.' I paused for a moment and wondered whether I ought to tell Pietro what I had really felt. After all, my actual motive was less noble than the one he was imputing to me. There have been times in the past when I have been presented with a choice between a convenient half-truth or a less comfortable truth. It is probably fair to say that I have more often opted for the former. I do not know why I didn't do so this time. Perhaps it was the morphine, or perhaps the bright earnest curiosity in Pietro's eyes. I see the turmoil of these recent weeks as originating with that moment, in that decision to tell the truth.

'I was angry because, well, because those gunmen thought I was totally insignificant,' I said. 'They didn't even bother watching me. When you are old people often don't see you, or they appear to look through you. You get used to it; after all, growing old is a slow process. But while I was in that shop I'd been thinking back to when I was young, at the end of the war.'

I paused for a moment. Since first arriving in Brazil in 1947, I had never mentioned my commendation for the Iron Cross Second Class. Even in my first interview with Feldmann Breweries, when asked about my experiences during the war, I had merely stated that I had defended my country. That was a standard response back then, and I had not been asked any more questions. However, on this occasion I felt impelled to tell the truth.

'I was commended for the Iron Cross Second Class. Hauptmann Brandhoff told me I was the youngest hero he had ever met. I hadn't thought about that for a long time. Then those men broke in and looked through me as if I were a ghost. That's what made me angry.'

'*Nossa*. I didn't know that. How old were you when you were decorated?'

'I was never actually decorated. I was commended for a decoration in February 1945 but our position was overrun by the Allies shortly afterwards and I never heard any more about it. I was 15 years old.'

Pietro was scribbling in his notebook.

'So young? What did you do to be commended?'

'I defended my country,' I said.

'How?' asked Pietro.

These are, of course, different times. It did not surprise me that Pietro wanted to know more. Nevertheless, I had to gather my thoughts to formulate a reply. When you have not spoken about something for over half a century, the words do not come easily.

'By eliminating the lead tank of the Allied 7th Armoured Division,' I said.

Pietro's eyes widened. 'Really? How did you do that?'

'I dug a foxhole in the road and hid in it overnight,' I said. 'Then I fired a Panzerfaust at the tank once it had passed overhead.'

'Panzerfaust?' queried Pietro.

'A Panzerfaust is a grenade launcher, specially developed for use against tanks. It looks like a stick with a bulbous head, about half a metre long.' I thought back to those strange, unwieldy weapons, halfway between a lollipop and a phallus. I had been small for my age; carrying a Panzerfaust over a long distance was torturous for me.

Pietro was looking expectantly at me, so I continued: 'Panzerfausts were simple to use. They had sights attached to them and you just lined up the target and pulled the trigger. You had to be careful there was no one behind you – the flames would shoot out the back.'

'And you were only 15 when you destroyed the tank with a Panzerfaust?'

'Yes.'

'But how did you know what to do?'

I took a deep breath. It felt strange to be talking about these things, using these words which now sounded so unfamiliar but which once represented almost the entirety of my existence. 'Well, I'd been doing military training since I entered the Jungvolk, just after my eighth birthday. I didn't learn how to use a Panzerfaust until I was in the Hitler Jugend – that was a bit later, when I was twelve. Before the war you used to have to be fourteen, but things were speeded up for us because of the need for manpower.'

'So you were in the Hitler Jugend when you blew up the tank?' asked Pietro, still taking notes.

'Technically yes, although by then I had volunteered for the Volkssturm.'

Pietro looked confused. He repeated, 'Volkssturm?'

I could see this was going to get complicated. I said, 'The Volkssturm was the People's Army, volunteers who were too young or too old for the Wehrmacht. As a member of the Volkssturm you were officially a soldier and therefore protected by the Hague War Convention. You were formally protected whereas other combatants, if taken prisoner, could be shot as partisans. That was one reason for volunteering. Also, we were told that we would be given a gun and allowed to use it.'

'Did all Hitler Youths volunteer for the Volkssturm?'

'No. As a Hitler Youth, you could volunteer either for the Volkssturm or to be one of the Flakhelfer who manned the anti-aircraft batteries. However, in both cases you were still officially a member of the Hitler Youth. But once you turned 16, you left the Hitler Youth and were recruited straight into the Wehrmacht. At least, that's what is was like for my generation, but we were one of the last intakes.'

'Why didn't you volunteer for the Flakhelfer?'

'I certainly thought about it, and a couple of my friends volunteered. It was a good way of avoiding the boring HJ duties.'

'Like what?'

'Like marching and drill, things we had been doing for years. Also, we all craved action back then, and as a Flakhelfer there was a chance that you might see some.'

'So why didn't you volunteer?'

'Well, I enjoyed the sports in the HJ, particularly the climbing. Flakhelfer were being recruited in the summer of '44, but I knew I had a chance of being chosen to climb the Matterhorn with an elite team that same summer, so I didn't want to volunteer before then. Then, after the summer, there was more pressure to volunteer for the Volkssturm, so that's what I did.'

'What was the Volkssturm like?' asked Pietro.

'I hated it,' I said. 'The Volkssturm was a ragtag army of elderly civilians who had never held a spade, let alone a gun. They were supposed to be enthusiastic volunteers, though in fact most of them had been conscripted. They were totally unfit to fight. The whole thing was shambolic. And then there were a few of us recruited straight out of the HJ. We'd been doing military training since we were eight years old. We could march better than we could walk.'

Pietro looked astonished. 'You learned to march when you were eight years old?'

'Yes,' I replied.

'But you can't have marched very far, at that age.'

'On the contrary. That's when I marched all the way to Nuremberg for the rally. 500 kilometers.'

Pietro's eyes opened wide. Even to my own ears it sounded astonishing, but that's the way it was.

'Did you spend all your time in the Jungvolk marching?' asked Pietro.

'A lot of time, yes. But we also played wargames. And we learnt how to dig a foxhole and fire a panzerfaust. That's why I later found the Volkssturm so ridiculous. The Volkssturm instructors were trying to teach us the same techniques, but they didn't have a clue. We knew much more about foxholes and panzerfausts than they did – we'd been training all our lives. It would have been funny, if we hadn't also known that the future of Germany lay in the hands of these incompetents.'

My jaw had started to hurt again so I pressed the morphine button once more. As I did so I reflected that I had not spoken about my life in Germany in this much detail since, well, since for ever really. But I did not find it unpleasant. Unfamiliar, yes, but not unpleasant.

Pietro had stopped writing. He asked, *'Como vai o Seu Otto?* Are you tired?'

'I am a little tired, but stay until you have to leave,' I said.

'If you're certain...' Pietro looked at me for confirmation. I nodded very slightly with my head. 'Well,' he said, 'I wanted to ask, how did you actually destroy the tank? What did you do? Who gave the orders?'

'The tank, yes. In fact, there were no orders. It was my own idea – that is why it was later considered an act of exceptional bravery. Many of the Volkssturm would have tried to stop me had they known. They didn't want to antagonise the invaders in any way. I can understand that now. After all, many of them had wives and children to think of. But it was different for us back then. We thought very little of our own lives. All that mattered was Germany. Germany had to be defended; we never questioned that. Already the enemy had crossed the Rhine – that was a heavy blow. The Russians were advancing in the east, raping girls as young as eight and women as old as eighty. The posters and the radio broadcasts left us in no doubt about that. For me, defending Germany was the same as protecting my mother from the barbarous Russians – that's how I saw it.'

'Did all Hitler Youths see it that way, do you think?'

'I think so, yes. You have to understand that we had been brought up to believe that Germany was everything, we were nothing. We had grown up with those songs.'

'Which songs?'

'The Hitlerjugend songs.'

'Like what? Can you remember one?'

'There were so many, let me think.' I closed my eyes. At first I heard nothing. Then, one by one, the melodies of my childhood returned to me. Once I had the melody, the words came easily. However, I did not want to sing them there and then; it would not have been right. So I recited for Pietro a few lines which I remembered:

'*Deutschland, du sollst leuchtend stehen, Mögen wir auch untergehen...* "Germany, you must shine even if we must die." That's one I used to like. There were many. Before I even joined the Jungvolk I'd heard them sung by the columns of Hitler Youths marching in the streets. My God, those boys were impressive, marching in step, singing in unison. We ran alongside the columns trying to pick up the words but we didn't learn them properly until we became Jungvolk ourselves. Then we sang them on marches and at the meetings. Later, when we went to the summer camp in the mountains, we sang them at night around the campfire.'

As I lay with my eyes closed in that hospital bed in Florianópolis, my jaw and hip fractured, my mind drifting on an opiate sea, I thought to myself how far away those campfires were. Another world, another life. And yet the memory was so vivid – my nostrils twitched in recollection of the scent of pine which used to be almost intoxicating, so clean and pure. Pine and the cool, cavernous smell of the Drachenwand, that mighty rockface above the campfire, where we climbed by day and above which a pale moon would nightly rise. Standing in front of the fire and facing us is Kurt Gruber, the 17-year-old leader of our *Schar* and a hero in our eyes. Theatrical as ever, he tells us once again the legend of the *Nibelungen*, this time the story of the slaughter of the faithful Burgundians in Etzel's castle. Siggi is sitting beside me, enraptured. Strange that he is the best climber of us all – his movements so natural on the rock – and yet he has told me that he prefers listening to the *Nibelungenlied* to climbing. His face is beautiful in the firelight. If only I could always remember him that way.

'Seu Otto?'

I opened my eyes and saw that Pietro was still beside my bed.

'And the tank?' he asked.

Yes, the tank.

Chapter 6

THESE ARE the worst of times. I am in the Volkssturm barracks at Wulfen. The wind whistles between the planks of the walls. We have used up our allowance of wood; the fire in the grate is out and it is as cold inside the building as it is outside. I am cleaning my boots for the hundredth time. I would prefer to be cleaning a gun but there are not enough to go around. Herr Weiss is sitting beside me. He was my maths teacher. Technically, he still is my maths teacher, but he has given up trying to teach me. He knows that I cannot concentrate on numbers. But he has a gun, because he is older than me. He doesn't even bother to clean it. He has no intention of ever using it, that is clear to anyone. He is like the other old men in this room: Herr Flach the retired chemistry teacher and Herr Seibert the baker. If the Americans walked into the barracks now, not a single one of them would fire a shot. They have no stomach for a fight. And yet they all have guns.

Herr Seibert is fiddling with the radio. We pretend not to listen, but we are listening. We have not heard the Führer's voice on the radio since Silvester. It is now February. That's two months. Why has he not spoken? He used to speak every week. So long as he is in control, Germany is not lost. The Führer will have a plan to get us out of this mess. But I wish he would speak.

The Volksradio reports small victories. Planes shot down over Köln. British airmen captured. But we also know that the Russians are advancing in the east. They want revenge. They are animals, raping women and murdering babies. And, in the west, the British have just crossed the Rhine. It has not yet been broadcast on the radio, but Max told me. He is a Flakhelfer and they know these things ahead of time.

Perhaps it is fortunate that Siggi is not alive to see these days. He would have taken it very hard. The Rhine, Germany's sacred river in which Siggi's namesake hid the *Rheingold*, has been crossed by an invading army. What would Siggi have done? He would not have sat here polishing his boots, that's for sure.

'*Otto, bist bereit?*' asks Herr Weiss. It is noon and we must cycle to the Flak batteries where Max, Sepp and the other boys work. Since they are still nominally part of the Hitler Youth they are still supposed to go to school. Obviously that is not possible at the moment – they are rarely allowed to leave the Flak batteries. Herr Weiss cycles out there to give a maths lesson during their lunch break. They pay no more attention than I do.

It's ridiculous that the Flakhelfer are still expected to attend lessons. The reason they signed up as Flakhelfer in the first place was because they were in a hurry to be done with the HJ. Siggi and I both wanted to join for that reason; we were impatient to be real soldiers. In the end we didn't, but that was only because we were given the opportunity to climb with an élite HJ team last summer; neither of us wanted to give that up.

Max and Sepp signed up as Flakhelfer as fast as they

could, but I'm not sure they really knew what they were letting themselves in for. They knew they would have to load and fire the anti-aircraft guns, but I don't think they knew how often the installations would get hit, and how little they could do about it. More importantly, they wanted to be real soldiers, but the other soldiers at the emplacements treat them like children. The officers refuse to give them razorblades and say they wouldn't know how to use them anyway. Their ration packs contain sweets rather than cigarettes. I think that's what annoys them most, and that's why I always bring them some cigarettes myself. Cigarettes are not hard to get hold of in the Volkssturm; all we do is smoke.

Herr Weiss and I get onto our bikes and start pedalling towards Borken. Our progress is slow – the dirt road is frozen in some parts and slushy in others. Herr Weiss's rucksack full of schoolbooks bounces up and down on his back. He is already out of breath. He was not made for this. Imagine if he had to fight, what a joke.

Briefly we cycle through the woods. The road is better here. The tall pines protect the surface from the weak winter sun and there is no thaw. Leaving the woods again, I can already make out the top of the Flak installations above the lip of the hollow in which they nestle. Once again the road is slushy and uneven. To the right and to the left of us stretch fields of snow.

Arriving at the installation, Herr Weiss and I let our bikes fall into the snow. There are soldiers standing around, stamping their feet and blowing into their hands. They look tense. Many are wounded veterans from the Eastern Front. They have thin, haggard faces. Faces marked by suffering. Max spots me from a distance and waves. His boyish features and curly blond hair could not be in greater contrast to these hard grey men.

One of the officers spots us.

'Jungs!' he shouts. *'Das Kindermädchen ist da!'* The other soldiers laugh. Max hears it too but he merely smiles. He has learnt the hard way that it is best to pretend he doesn't care.

I give Max the cigarettes I have brought. He claps me on the back. Other boys arrive in twos and threes. Some of them I know from the HJ at Borken. Others I know from the summer camp in the mountains. Some I have met through Max. A few I do not know at all.

'They say it will probably come tonight,' Max whispers to me.

There have been rumours of the advance of the 7th Armoured Division for a number of days now. That's why the atmosphere is so tense. There will be air raids to prepare the way for the column. Borken is a gateway to the Ruhr and there is little doubt that this installation will be in the thick of it. What's more, the information which the Flak installations receive is usually reliable. If they think there'll be a raid tonight, then it will probably happen.

'But you have an important game of dominoes tonight, I have no doubt,' says Max, elbowing me in the ribs. For some reason everyone thinks that the Volkssturm just play dominoes. It's true that we don't do a lot, but I have never played dominoes. Not once. I usually have to shine my boots.

'No,' I say.

Sepp chimes in: 'So Otto, what will you be doing tonight? Shining your boots?'

I look at Sepp. He has dark rings under his eyes. I know he barely sleeps when he is at the battery. He is very frightened. I feel for him. He was with us at the summer camp; he was a good friend then. Now he channels his fear into sarcasm. But really, it is not right that he should be here fearing for his life, terrified of the next raid, while I shine my boots. That is never how it was supposed to be. It is not what I want. Not what Siggi would have wanted. But what *would* Siggi have wanted?

'Or maybe you can climb the Volkssturm flagpole tonight?' says Sepp. That is a cheap shot. A few of the better climbers at the summer camp once shinned up the flagpole for a dare, but that's not why we were chosen for the elite team. And I certainly did not join the elite team in order to avoid the Flak batteries. But Sepp knows that.

Herr Weiss calls us. We go over to him. There are about twelve of us. He knows we won't pay attention to the lesson. In fact, we could just walk off if we chose. But we don't walk off. Herr Weiss is not a great teacher, and the subject is tedious, but it reminds us all of better times. Other classrooms in warmer, sunnier places. Times when the breaks between lessons were filled with excited chatter about the latest victories. Even back then the Führer said there would be dark days ahead. Well, they are here now. And this is the real test of our courage. We must not be found wanting.

Herr Weiss attracts our attention as best he can, but we are all daydreaming. Most of the time we dream of food. But I have smoked three cigarettes and I feel a little sick. I think about the summer camp, high in the Bavarian Alps. I think about the hot summer sun and the cold, clear waters of the lake. I think about Siggi. Then I have an idea.

Herr Weiss collects our books. The other boys return to their stations. I grab Max by the sleeve. Sepp is next to him.

'Listen,' I say, 'I need your help. I can't shine my boots tonight. There is something I want to do.'

'What?' asks Max.

'Something big,' I say. 'Something that would make Siggi proud. But I need your help. Will you meet me by the edge of the woods when you come off duty?' I know the Flakhelfer get four hours off to go home and sleep before the night shift.

'What do you want to do?' repeats Max.

'I want to dig a foxhole in the Heiden-Borken road,' I say. 'So if the advance comes tonight or tomorrow, I will be ready.'

Sepp narrows his eyes as if he doesn't believe me. 'You're crazy,' he says.

Max also looks at me quizzically. There is silence. They are both waiting for me to reply.

'The harder a task is, the greater its value as a dedication and an offering,' I quote from the Führer's speech at Nuremberg. Still they are silent. 'So, at five o'clock, at the edge of the woods?' I say again.

Max places his hand on my shoulder. '*Bis dann*,' he says.

*

I cycle back to the barracks at Wulfen with Herr Weiss. I think about what I have just committed to. I know all about digging foxholes. I have dug more foxholes than I can remember. It is a central part of HJ training. Even the Volkssturm instructors have us digging foxholes. The foxholes they make us dig are designed for grown men. They are far too wide. They would cave in if a vehicle passed anywhere near them. If the situation were different, the incompetence of the Volkssturm would be funny. As it is, it is tragic.

In the HJ we were trained to dig a foxhole no wider than fifty centimetres. It is lucky that I am thin – I can lie in one of them without any problems. But I have never put the training into practice. I know that the 12th SS Panzer Division under Panzermeyer had many successes with foxholes in the defence of Caen last summer. It is not surprising – the regiment is composed entirely of Hitlerjugend. The boys on the Eastern Front have been using them too, but the Russians have grown wise to them. They now travel in closely packed convoys so there is no room to spring out once a vehicle has passed overhead. In the past, the drivers were more frightened of landmines; they used to leave larger gaps. At least, that is what I have heard. I have also heard that some HJ boys have started destroying tanks by firing the Panzerfaust vertically upwards, out of the foxhole. Often this kills the boy too. They are very brave on the Eastern Front.

Panzermeyer. Now he is a real hero. Strange that we have heard so little of him, of late. His real name is Kurt Meyer. SS BrigadeFührer Kurt Meyer. They call him Panzermeyer because, when he was training to be a policeman before the war, he wanted to play a prank on a friend and climbed onto the roof of a two-storey building to empty a bucket of water on his friend's head. Meyer slipped and fell, landing on his feet but suffering over twenty fractures. The doctors did not expect him to survive, but he did survive. They called him 'Panzermeyer' because he was as tough as a tank. He went on to fight in the Balkans, in Greece and at Kharkov, proving his bravery time and again. He was awarded the Swords to the Knights Cross with Oakleaves – that is very rare. He was one of our heroes in the Hitler Youth. Now he commands the 12th SS Panzer Division Hitlerjugend, composed entirely of HJ boys born in 1926. What an honour it would be to serve under him! But instead I am in the cowardly Volkssturm, cycling down a muddy road with an old schoolmaster. Well, tonight I will show them.

We return our bicycles to the bicycle storeroom. Herr Weiss makes his way to the mess tent. I pretend that I have to fix a puncture. I get the keys to the storeroom from Volkssturm main office. No one can be bothered to accompany me, as I expected. I take three spades and just about manage to tie them to my rucksack. 'Guns of Peace', we used to call them before the war. Then I break open one of the rectangular wooden crates at the back of the shed and remove a Panzerfaust-30. It is one of the earlier models, but it is the one I have fired most often. I remove my leather belt and strap the Panzerfaust to the horizontal bar of my bicycle. I return the keys to the main office. Now I just have to wait.

I am not hungry. I am too excited to sleep. I smoke one cigarette, then another. It is only four o'clock but already the washed out winter light is fading from the sky. There is a faint red glow in the west but it is nothing like the spectacular sunsets of autumn. Just a tentative reminder of how gloriously the sun can set, no more than that. Everything these days seems like a reminder of past glories.

I get on my bike and cycle back towards the Flak installations. I am weighed down by the three spades and the Panzerfaust. The poor light makes it hard to see the ruts and holes in the road. My progress is slow, but the fact that I have to concentrate so hard means that I do not think about the task ahead.

I arrive at the edge of the Teutoburger woods a little early. The tall pines rise up either side of me. If I stare at their tops the whole world appears to spin. I look across the snowfields towards the hollow where the installations are. I see two small figures on bicycles cycling towards me.

Max and Sepp have brought their rucksacks. I give them a spade each. We continue through the woods, towards Borken. This is the road along which the advance is predicted. Coming out of the woods we can see a long way in every direction. The road itself is not wide but the land either side is flat and firm; good terrain for an advancing division. Though we are out in the open now, the woods continue to flank the road fifty metres away on the right hand side. We stop where a small finger of trees sticks out closer to the road.

'Here is good,' I say.

I look at Max and Sepp. They are very quiet. It had crossed my mind that they might try to dissuade me, but they are too tired for that. What is more, they have to be back at the battery in a few hours for the nightshift. If the advance happens as predicted, then the bombardment tonight will be heavy. And if they are discovered away from their posts after the appointed time, then there is a chance that they will be shot as deserters. We have all heard stories of HJ boys who have been shot as deserters.

Max and Sepp leave their bikes by the side of the road. I hide mine under a bush, just a few metres from the woods. Then I mark out a rectangle in the middle of the road. We begin to dig. The Heiden-Borken road is narrow; that is good when you dig a foxhole. If the road is wide you don't know exactly where the vehicles will pass. A lot of HJ boys have died when a tire or tank track went directly over a foxhole and collapsed it. Of course, the narrower the hole, the less chance of that. Fortunately, I can fit into a very narrow hole.

From time to time one of us shovels the earth into a rucksack and carries it to the nearby woods. Here, behind a tree, we empty it. Important not to leave any traces. When the hole has been dug, I climb in. I lie on my back with my arms folded and my hands touching my shoulders, like a young Pharaoh. I practice sitting up quickly and climbing out; the hole is just wide enough. Then I lie down again and Max places the Panzerfaust on top of me. Max and Sepp cover the hole with sticks, then cover the sticks with earth. The occasional small clod falls on me. I think to myself that there must be skeletons interred like this all round Germany – boys who were buried alive when the hole collapsed. It is not a good thought and I try to banish it from my mind.

Max and Sepp continue to scratch around on the surface for a while. 'Cover the tracks well,' I say.

'*Keine Angst,*' says Max. His voice comes to me muffled through the sticks and the earth above me. Then they both wish me good luck. 'See you tomorrow,' I say. '*Na klar,*' they reply.

*

It is very cold in the foxhole. Water starts to gather beneath me and to seep into my overcoat. I'm wearing all the clothes I own but it is not enough and I soon start to shiver. It is impossible to sleep. Nor can I tell the time, though after a while I hear the drone of aircraft high overhead. They must have begun the bombardment. I think of Max and Sepp in their snowy hollow, sitting ducks for the big American bombers.

Now I am afraid. I remember the speech given by the wounded Officer who presented Siggi and I with our daggers after we won the climbing competition. 'Only a fool does not feel fear,' he had said. I am afraid of pain. I am afraid of dying in this little hole. But even more than that, I am afraid of doing nothing. Of watching while Germany falls. I am afraid of being ashamed of myself. I am afraid of being unworthy of Siggi's memory, of being a coward, of ending up like Herr Weiss. Or like my father.

My mind begins to wander. I try to think pleasant thoughts. I remember standing pressed against the granite of the *Drachenwand*, the hot sun on my shoulders. I remember the sweat trickling down my back. I remember the false route I took, and having to track back. I remember hauling myself onto the ledge beside Siggi. There is no reproach in his eyes, though my error might have cost us the competition. Rather, he beams at me before setting off to lead the last pitch. He is in his element. How naturally he moves on the rock, his hands merely flitting over the craggy surface. The smell of morning dew and moss still in the shady cracks. The smell of pine growing stronger as we near the top of the cliff.

There is no way for me to measure the passing of time.

The aeroplanes continue to drone overhead. From where I am lying, it is impossible to tell whether they are coming or going. My teeth are chattering. It is bitterly cold in the foxhole but I have long since ceased to feel my limbs. I have tucked my gloved hands beneath my armpits and the Panzerfaust lies heavy on my chest. More droning, then silence. Utter silence. The silence of the grave.

*

I notice the merest hint of a grey triangle between the sticks above me. The triangle solidifies; the pale dawn filters through the cracks. And now, in the distance, I hear the sound of machinery; a menacing hum, like a beehive high in a tree. Minute by minute the hum grows louder. The hum becomes a roar and the earth around me begins to shake.

The vibrations dislodge a few of the sticks above me and small bits of mud fall onto my face. Now the roar is a howl, the deafening howl of a tank at close range. For a second the strips of light above me disappear and I realise that the tank has passed over me. I sit up and thrust the Panzerfaust through the sticks and mud above me. My arms move sluggishly but they lift me out of the foxhole. In front of me I see the back of the tank which has just driven over me. Looking back, I am surprised to see the rest of the column a hundred metres behind. Perhaps they were expecting landmines; whatever the reason, I have been granted a few vital seconds before the next vehicle is on top of me.

I raise the Panzerfaust until the tube is under my armpit, then I line up the lower back panel of the tank with the rim of the warhead and the rear sight. I pull the trigger. The warhead appears to travel in slow motion but its flight is true. It strikes the tank square in the middle of the weak rear plate. The tank explodes in a ball of flame and a rush of hot air blows over me.

I am dazed by the explosion. Everything seems unreal. I cannot hear anything. I run towards the bush where my bicycle is hidden. I wrench the bicycle free. Not far in front of me the earth is being torn up by volley after volley of machine gun fire from the vehicles behind. I am about to leap onto the bicycle when I see a German officer standing at the edge of the wood, just twenty metres away. He waves frantically. He wants me to follow him. But I don't want to leave my bicycle behind. I am in two minds. Then my hearing returns and I become aware of the rattle of artillery. The officer waves one more time before diving into the woods. I see a number of other German soldiers retreating. I throw my bicycle to the ground, then I run for the margin of the woods.

We run for almost an hour, until we reach the Wehrmacht HQ outside Heiden. I am a good runner and the distance is not a problem for me, although the snow makes it hard work. When we reach the HQ I am sweating despite the cold. And I feel weak. The last soldiers to arrive are bent double, hands on knees, trying to catch their breath. I can see from their uniforms that they are from an elite unit. I am proud that I was able to keep up with them, though unlike them I am not weighed down with a weapon or a pack.

Clouds of condensation rise from the soldiers. They remove their helmets which steam in the cold morning air as if they contained hot soup. Other soldiers come out from the HQ to meet us. They are accompanied by a number of shepherd dogs who similarly send up little puffs of condensation. Two of the soldiers pull out packs of cigarettes. They each place one in their mouths and pass round a box of matches. Then they lean back against the broad trunk of a pine tree and exhale slowly. The smoke is caught in the sunlight that has started to filter between the branches. The soldiers stamp the snow from their shoes and say something which I do not catch. Then the taller of the two looks over at me. '*Gut gemacht,*' he says and throws me the pack of cigarettes with the matches inside. I feel very proud.

Chapter 7

B Y THE time I get home it is too dark to go surfing. I am disappointed – I haven't felt like surfing for a while, but I do right now. Perhaps it is because of the long conversation I had with Seu Otto. I asked him what made him strike the gunman in the store. He told me that he was angry that they thought he was of no consequence. The cover of a magazine had made him think about his childhood in the Hitler Youth. He was even commended for the Iron Cross second class; he told me how he destroyed the lead tank of the 7th Armoured Division. I can't stop thinking about it. Sometimes, when I have ideas spinning around inside my head, it can help to paddle out and sit on my board in the ocean. Things often seem to fall into the right place when I do that, and it barely matters whether I catch a wave or not. Though of course, that's not the way my sponsors would see it.

I am in awe of Otto's bravery when he was only fifteen years old. Perhaps it is easier to be brave when you are younger; you don't think of the consequences. There are certainly waves that I used to ride a few years ago which I wouldn't ride now. Surfing can be dangerous too, but it is dangerous in a different way. For one, the choices you make are your own. No one forces you to surf.

The way Otto described it, no one forced him to spend

the night in the foxhole or to blow up the tank. That's why he was commended for the Iron Cross second class. It's true that he'd been training for just such an opportunity for years, but it also seems he was driven to do it, just like he was driven to strike the gunman in the store.

*

Tomorrow is my night at Divino, so I drive into Lagoa to hand out fliers. I wander up and down the main street. There are many tourists, mostly drunk. I give them the fliers and watch as they take one look before letting them drop to the street. Usually I would find that depressing, but tonight it doesn't seem to matter.

I still cannot stop thinking about Otto. It is strange that the cranky old man is the same person as the brave young warrior. I suppose the incident in the shop proves it, but still, it is hard to picture. It makes me wonder about all the other old people I see wandering about – they all have pasts and histories which may be very different from the present. Unlikely to be as extraordinary as Otto's, but nevertheless, still not as predictable as I usually assume.

Marina returns home shortly after me. It is early, for her. She tells me there was a fight in the bar and the police closed it down for the night. Then she asks about my meeting with Seu Otto.

'It was very interesting,' I say.

'Tell me,' she says. But for some reason I don't want to. It is too early, I don't yet know what to think.

Marina is disappointed. She thinks I am refusing to tell her in order to spite her.

'I promise I'll tell you when I'm ready,' I say. She nods, unconvinced. 'He is an extraordinary man,' I add.

'Well, have you worked out how you are going to make any money out of this?' she asks.

'No,' I say. 'Not yet. But it's not just about the money.'

Marina laughs, though it comes out as a snort. It is not an attractive sound. 'Look Pietro,' she says, 'I am happy that you are enjoying yourself with your Seu Otto, but that's not going to help you get a job, or a degree, or stop losing money at your damn nightclub.'

She spits the last words out and I am surprised by her vehemence. Then I think to myself that she is probably still angry because of the rumours about Sara.

'I know, I know,' I say. 'I'll work something out.'

'What?' she asks. 'What will you work out?'

I am not sure what I will work out. But it feels as if Seu Otto holds some secret, something I must find out. It's not that I think he's hiding something from me. Maybe it's just that I admire his courage, his willingness to dedicate himself to something. Maybe I could use some of those qualities myself. Talking to him certainly makes me wonder about the way I live my life.

'I'm sorry Pietro,' says Marina. I notice that her eyes are glassy.

'Are you ok?' I ask.

'I didn't mean to nag,' she says. 'It's just that I want you to be the best you can be. And you're better than this, than the girls at Divino and handing out fliers and promoting.'

Now she really does have tears in her eyes.

'This could be your big break. You could write a story, sell it to a paper, clear your debts. It could help you get a job, something with a real future, away from this damn island.'

I wrap my arms around her. I don't understand why she is crying, but girls can be like that. But she's right too. This is a big opportunity.

Chapter 8

WHEN I awoke, the ward was bright with sunlight. My jaw and my hip both hurt much more than on the day before. I reached up for the button on the morphine drip but the drip was gone. I rang for the nurse. As I waited for her to arrive, I noticed a pile of cards and flowers on the table next to my bed.

Fernanda came in carrying a number of parcels in her arms. She placed them on the table.

'*Bom dia, Seu Otto,*' she said. 'You are popular.'

'They are all for me?' I asked.

'*Sim, com certeza.*'

'Who from?'

'I don't know, they arrived in the post,' replied Fernanda. 'How do you feel?'

'Not so good. Everything is hurting.'

'I can give you another morphine drip. But have a look at all your cards, Seu Otto. You are very famous. And you had a visit from a very sympathetic boy last night.'

'Yes, he is sympathetic. So you met him?'

'Oh yes, I spoke to him after you had fallen asleep. He said he was going to write about what a hero you were during the war.'

I suddenly felt a little flushed, though not with pride. I am not usually as outspoken as I had been with Pietro. In fact, I rarely speak about the war. It is not good to talk too much of one's own achievements. In any case, unless you were there you cannot understand how things were.

Fernanda pushed my shoulders forward and plumped my pillow.

'Did you not enjoy the visit?' she asked. 'You look very thoughtful.'

'I did enjoy it, but I fear I may have said too much. I do not usually talk so much.'

'You can never say too much,' said Fernanda. 'Talking is the best cure. The patients who talk the most recover the fastest. Keeping things bottled up inside is what kills people. I've seen it happen.'

'Really?'

'Yes, I promise you. Now here are two painkillers for you to swallow, and here is your water. I will see about the drip. Dr. da Silva will be here soon and he will tell you about the operation tomorrow.'

*

I started opening the letters piled on the table beside me. A couple were from acquaintances, but the majority were from people who had seen the footage on the news – the channel had also announced which hospital I had been taken to – and wanted to wish me well. One parcel contained pictures drawn by a class of school children whose teacher had shown them the footage in order to 'subvert common stereotypes of the elderly.' Good luck to her. In any case, I was just leafing through the drawings, ranging from stickmen cartoons to technicolour abstraction, when Dr. da Silva arrived.

'Ah, Seu Otto, your notoriety is causing problems for our internal post,' he said.

'I'm sorry.'

'*Não há de quê*. It is not everyday that we have a real-life hero in the hospital.'

Dr. da Silva turned to the back-lit screen beside the bed and pointed to the x-rays that had been taken when I first arrived. He explained to me the procedure for the hip replacement. He would make an incision over the buttocks to expose the hip joint, then he would cut out and remove the broken head of the femur and clean out the remaining cartilage. After that, he would implant the new socket and insert the metal stem into the femur before fixing the artificial components in place with a special cement. Then the muscles and tendons would be laid back against the bone and the incision would be closed. After surgery I would be back on a morphine drip for up to three days, and I would also have IV lines in place for fluids and nutrition. I would wake up wearing inflatable pneumatic compression stockings to prevent blood clots; I did not like the sound of them at all. Dr. da Silva said I would have to try to move the joint as soon as possible after surgery, already on the first day. I would have physiotherapy for the next five days before leaving the hospital and would continue the programme from home, coming in to see the therapist daily. The operation was booked for the following afternoon; I was not allowed to eat anything beforehand.

I confess that I was apprehensive about the operation. Nevertheless, I think it is important to remind oneself of the advances that medicine has made; it is too easy to take them for granted. What is more, Dr. da Silva said that the results of hip surgery are excellent, that over eighty percent of patients need no help walking. And I would almost certainly be able to swim as well as before.

Anna-Maria arrived later that morning and began to fuss in a most exhausting manner. Perhaps I was just tired, but I found myself being quite short with her. However, she told me that Pietro had enjoyed our conversation the evening before and that he hoped he could visit again that very afternoon. Earlier that morning the recollection of laying bare the past had left an unpleasant taste in my mouth, and I had resolved not to repeat the mistake. However, hearing that Pietro was so keen to come again made me reconsider. I did not wish to disappoint him and, what is more, his presence would enable me to escape from Anna-Maria's excessive solicitude. The well-meant ministrations of women can be so trying.

*

A nurse came in to replace my morphine drip after lunch. I may have celebrated its return a little too enthusiastically since I subsequently had a very peculiar experience. I was slipping in and out of pleasant dreams when I saw the door to the ward open and Siggi himself came in and sat by my bed. He looked young and healthy. I knew I was dreaming, but it was such a pleasure to see him, and to remember his features so clearly, that I wanted to extend the dream indefinitely. After a while, Siggi said, 'Seu Otto, are you awake?'

This surprised me. The characters in my dreams do not usually inquire as to the state of the dreamer. I was also surprised that the voice sounded like Pietro's, not Siggi's.

I was about to reply when I saw that Siggi's face was

dissolving into Pietro's, as if they had previously been layered on top of each other.

'Seu Otto, are you ok?' asked Pietro, for it was clearly Pietro who was now addressing me.

'Yes, yes, I'm fine,' I replied.

'Thank you for talking to me last night. I was wondering…'

I couldn't concentrate on what Pietro was saying. The image of Siggi sitting in that very chair was still so fresh and vivid in my mind. What was the meaning of this?

There is certainly a strong physical resemblance between Pietro and Siggi, but I think it is more than that. Siggi was always very curious, always asking questions, as Pietro is doing now. Asking questions was not encouraged in the Hitler Youth, and Siggi would have got into more trouble if it hadn't been for his natural charm, which meant that even the strictest instructors treated him with a degree of indulgence. Pietro has natural charm too – I don't think I would so willingly subject myself to this interrogation if it weren't for that quality. Vague as this may sound, the way I feel when talking to Pietro reminds me of the way I felt when I was with Siggi all those years ago. It is a very pleasant way to feel.

Indeed, I cannot shake the sense that there may be a real connection between Pietro and Siggi, something more than merely a projection of my own mind. Could Pietro be related to Siggi? Hadn't Pietro's grandfather Horst been born here in Brazil without knowing who his father was? Could Siggi have been Horst's father? Extremely unlikely, but perhaps just possible.

'Seu Otto?'

'I'm sorry Pietro, I'm a little distracted today. What were you asking?'

'I was just saying that I'd really like to write an investigative piece on the Hitler Youth – how it worked, who was involved, what it was like. I think I could get a very good grade with that. And then I have the chance of getting a decent job.'

'I see.'

'So, would that be ok?'

I thought for a moment. I had been worried that Pietro was going to ask to do a piece all about me. In fact, I'd been preparing to tell him that I wasn't entirely comfortable discussing my own achievements. But that no longer seemed necessary. I could explain to Pietro how in the beginning we joined the Jungvolk, and about the attraction it held for us. I could tell him about the initiation at Marienburg and the long march to Nuremberg. I could tell him all this without having to dwell on my own achievements.

'Yes, we can talk about that,' I said.

'*Beleza.*' Pietro took his notebook from his bag, then he sat back in his chair, his silver pen poised. 'So,' he said, 'how did you come to join the Hitler Youth?'

'Hmmmm,' I said, 'that is a very big question.'

Chapter 9

I GREW up in a suburb of Bochum, in the industrial Ruhr. Everyone was very poor in the 30s; it was the depression. My father was an engineer but even for him there was no security until the Führer came to power. I had an older brother who died of tuberculosis before I was born. I know my mother thought that he would not have died if we had been richer, if she had been able to take him away to the mountains or to the sea.

I do not have many happy memories of the small house I grew up in. There was always something sad about it, and about my parents. I spent as much time as I could out of doors, playing in the streets and around the workshops. As far back as I can remember, I used to see the Hitler Youth boys marching in the streets and singing. They were purposeful and impressive in their uniforms, and I hoped that one day I would be like them.

At school we were encouraged to volunteer for the Jungvolk. The government had decreed that all teachers had to belong to the National Socialist Teachers' Alliance. They had to wear swastikas on their lapels. Teachers who didn't join were dismissed. A couple of the older teachers at my school refused to join; they had fought in the trenches in the First War and they distrusted the Führer. They were removed from their posts and replaced by much younger men who were handsome and athletic and encouraged us to sign up. The teachers who left had been old and stuffy; the ones who now arrived were dynamic and inspiring.

At that time there was a sense of shame in the air. Shame of being poor, of having lost the war, of the humiliating dictates of Versailles. When the Führer came to power and his policies started to create jobs and wealth, people became optimistic about the future. My father bought a Volksradio. Neighbours used to come round to listen to the Führer's weekly broadcasts in our kitchen. We all crowded around the Volksradio, although there was often so much static that you could barely make out the words. One of the first broadcasts I heard was about the remilitarization of the Rhineland. I remember my father embracing me then – that was very unlike him. I felt proud that once again there were German soldiers on German soil. I was only six years old and already I loved the Führer.

A couple of years later I joined the Jungvolk. I didn't know anything about politics but I knew this was what the Führer wanted; that was enough. My friends all joined and the new teachers praised us for it. Also, we were happy to be connected to the National Socialists. It's hard to imagine now, but at that time 'Nazi' was not a bad word. The National Socialists were the most modern, the most efficient, the most stylish of the political parties. They were very appealing. I wanted to be one of the boys marching in the streets; I wanted to be like the young athletic teachers who had replaced the two old fuddy-duddies. What is more, joining the Jungvolk gave us a form of freedom, freedom to oppose the older teachers and our own parents.

If you were in the Jungvolk you didn't have to go to

school on Saturdays – you played war games instead. There was nothing the teachers could do about it. The meetings were called *Dienst* and the place we met at was our *Heim*. You couldn't get into trouble for not doing homework if it was because of *Dienst*. My parents didn't like me going out alone at night but they couldn't stop me. In our Jungvolk uniforms we were no longer treated like children; we did not always have to obey adults. It was intoxicating.

In fact, nothing was more intoxicating than the initiation into the Jungvolk itself. It was on that occasion that I first felt a sense of history, and greatness, and solemnity. The initiation took place on the same night every year, the 19th April, the eve of the Führer's birthday. That was no coincidence; it was a birthday present - Baldur von Schirach delivering Germany's youth to their Führer. The Volksradio used to broadcast the ceremony from inside Marienburg castle. I had first heard the broadcast in 1936, when I was just six yeas old, and it had sent shivers down my spine. Of course, I did not know then that I would be one of the boys chosen to be initiated at Marienburg two years later.

Germany was divided into *Gaue*; each *Gau* sent a contingent of boys to Marienburg. I was part of the East Ruhr contingent. I do not know whether our names were picked out of a hat, or whether the HJ instructors, who were also teachers at the school, had selected us personally. I remember standing in assembly one morning and hearing my name read out. I was given a letter to bring home to my parents and a week later my mother accompanied me to the train station in Bochum. Ten or so of my classmates, whose names had also been read out, were already there, as were the two young teachers.

We took the overnight train to Danzig. I was eight years old and this was the first night I had ever spent away from home. We climbed into the narrow bunks of the sleeper compartment as soon as it grew dark, but we were too excited to sleep. We whispered to each other late into the night. We had all heard the broadcasts of past initiation ceremonies but most of us had never left Bochum before and we had little idea of what to expect.

We arrived in Danzig on the morning of the 19th April. It was a beautiful spring morning, very sunny and breezy. Herr Reiter – one of the young teachers accompanying us – had grown up just outside Danzig. He led us from the train station through the narrow, twisting streets of the Old Town. The corners and doorways were decorated with carved stone gargoyles which fascinated and frightened me in equal measure. We walked around the dark, brooding tower which housed the torture chamber in medieval times. Herr Reiter told us about the thumb screw, the Judas cradle, the pear of anguish, the brazen bull and other medieval torture devices. By the time he'd finished we were all quite pale. From the tower he led us down to the river to see Europe's largest wooden crane. Normally this would have bored me but now I found it a pleasant relief.

In the afternoon we returned to the railway station and took a train to Zoppot, ten minutes away to the north. In the 20s and 30s Zoppot was a fashionable seaside resort where many politicians and industrialists used to spend their holidays. On the train Herr Reiter told us that Zoppot had Europe's longest pier. It seemed to me that everything I was coming into contact with was the biggest and the best.

I had never seen the sea before. Only one or two of my classmates had; they were boys whose parents were wealthy and had taken them on holiday. So, I was very excited when the long white wooden pier came into view. Herr Reiter said we could have a race; we ran towards it as fast as we could. When the instructors had caught up with us, they led us down to the beach. I didn't know how to swim then, though of course I had to learn as soon as I joined the Jungvolk. Later I became a good swimmer. But on that sunny morning the instructors let us take off our shoes and socks and walk in the surf. The water was very cold but I liked the feeling. My feet hurt at first but soon they started to warm up from within; I had never experienced that before.

After a while I left the others in the surf and wandered barefoot up the beach. I wandered a long way. I would certainly have been in trouble if the instructors had realised that I had gone so far by myself. But I was so absorbed watching my own naked feet on the sand that I lost all sense of time. After a bit the wind started to pick up and the fine white grains swirled over the surface and whipped at my ankles. At times I even lost sight of my feet. I was staring very hard at my toes, trying to distinguish them among the swirling sand particles, when I saw a small, round stone – almost a perfect sphere. I picked it up; it was very light. I spat on it, rubbed it against my shorts and then held it up to the sun. Frozen in its honey-coloured centre I saw the delicately veined wing of an insect. I walked back to the others and showed the stone to Herr Reiter.

'That, Otto, is a piece of amber,' he said.

'From someone's necklace?' I asked.

'No. Amber is used in jewellery, but really it is fossilized resin from the pine forests which used to cover northern Europe and Scandinavia.' Herr Reiter held the piece of amber up to the sun. 'In prehistoric times, this insect landed on the resin and got stuck. Eventually the resin encased the insect. When the tree fell it was carried by rivers to coastal regions. Over millions of years the tree was covered with sediment and the resin hardened into amber. Pieces are often washed up here on the Baltic coast. Danzig is famous for its amber craftsmen.'

Herr Reiter returned the stone to me and I put it in my pocket. That piece became my talisman. Sitting in the train on our way back to Danzig, we were all apprehensive about the initiation which we would be undergoing that evening. However, touching that small, smooth, ancient piece of amber gave me confidence. When it was warm I could just make out the faint scent of resin – the scent of the pine forests of the north.

*

We arrive back in Danzig station and board one of the special buses bound for Marienburg. The journey takes two hours and leads through flat farm country. It is dusk by the time we arrive. Descending from the bus, I have never seen so many vehicles and people in one place. Small contingents of eight-year-old boys accompanied by their instructors have been arriving all day from all over Germany. The surrounding fields are full of tents. Beyond the tents, on the other side of the river, loom the walls of the castle. Herr Reiter explains that Marienburg is the largest brick castle in the world. It was founded by the Teutonic knights in the thirteenth century and once housed three thousand men at arms. Herr Reiter takes me aside and tells me that the Teutonic knights used to regulate the amber trade on the Nogat river – it became a lucrative monopoly. It is the first time I hear the word 'monopoly'. I repeat it. It has a fine ring to it. Monopoly.

The castle is enormous and made even more imposing by the fact that it is lit entirely by flaming torches. There are three separate sections – the High, Middle and Low castles. Each section is separated by moats and towers and each is more heavily fortified than the last. We enter by the main gate in the Low castle and cross two moats to get to the High castle. Twice we are stopped by the black-clad soldiers of the Schutzstaffel – the SS – Hitler's bodyguards. They are enormous men. In the flickering torchlight their dark eye sockets and chiselled jaws make them seem like a race apart – like the race of supermen we would later hear so much about. We stand in a long line waiting to show these men the folder of papers which each of us is holding in our trembling hands. The folder contains affidavits of racial purity, statements of physical fitness and school reports.

I hand my folder to the SS man in front of me. He glances through the sheets of paper and ticks a number of boxes against my name on a list on his desk. I am very nervous in case something is not in order. He removes the affidavits and passes the rest of the folder back to me. He notices my trembling hands and the suggestion of a smile tweaks the corner of his mouth.

'*Keine Angst*,' he says. 'One day it will be you sitting here, and my son in front of you. You always have to start at the bottom.'

I salute as we have been taught to do, then I rejoin the rest of my group who are waiting with Herr Reiter in front of the gateway to the High castle. I touch the amber in my pocket and feel proud of what the SS man said to me.

Despite the warmth of these spring days, the nights are still cold. I can see my breath condense in front of me as we make our way to the Great Hall. Now there are SS men lining the walls either side of us, all the same height, all unblinking in the torchlight. From the Great Hall I can hear the sound of music, but I do not hear high joyous voices singing the Hitler Youth marching songs which I already know so well. Instead I hear music of great solemnity, traditional hymns and ancient Germanic chants delivered in a deep liturgical monotone. The effect of the music and the torchlight is haunting – it sends shivers down my spine.

Wherever I look in the Great Hall there are enormous Swastika flags – against the walls, draped from the dark vault of the roof far above, flanking the distant stage at the end of the hall. The flags too are lit by flickering torches. After the last group of boys has been led in, the huge iron gates of the hall are closed. They make a noise of tremendous weight, tremendous finality. I feel that what happens in this place cannot be undone. Then the singing begins to change in character. We are too far away and it is too dark to see the choir, but there must be a women's choir too. Above the deep incantations rise ethereal voices. Years later Siggi would tell me about the ships which were lured onto the rocks by the voices at Lorelei; these were just such voices. I feel the amber in my pocket and think to myself how it is this music, these songs, that would have been sung when that delicate fly's wing was caught in the resin of an ancient tree.

The singing grows in intensity, male and female voices intertwining. A man climbs onto the stage at the far end of the hall – Baldur von Schirach, Reichsjugendführer and head of the Hitlerjugend. Even at this distance I am able to recognise him – I have seen his face on many posters. He looks like a movie star. Then the singing stops and von Schirach begins to speak. At first he speaks very quietly, so quietly that I find it hard to hear. He describes the *Nibelungentreue*, the fidelity of the Burgundians who were slaughtered to a man at Etzel's castle when they refused to hand over Hagen, the vassal of King Gunther. He speaks about the Order of the Teutonic Knights who built the Great Hall in which we are standing – the knights who had defended Acre against the siege of the Seljuk Turks. Then the singing begins again, quietly at first then louder and louder until the enormous gates behind us open and a cohort of the black clad Schutzstaffel march in bearing the *Blutfahne* – the blood flag.

'*Jungs!*' shouts von Schirach, 'This is the *Blutfahne,* the most sacred object of the party. As you know, it is this very flag that was drenched in the blood of the martyrs who died at the Hitlerputsch. It is this flag upon which poor Herbert Norkus breathed his last, having left a bloody trail from door to door after the Communist pigs stabbed him through the heart. Let us never forget the bravery of those men who have given up their lives to make our dream come true. Let us celebrate their courage and emulate their faith. In the years ahead, it may be that you too shall have the privilege of dying for the Führer. If such an opportunity should fall to you, may you seize it with joy in your young hearts. In the presence of this flag, let us repeat the oath together.'

There is a moment of silence before we all repeat in unison the words which we have spent our evenings committing to memory:

In the presence of this blood banner which represents our Führer, I swear to devote all my energies and my strength to the Saviour of our country, Adolf Hitler. I am willing and ready to give up my life for him, so help me God.

There is another minute of silence before von Schirach speaks again. 'Let me be the first to congratulate you on becoming members of the Jungvolk. You are Germany's future; may you make the Führer proud.'

*

It is not quite true that I was a member of the Jungvolk from that moment on. There was a trial period of a couple of months during which you had to pass a number of exams. You also had to receive your *Ahnenpass* – the document that proved your racial heritage. This was based on the affidavits we had handed to the SS man. If you were denied an *Ahnenpass* for whatever reason, then you were expelled from the Jungvolk. We were all nervous about this, even those boys with blond hair and blue eyes. By the time we were eight years old we had already had countless hours of lessons on race theory; it was one thing they could not teach us enough of. We all knew exactly how to recognize a Jewish nose or a Slavic skull. We had also learned that entry to the SS required proof of perfect Aryan blood back to 1650, sometimes as many as 12 generations. The Jungvolk was not as strict as that, but we were eight-year-old boys – most of us had no idea about our more distant family history and we knew that there would be people investigating us. That was a little frightening, though in the end I need not have worried. I passed and officially became a member of the Jungvolk in June 1938, shortly before my 9th birthday.

Chapter 10

I HAVE to leave Seu Otto when the nurses arrive with the dinner trolley. They say I can come back after he has eaten, so long as it is ok with him. Otto says that's fine, so I say goodbye and make my way to the hospital car park. I have a couple of hours to kill. I decide to go and pay João a visit. Talking to Seu Otto has made me think about my own childhood, and tonight I would like to see João.

João is one of my oldest friends. We have been surfing together since we were little kids. In one way or another, he has been a part of most of the adventures of my childhood. We are still good friends but it's fair to say that in recent years we've grown apart. I think he doesn't push himself enough. He doesn't understand why I am not content just to surf and to hang out on the beach. João dropped out of university and barely ever goes out, so we don't see much of each other anymore.

João is working a summer job at the sand dunes before you get to Joaquina beach. He rents sandboards to tourists and teaches them the basics of sandboarding. He says it's not as competitive as the surfing industry; I'm sure that's right. The sand dunes are not far from the hospital and this is a good opportunity to see him.

I park my car at the bottom of the dunes, on the side of the road. Joaquina beach is a few minutes further on and there are no buildings here, just a couple of stalls where you can rent sandboards. I hope João is on top of the dunes and that he has a sandboard he can lend me. I start to climb. The dunes rise steeply from the road and the sand makes it heavy going. I pause to catch my breath and admire the sunset. At moments like these, I understand why photographers and filmmakers are fond of dawn and dusk – the light is soft and warm and and the shadows cast by the dunes are gentle and undulating.

I have removed my *chinelos* and I watch my feet kicking into the sand at every step. Strange to think of Otto walking barefoot on the beach at Zoppot all those years ago. Strange also that on those northern European beaches you can find pieces of amber with insects frozen inside. I think back to Otto's description of the initiation ceremony at Marienburg. It is almost too theatrical to be believed. But then Otto doesn't seem the kind of person to invent things. What's more, he himself said that the Nazis were obsessed with style. Maybe their theatricality was just another aspect of that. I make a mental note to check the facts about the Jungvolk initiation when I return home.

The top of the dune forms a ridge. A narrow path has been forged by feet walking along it but in the distance it is hard to make out the path and the ridge appears pointed and sharp. There is a group of figures up ahead and I look for João. The wind contains particles of sand and I have to squint to protect my eyes.

'*Oi*, Pietro!' I turn round. João is directly behind me. He is carrying a number of sandboards. '*Tudo bem?*' he asks.

We embrace. Although we have grown apart, João is still an old friend.

'What are you doing here?' he asks.

'Nothing. I came to see you. I had some time to kill – I'm visiting a friend at the hospital. How are you doing?'

'*Tudo joia,*' says João. 'Enough business, but not too much. I have time to surf in the evenings. Hey, are you entering the Joaquina contest?'

The Joaquina comp is one of the smallest on the island. In the past I was one of the organisers. I've won it too, two years ago. This year I will not be organising, but I should take part. It would be a good way back into competitive surfing.

'Sure, I'll enter. Are you organising it?'

'I'm helping,' says João. 'We're still short of judges so if you know anyone…'

'I'll think about it,' I say. There are plenty of pros on the island who would be happy to judge, but most would want to be paid. A small contest like this does not have the money to pay judges. There is barely enough for the prizes. In any case, judging is not hard. Pretty much anyone can do it. Often it's best to attract someone prestigious; that way the contest may get some media coverage. That is really more helpful to aspiring surfers than a strict interpretation of the rules.

'Well, let me know. Time is running out. I should send out a press release in the next few days,' says João. He extends one of the sandboards towards me. 'Ride?' he asks.

'Thanks,' I say, taking the board from him. I lay it down where feet have flattened the top of the dune. I put my feet into the foot supports and tighten the ratcheted clips. I jump a couple of times until I am on the edge of the lip. The jumping motion throws up the sand from the top of the board and the wind catches it and blows it straight into João's face. He turns around and spits out the sand in his mouth.

'Sorry,' I say.

'*Tá bom*,' he replies, his face still a little contorted.

I jump once more and land on the face of the dune. The board has been well waxed and I begin to accelerate immediately. I make a couple of speculative turns; the board responds well. I begin to carve more deeply into the sand. The grains make a crunching noise that at times verges on a squeak. It is a very different sound to the hiss of surfing. I continue to dig the edge of the sandboard into the side of the dune. Suddenly something catches and I am thrown forwards. I land face first on the surface of the sand and just manage to protect my face with my hands. My body flips over in a somersault, then I roll sideways a couple of times before eventually coming to a stop.

There is sand everywhere. In my mouth, my ears, my eyes, my nose. I sit up and spit and snort and rub my eyes, which doesn't help at all. My neck aches a little but that is all. There is no serious damage. Well, no serious damage to me. But the board's rear binding is only loosely attached to the board itself. The binding's two front screws have been torn out of the board and the binding flaps up and down at the front. I look around me but there is no sign of the missing screws. The chances of finding a screw in a sand dune are not high.

I walk back up the dune carrying the damaged board under my arm. The group on the crest has thinned out. João waves to me. I signal to him with a thumbs down sign. The board is not beyond repair but I'll have to drive to my father's garage to use his tools. I need to drill new holes to re-attach the binding. If the old holes show, then I'll have to fill them with a resin filler, then sand the resin and respray the area.

I am out of breath when I reach the top of the dune. I show the board to João and explain how I can re-attach the binding. He's not angry but he wants me to fix the board tonight, otherwise he will lose a day's earnings on it tomorrow. I start jogging back down the dune to the combi. I must get to my father's garage before he closes up. If I'm fast I'll still get to see Seu Otto before visiting hours are over.

*

I pull into the dusty parking space in front of my father's garage. The garage door is already closed and bolted but I see that my father is still attending a client in the little room that serves for an office. I pick up the sandboard and slip into the office. My father is mid-sentence. He raises an eyebrow at my entry but does not stop talking. As I close the door behind me, I hear my father say, 'If it were me, I'd change all four pads. These ones might still last a little longer, but when your daughter's safety is at stake…' The other man mumbles a reply. I cannot make out what he says but he is probably agreeing. My father is a good businessman.

I have already drilled the new holes when my father enters the workshop. He watches me silently for a bit. My father is not a communicative man. 'How's business?' I ask, to break the silence.

'Too easy,' he replies. 'Men with daughters, you can sell them anything if you use psychology. The brake pads on that car were practically new. What a fool.' My father snorts derisively, then he asks, 'How's business with you?'

'So so,' I reply. I do not like to tell him that things are not going well.

'I hear that you are running a night at Divino? That's a tricky business. Lots of people go into it just to get laid, but it's not easy to make money. What are you making?'

My father likes to talk about money. 'I'm losing money at the moment,' I say.

My father almost smiles. He also loves to be proved right. 'I could have told you that would happen,' he says. 'But you have your sponsorship money.'

I have explained to him many times that the sponsors give me surfing equipment but they no longer pay me. I don't know why he can't remember that.

'I've told you before, they stopped paying me,' I say.

I start to sand down the new holes. I am careful to scuff the paint as little as possible. Then I position the binding over the new holes and insert the screws.

'You know I can't help you out,' says my father. 'I'm still paying off the loan, and you're already living in my apartment rent free.'

'I know,' I say.

'I wish I could help you, but sometimes you have to learn the hard way.'

I have forgotten to reset the direction of the drill. I attempt to tighten the first screw but I loosen it instead and it comes popping out.

'You have to set the direction of the drill,' says my father. I move the switch to clockwise and tighten the screws. My father watches my progress. I find it annoying.

Then he says, 'You know I need you to move out of the apartment in a few months. That was our agreement.'

'I know,' I say. It's true. He said I could live in the apartment until he could afford to do it up. Then he plans to rent it on the open market. I don't really want to tell him about Seu Otto, but I suppose he ought to know. After all, it is relevant to his dreams of a property empire. 'You remember Seu Otto, Vovó's employer?'

My father nods.

'He was on the news because he tried to stop two gunmen holding up a store. He got hurt and he is in hospital now. I've been talking to him and interviewing him. I want to try to sell his story, if he agrees. It might also help me to get a job when I graduate.'

My father ponders this. 'There's a lot of money in media,' he says, somewhat vaguely. 'If you're clever about it, you could make a packet. But make sure you pin Seu Otto down. Get him to agree to the idea and don't allow him to back out. Use psychology. Make sure he feels indebted to you. You could make a packet.'

My father is a good businessman. I know his advice is sound, but still it annoys me.

'I'll do that,' I say, hoping that he'll leave now.

'If I'd had the opportunities you have, I'd be a tycoon by now. Like Roberto Marinho.'

I tighten the last screw. 'I've got to go now. Seu Otto is expecting me,' I say.

'Well, pin him down,' says my father. He returns to the office and takes the money out of the till. We don't kiss or embrace – we never have. When I pull out of the car park he isn't even watching.

Chapter 11

FERNANDA REMINDED me that I would not be able to eat the next morning because of the operation; she said I should eat as much as I could now. I would gladly have followed her instruction but the hospital cuisine was very disappointing. Even the *feijão* was tasteless and watery. Who has ever heard of tasteless *feijão*? What an embarrassment. However, the man in the bed next to the window was less discerning. I had been watching him spoon in his meal with considerable enthusiasm and not a little noise. When he saw me put down my knife and fork and push the food tray away, he said:

'*Ó Senhor Eisinger*, will you allow me to finish your dinner? It is good enough for me.'

I observed him laboriously lift his pyjama-clad body from his bed into the wheel chair and wheel it towards me. We exchanged dinner trays and he wheeled back to his own bed. He polished off my meal with similar enthusiasm and I wondered how, with such an appetite, he could be so gaunt. Then Fernanda reappeared and collected our trays.

'Seu Otto, you are hungry tonight,' she said as she saw the spotless plates on my tray.

'Yes, very hungry,' I said. And that was not a lie, I was very hungry.

*

Pietro returned after dinner.

'*Seu Otto, comeu bem?*' he asked as he approached my bed.

'The truth is that I did not eat at all. But it doesn't matter. I am more interested in what you have been up to.'

'When?' asked Pietro. 'You mean now?'

'Yes,' I replied, 'while I have been watching the others eat.'

'I went to visit my friend João at the dunes,' said Pietro, 'but I accidentally broke his sandboard and had to go and fix it in my father's garage. At first the nurses didn't want to let me back in to see you but I said we still had important things to discuss.'

'I see,' I said.

'I hope you don't mind.'

'No. But what do you want to talk about?'

'Well,' said Pietro, 'I'd like to know about how you graduated from the Jungvolk into the Hitler Youth, and how your parents felt about that. What was your family like? Did you resent having to spend so much time away from home, or did you welcome it?'

I thought for a moment. Did I want to talk to Pietro about my family? They were not happy memories. When I think about my parents now, I feel that I should have loved them more, that I was an ungrateful child. Did I really want to share these thoughts with Pietro? But then, I could tell him as much or as little as I wished: I could just tell him how things were at the time. There was no need to 'explore my feelings', as the psychologists would have it.

'I was not very close to my own parents,' I said. 'In fact, that was one of the attractions of the Hitler Youth. It meant I could spend long periods of time away from home. Home for me was always a sad place.'

'You mean you could go to the summer camps in the mountains?'

'Yes. Well, partly. That came later. The first time I really felt that I had escaped from my parents was when we marched all the way to Nuremberg for the last of the great party rallies. That was in 1938. It was quite something.'

'Why?'

'Well, for one, it was a huge distance. Remember, I was still only eight years old. Nuremberg was about 500 kilometres from my home. We walked 20 kilometres a day; it took us a month. At the beginning I found it exhausting, though by the end we were much tougher. Hitler Youth *Gefolgschaften* from all over Germany were marching to Nuremberg for the rally... we bumped into contingents from as far North as Lübeck and Kiel. Often we heard them before we saw them; each *Gefolgschaft* had their own band and most of the time we sang as we marched. Sometimes we camped in the same places and made friends. Other times we were invited by farmers to sleep in their barns – often they would feed us too. Sometimes we helped them with their farm work for a couple of hours before we left in the morning. We could do in a morning what would have taken them weeks.'

I closed my eyes for a moment and saw again the rolling countryside stretching from Dortmund in the north, past Frankfurt am Main and Würzburg to Nuremberg. I remembered the long, hot summer of 1938. We marched throughout August and it didn't rain once. Sometimes we would see the columns of other *Gefolgschaften* in the distance; the boys' feet kicked up clouds of dust which trailed behind them. And always there were flags, flags of all sorts: regional flags, Jungvolk flags, Hitler Youth flags, Nazi party flags, all fluttering above the dust and the marching columns. Singing and flags, that's what it was like in those early years.

With my eyes closed, one image triggered the next. I thought of the *Jungmädel* who accompanied us on the march, the girls who were our age and who would graduate to the *BDM*, the *Bund Deutscher Mädel,* when we graduated from *Jungvolk* into *Hitlerjugend.* We spent a lot of the time fighting with the *Jungmädel.* We did that mostly to impress the older HJ boys whom we were accompanying – they thought we were weak and insignificant and we wanted to prove them wrong. We never got very far; the HJ boys were much more interested in flirting with the *Jungmädel* than in paying any attention to our boisterous displays.

It was on that march that I first talked to Christiane. I had seen her before at the occasional *Dienst* meeting in Bochum. However, she was a couple of years older than me and our paths had not crossed frequently. I found her very attractive – in fact, I was infatuated with her – and yet she had dark hair and light brown, almost golden eyes. I remember finding that very strange. I had been brought up to think that blond hair and blue eyes were a prerequisite for beauty, but she disproved that.

I remember how surprised I was when I found out that Christiane was a vegetarian; that was very unusual too. The other BDM girls teased her because of it – it was thought that being vegetarian would make you sickly and infertile. They accused her of being unpatriotic – of not wanting to bear children for the Führer. But really they picked on her because they were jealous of her, because the HJ boys paid her the most attention. When the HJ boys in their turn picked on us, Christiane would stand up for us. I suppose that was because she knew what it was like to be a victim. In any case, we adored her for it.

'Seu Otto?'

I had forgotten that Pietro was sitting next to my bed. I opened my eyes. He was staring at me. 'Are you alright?' he asked.

'I'm sorry,' I said. 'I think it is the morphine. It makes my mind wander. What were we talking about?'

'The rally, but if you are very tired…'

'Ah yes, the rally,' I said. What a show that was! 'The rally of 1938 was the biggest yet. Over half a million party faithful had come from all over Germany. When we arrived, the surrounding fields and hills were covered with tents; at night thousands of small fires lit up the landscape. The organisation was astounding; every delegation had been allocated an area in which to put up their tents and we had all been given precise instructions as to where to dig our latrines in order to maintain the highest standards of hygiene.'

I closed my eyes again. The images came more fluidly when I had them closed. But this time I kept talking.

'I remember the sports track. We spent most of our time watching the athletics competitions there. Even at that age we were crazy about sport. Two years earlier Germany had won almost twice as many medals as the next placed nation in the Olympics. We were very proud of our athletes. To win at Nuremberg meant you were the best in Germany and therefore, probably, the best in the world.'

I saw the tents on the hillside. I saw the small fires

lighting up the night. I saw the sports track and the glistening muscles of the runners. But somehow it felt as if these images were just a facade. The real significance of the rally was much greater. It was at that rally that I saw the Führer. Not just that I saw him; that he looked into my heart. But could I tell Pietro? Would he understand?

'I was part of the parade that marched through the centre of Nuremberg,' I said. 'The town was packed to bursting with spectators. It was hardly possible to see the buildings behind all the flags and the wooden tribunes. We started at one end of the town and marched to the other, passing through the Adolf Hitler Platz in the middle. The cheering in the square was deafening. The largest tribune was right in the middle of the square and on it stood Baldur von Schirach, whom I recognised from Marienburg and also from countless posters, and next to him the Führer himself. As we marched past we looked towards the tribune and raised our right arms in the salute, without breaking step. We had practised this many times on the way to Nuremberg, using trees or buildings to represent the tribune.

'Before I had even looked at the tribune, I felt the Führer's eyes upon me. When I looked up I saw that he was staring straight at me; I can't tell you what that was like. He was like a God to us. Try to imagine being eight years old and coming face to face with your God – it's impossible. In that one moment I felt that he looked right through me, that he knew the secrets of my heart. I also felt unbounded love for him, and I wanted to be loved by him, and I knew that he would love me if I pledged my life to him. That was what we had been taught; those were the oaths we had taken. I had already pledged my life to him, and I had meant it, but never so much as in that moment. And I realised with mounting joy that there were no secrets in my heart, or at least no secrets from him. I had dedicated myself to him. To him, to Germany, to everything around me: to my *Kameradschaft,* to the jubilant crowds, to the fluttering flags. I realised that I was a part of something much, much greater than myself. It was a very significant moment for me.

'When we gathered again on the other side of the town I was dazed; I think we all were. And that was another strange thing: all of us felt that the Führer had looked directly at us, that he had looked into us. For five and a half hours he had stood there on the tribune whilst Germany's youth paraded past. For five and a half hours he had looked into our hearts.'

Lying in that hospital bed almost 70 years later, I am powerfully affected by the recollection of the moment in which I felt the Führer's eyes alight upon me. Go through me. What I feel now is a brief reminder, a fleeting shadow of the excitement and optimism of those days. We believed in a cause and that gave us a sense of purpose; everything else was secondary to that. Is it too much to say that we were in love with the world back then? Perhaps not. But everything since then has been so different. Personally I cannot complain, I have led a good life, by the standards of today. And yet, when I compare it to those early years, has everything since not rung a little hollow? What has it all been for? Perhaps those are doors best left shut.

I swallowed involuntarily once or twice. Pietro replenished my water glass before passing it to me. To tell the truth, I was a little taken aback by the strength of these feelings. Why this sudden sense of loss about that far distant world? Well, perhaps I do not usually allow myself to think about the happy times. But Pietro's earnest curiosity, and his similarity to Siggi, have encouraged me to open the box of the past which has long been closed. Nor should I discount the effect of the morphine which makes it so easy to flow from one buried memory to another. And then I am anxious too, anxious about tomorrow's operation.

There was a time in the early 1970s when I had just been promoted to a prominent role in the Feldmann brewery in São Paulo. My responsibilities had increased considerably and at the same time profits had slumped. I remember all too well the feeling of stress, of being wound up inside like a clockwork toy. A peculiar side effect was my tendency to weep during any film I watched during that period, no matter how clichéd or sentimental. At the time I was told by my doctor that all emotions need to be expressed and that, if they are unable to find an outlet in the subject's real life, then they will do so as soon as his guard is let down, by empathising with a fictional character for instance.

My doctor wanted me to see a psychotherapist. The idea did not appeal to me – I have always seen psychotherapy as a forum for complaining. The process seems to me to encourage an unhealthy obsession with oneself, and a good deal of whining. Nevertheless, my own unpredictable tears were not a symptom I could easily ignore, and so I followed my doctor's advice and went to see an American psychoanalyst in São Paulo by the name of Dr. Greenbaum. From the very moment I entered Dr. Greenbaum's practice, I felt ill at ease. It seemed to me that Dr. Greenbaum had moved from his native New York in order to create his own sun-kissed harem: the other clients I saw arriving and leaving were the cream of Brazil's society ladies. If Dr. Greenbaum was disappointed that a middle-aged male had slipped through the net, he was kind enough to disguise that emotion. In fact, he disguised every emotion; talking to him was like talking to a brick wall. However, in our first meeting he insisted that he would require me to 'explore my feelings'. I replied that I had no interest in exploring them, I just wanted to return to the way I had always been. Over the course of a few sessions, Dr. Greenbaum became increasingly insistent. Then, fortunately, I had to leave on a business trip.

One of the results of the business trip was the amelioration of my work situation. Feldmann's international sales increased and profits consequently went up. My own symptoms diminished – I was no longer overcome by waves of emotion at inopportune moments. This confirmed what I have always believed, that the only true healer is time. Following my return from the trip, I had my secretary cancel all future sessions with Dr. Greenbaum. I imagine he was as relieved as I was, though of course he would have disguised that emotion too.

But why were the memories of my childhood crowding in upon me so vividly as I lay in that hospital bed?

'Seu Otto, would you like some more water?' Pietro interrupted politely.

'No, no thank you.' I put the glass back down, then Pietro asked, 'You said earlier that you saw the *Blutfahne* twice – the first time was at Marienburg. When was the second time?'

'That was when I heard the Führer speak at Nuremberg. It was on the last day of the rally, a week after we had paraded past him in the Adolf Hitler Platz. Towards sunset we made our way to the Zeppelin Field.'

Again I closed my eyes, and again I could see before me the overpowering enormity of the Zeppelin field. How to describe it to Pietro? How to convey the impact it makes on you as you enter the gates?

'The Zeppelin field was an area the size of 12 football pitches,' I said. 'It was a vast rectangle. On three sides it was surrounded by tribunes for spectators; that is where our seats were. Opposite us was the monumental main grandstand. The Führer's rostrum stood in the centre and two tribunes supporting double rows of white columns stretched away into the far corners of the field like the wings of an enormous bird. It was magnificent, like a Greek temple but many times bigger.

'We found our block of seats. Being the youngest, we had to sit furthest back. The HJ boys sat at the front of our block. The block next to ours was for the girls – BDM at the front and the *Jungmädel* behind them. The BDM were even more excited than we were – they hadn't marched past the Führer as we had and many of the girls were crazy about "our dear Adolf", as they liked to call him. Christiane was there too; she was sitting in the row in front of me, just on the other side of the narrow walkway that divided our two blocks. I liked Christiane a lot. In fact, I was sweet on her.'

Pietro smiled briefly. I don't think he expected me to be up to date with *Jugendsprache*.

'I wanted to attract her attention,' I said, 'but she was

just out of reach. In any case, her attention was riveted to the vast open expanse of the Zeppelin Field in front of us. The tribunes were beginning to fill up with spectators – many of them were Hitler Youth from other parts of Germany, others were ordinary civilians. Everywhere people were joking and laughing and passing around food and beer. As the sun dipped behind the horizon, the white stone of the Führer's rostrum was caught in the red glow. For a few moments the crowd hushed. Then the glow faded from the stonework and 200 Hitler Youths in Rhönrads came rolling through the gates.'

'In what?' asked Pietro.

'In Rhönrads. They were a type of gymnastic toy, very popular with the HJ. Imagine two metal rings, each the height of a man. The rings were fixed parallel to each other and held apart by six metal bars each about the length of a forearm. Each bar had a grip attached to it on the inside, two grips for your hands and two for your feet. By placing your hands and feet on the grips you could stand between the two outer rings. By shifting your weight left or right you could make the Rhönrad roll forwards or backwards. That was the easy part. The hard part was steering. By pushing your belly or your bottom either in or out you could, in theory, turn corners.'

'Have you tried it?'

'I've played around on a Rhönrad, yes. It's fun, though it always made me a bit dizzy. But the few rotations I managed were a far cry from the HJ Rhönrad display which I saw on the Zeppelin Field. They just kept rolling in through the gates, four abreast. When there were 200 Rhönrads inside the Zeppelin Field, they started performing the most intricate manoeuvres with unerring accuracy. It is hard enough to turn a corner in a Rhönrad, let alone describe concentric arcs and rings and parabolas in concert with 199 others. It was like watching the tiny interlocking cogs spinning inside a wristwatch, except that each cog was moving freely and had to be controlled by the boy inside. When they finished their display the crowd erupted, and at the same moment a squadron of fighter planes flew over the Zeppelin Field in the formation of a swastika. In those days we were constantly being astounded, and I don't think it was just because we were young.

'The Rhönrads and their HJ pilots occupied a tiny area at the very front of the Zeppelin Field, closest to the Führer's rostrum which was still empty. Then came the contingents from the Reich Labour Service. Before the war, you left the HJ at 18 and then spent six months with the Reich Labour Service, working the land. Boys were sent to the farms and rural areas of Germany to work for free. You were given your uniform and a spade – 'guns of peace', as the spades used to be called. Company after company of the Reich Labour Service now came marching into the Zeppelin Field. They carried their spades like rifles on their shoulders; the metal was polished mirror-bright. When thirty thousand young men had marched in and a third of the field had been occupied by the neat rectangles of their companies – each with its own flags and banners – they performed the military salute with the spade before standing at ease with both hands resting on the handle. All these movements were once again carried out with the utmost precision. As one hand came down on the other on the spade handle it rang out as one clap. The spectators enthusiastically applauded the neatness of each movement.

'For the next half hour the rectangular units of black clad SS soldiers streamed into the Zeppelin Field... row upon row of them, marching with perfect uniformity. Their columns stretched from just in front of the tribunes where we were sitting right up to the Führer's rostrum on the other side of the field. There were 70,000 of them, one quarter of the entire number of SS at that time. It was dark by the time the last company had entered the field. Then we heard a low murmur and one after another the enormous searchlights around the outer edge of the grandstand came on, beaming bright columns of light into the night sky. The Zeppelin Field had been designed with this in mind; it was also know as the 'Cathedral of Light'. Such a thing you cannot imagine.

'I heard the blast of trumpets and then other searchlights picked out the enormous red, white and black swastika flags that were draped all around the tribunes of the Zeppelin Field. The music grew louder and a number of searchlights were trained on the figure of one man in the far distance; the Führer was ascending the steps to the rostrum followed by a small group of other men, one of them carrying the *Blutfahne*. The loudspeakers all around played the Horst Wessel song while the flag bearers of newly formed SS regiments carried their flags up to the Führer. The Führer held the material of the *Blutfahne* in one hand and touched it to the material of the new flags that were presented to him, consecrating the new flags with the blood of the martyrs.

'Then the music stopped and the Führer began to speak. I don't remember all of his speech and I certainly didn't understand it all, but I do remember the beginning. '*Die*

Zukunft Deutschlands ist ihre Jugend,' he said. Germany's youth is her future. Of course we all applauded at that. Then he explained what he expected of us: total, unquestioning loyalty. Only on that basis could the Thousand-Year Reich be built. *Unsere Ehre ist unsere Treue* – Our Honour is our Loyalty. The sea of SS soldiers cheered at that; it was their motto. The more he spoke, the more impassioned he became. He said that there would be dark times ahead and that we would have to do difficult things, but that the value of an action is directly proportionate to its difficulty. 'The harder a task is, the greater its value as a dedication and an offering'; those were his words. Then he said that the generation of our parents would not understand this, that they did not love Germany the way we did and that they did not truly understand the meaning of devotion. The future lay in our hands. Even the youngest of us – that was me – had a vital role to play. And that role was simple: we had to place our trust in the Führer completely. We had to follow every order we received. And together with Germany's beautiful girls, the most beautiful in the world, we had to people the Thousand-Year Reich. When he said that, a great high-pitched cheer went up from the rows of BDM girls, many of whom were now crying with emotion.

'As the Führer spoke those words and the loudspeaker projected them over the Zeppelin Field, Christiane turned round and looked me straight in the eye. She had never looked so beautiful to me as she did right then, her eyes shining with devotion, her pupils wide, her features soft in the reflected glow of the searchlights. Later I came to understand that that look was a kind of promise. Of course, at the time I was only eight years old; I did not know what it meant, and probably neither did she. When your heart is close to bursting it is hard to comprehend your emotions, all the more so when they are emotions you are feeling for the first time.'

I took a deep breath.

'*Nossa, Seu Otto,* you remember it all so well,' said Pietro.

To tell the truth, I too was surprised by how vividly I was able to recall these events. It was almost as if they had retained their original colour by having been kept in the dark for so long, or as if they had been preserved in amber, untouched by the passing of the years.

Pietro's voice dragged me back into the present. 'You still haven't told me about your family,' he said. 'Can you tell me about your parents?'

At that moment the door to the ward opened and Fernanda appeared in the doorway. 'Still here?' she asked. 'How our hero must talk, to keep a handsome boy by his bedside on a Friday evening.'

Pietro smiled. 'I'm very grateful to Seu Otto,' he said.

'And I will be very grateful to you if you leave now,' replied Fernanda, swatting at Pietro like a fly. I could see that Pietro was reluctant to leave.

'I'll tell you about my family another time,' I said. '*Boa noite.*'

Pietro waved back from the doorway. As he did so, I again had the fleeting sense that there might be a real connection between him and Siggi.

Chapter 12

ONCE PIETRO had left, Fernanda turned her attention to the man at the end of the ward. He was surrounded by a tight circle of family members including children and grandchildren, or so I assumed. They were all leaning in to listen to him. I couldn't hear what he was saying but it was obvious that his listeners were hanging from his lips. Even Fernanda seemed unwilling to inform the happy gathering that visiting hours were over. She busied herself for a while fiddling with the window lock, then she spoke briefly to the other two patients. By now the speaker had come to the end of his story and the family around him – even the young children – were laughing. I wondered what he had told them.

Families. What a difficult business. And yet how greatly they influence us, whether by their presence or by their absence. Seeing that smiling family filter out of the ward made me think how very different my own family had been back in Germany. I had not deliberately avoided Pietro's question, but I do not like to dwell on my own family relationships. I was rather ashamed of my own father. And now I suppose I am ashamed of having been ashamed. How devilishly these things feed themselves.

My father was an engineer; because of this he was excused military service. He did not believe in the Führer, that much was obvious to me from a young age. The fathers of many of my friends had signed up enthusiastically for the *Wehrmacht*. Other friends had parents who were older and who had served in the first war. Many were decorated, several had been wounded. Many were opposed to another war, but at least we knew that they were not cowards. I suspected that my father was a coward. Once I asked him why he had never been promoted in his *Gusstahlfabrik* – the metalworks where he was employed. He said that if he were promoted he would be responsible for other people and he did not want that.

Because my father avoided promotion we never had much money. I did not go hungry but there were few luxuries. As I grew older things improved. I learnt at school that this was due to the Führer. It was because of him that the factories in the Ruhr were functioning once again, that roads and railways were being built and that workers no longer had to worry about whether they would be able to feed their families.

I had an older brother who died from tuberculosis before I was born. I think it is true to say that my parents never recovered from his death. There was no joy or laughter in our home. The three of us usually ate in silence while my father read a book using a device he had built that turned the pages without the need for him to touch them directly. When I joined the Jungvolk I was delighted to be able to stay out later and later, to spend as little time as possible with my parents. I preferred going to the Jungvolk *Heim* to staying at home, even on nights when all we did was sing songs and practise the salute.

My parents thought I spent too much time away and that they were being denied the opportunity of bringing me up the way they wished. Maybe they were desperate to protect me from the outside world because they had already lost one son. At the time I did not understand that.

There were occasions when they tried to coerce me to stay in after dinner; at first they offered me incentives – sweets, even money. Following an argument they once even locked me in my room. The next day my form teacher asked me why I hadn't been at *Dienst* that evening. I told him that I had wanted to go but that my parents had locked me in my room. He must have reported this to the leader of the HJ because that same afternoon, as I was walking home after school, I saw a senior HJ leader close our front door and drive off on a motorbike. When I got home, both my parents were sitting silently at the dinner table. My father was staring at the pepper pot. My mother stared at me. I announced to them that I had drill practice with the Jungvolk. Neither of them responded; they just kept staring. I remember going upstairs and changing into my Jungvolk uniform with a sense of triumph.

I wasn't one of those treacherous children who delighted in shopping their parents to the authorities. It was just that, from a young age, I believed that my parents were misguided. They seemed to me to be old-fashioned in the extreme. I believed that it was the attitudes of their generation that were responsible for the loss of the First War and for the hated treaty of Versailles, beneath the shame of which we still laboured. Also responsible, of course, were the secret activities of European Jewry, intent on Germany's destruction. Well, that is what we had been taught, and what we all believed at the time. On the other hand there was the Führer, the Nazi party and the Hitler Youth; together they represented everything that was modern and optimistic and forward-looking. They promised a new world, a new order. My parents simply did not understand that. I did not hate them for it, but I pitied them. And I decided that I would spend as little time as possible in their company.

Because he had been educated at a university and had a profession, my father considered himself superior to many of the other families who lived in the same area. He was a snob. I am sure that was one of the reasons why he was unhappy that I was a member of the *Jungvolk*. He did not like me mixing with the sons of labourers.

For us, the fact that adult social criteria did not apply was another of the attractions of the HJ. As eight and nine year olds playing war games, we chose our friends and made enemies as we saw fit, basing our judgements entirely on the qualities of the individual. The qualities in our peers that attracted us were predictable – success, confidence, humour – but where someone lived, or who their parents were, well, that was quite unimportant. Probably those things are unimportant for young children anywhere; perhaps the remarkable thing about the Hitler Youth was that they continued to be unimportant all the way up.

Had it not been for the HJ, I would certainly never have met either Siggi or Christiane. Or, even if I had met them, we could not have been friends. Siggi's father had moved to Bochum because his reputation as a drunkard had made it impossible for him to find work in his own hometown. Siggi told me that one winter's night his father had been found lying in a blizzard after an evening in the *Bierhalle*. He hadn't even put on his gloves and his two little fingers had to be amputated because of frostbite. Whenever I saw him, I was fascinated by these two amputated stumps, like tiny uncooked sausages. As well as being a drunkard, he had been a famous bar brawler. In the early days those were exactly the qualities which were sought by the brownshirted Sturmabteilung – the SA. But after the Night of Long Knives, when the leaders of the SA were executed, the brownshirts were either marginalised or absorbed into the more disciplined SS. The SS had no use for undisciplined brawlers like Siggi's father, so he started to drink more than ever. Nevertheless, it was a source of great pride to him that his son Siggi was such a widely admired member of the Hitler Youth. When he heard what happened to Siggi, he drank himself to death in three weeks.

As for Christiane's background, that was quite different. She went to a private school and lived in a part of town where the houses were enormous and set back from the river. I went there once, not long after I had first seen her. It was summer, and at that time I used to attend meetings at our *Heim* in the fervent hope that she would be there. We had not yet spoken; it was enough for me just to see her. Since she only rarely came to *Dienst*, I was frequently disappointed.

After yet another *Dienst* meeting without her, I chose to stay behind in the *Heim*. I sat by the open window while the others filed out. The afternoon sun poured through the window. There was honeysuckle climbing up the wall and its tendrils tapped against the wooden window frame. Its fragrance enveloped me and filled the room. I drunk it in and pretended to myself that it wasn't the scent of honeysuckle but rather the essence of Christiane herself which I was inhaling.

Perhaps the honeysuckle intoxicated me. After I had sat by the window for a while, I decided to cycle to Christiane's house in the hope of seeing her. We all knew the street she lived on – it was one of the most famous in the city – but I didn't know the number of her house. Between the houses and the river there was a path where the sunlight filtered through the *Linden* trees. I cycled up and down the path for a while, then I sat on one of the benches which had been positioned to afford a view of the river. I never saw her.

There were other Hitler Youth *Heime* in Bochum to which Christiane could have gone, but ours was the largest and we had the best relationship with the *Gauleiter*. That was why some of us were initiated at Marienburg, and also why our summer camps took place in the Bavarian Alps rather than in the flat countryside surrounding Bochum. Because of these advantages, Christiane's father wanted his daughter to be a member of our *Heim*. When she did attend meetings, he would drive her in an open-topped black BMW – he was a wealthy Bavarian and a big fish in the automotive industry. Christiane had grown up in Munich until her father was transferred and the family moved to Bochum.

Christiane had an older brother of whom she was very ashamed. He was a painter in his mid-twenties and lived in Hamburg. Once, during a secret rendez-vous at the summer camp, she confessed to me that her brother was opposed to the Nazis. When I think about it now, it seems to me that Christiane's devotion to the Führer and her outstanding record in the BDM were an attempt to atone for her older brother. I did not realise that at the time.

The Hitler Youth complicated family relationships, there is no doubt about it. It certainly drove a wedge between my parents and me. When I was 14, a few months after I had joined the Volkssturm, I was informed of my father's death in the bombing of the factory where he worked. I remember I was helping Herr Weiss to clean his gun, a procedure about which he had not the faintest idea, when one of the orderlies entered the hut and instructed me to accompany him. We walked across the frozen parade ground to the hut belonging to Kompanieführer Zaun, the austere elderly Captain of our company. The orderly remained at the door while I entered the hut.

Kompanieführer Zaun had been a tanner in civilian life and, as I recall, his wrinkled skin had a suitably leathery appearance. I found him frightening. When I entered the hut, he was sitting at his desk, facing the door. The hut was warm inside – there was a brazier in the centre of the room and Kompanieführer Zaun had plentiful access to coal. I closed the door behind me and clicked my heels. Kompanieführer Zaun continued writing for several minutes before looking up.

'Volkssturmmann Eisinger,' he said, 'your father is dead.'

'Sir.'

'You may take compassionate leave.'

'Sir.'

He returned to the papers on his desk and I let myself out of the hut.

I am not proud to admit it, but I cannot say that I was particularly saddened by my father's death. There was nothing I admired about him – he was not a soldier or a hero. In all honesty, I was ashamed of him: a cowardly engineer hiding in a metal factory. When he died I realised that I was now the only remaining male Eisinger; I liked the fact that the future of the family name lay entirely in my hands.

I was given a week of leave to attend the mass funeral in Bochum but I didn't go. I was afraid the Allies might roll into Germany while I was away from my post. That may callous, but in many ways I had ceased to see him as my father long before then. We were encouraged to view the Führer as our father and I was more than willing to do that. Now, of course, I do wish that I had known my own father better, or at least that I had known him before the death of his first son robbed him of any ambition he may have had. My father was a broken man, and as a young boy I believed that one should despise things that are broken.

After my father's death, my mother became even more withdrawn. She seemed to be afraid even to leave the house. At the time this did not concern me; it meant that I could come and go as I pleased. Later, after the war, and after my 'denazification', I suggested to her that we emigrate. She said she preferred to remain in Germany; I did not try to persuade her. I was confident I could get to Brazil and make a new life for myself with the help of relations of my father's who had emigrated before the war.

Eventually I had all the necessary papers. I left Germany in 1947, bound for Brazil. My mother stayed behind. I was not sorry to say goodbye. If anything, it reinforced my sense of a new beginning. That was what I wanted more than anything.

Chapter 13

FERNANDA CHASED me out of the ward just as Seu
Otto was about to tell me about his family. As I drove
through the dark streets back to my apartment, I realised
that was what I really wanted to know. It's strange because
that's not the angle that will sell Seu Otto's story. I mean, I
am interested in the Hitler Youth and the parades and the
camps in the mountains too, and I can see how attractive
that must have been to a young boy. But to me it feels like
a different world, one that I can only see in jerky black and
white. Seu Otto's feelings about his parents, on the other
hand, and his sense of difference from them, well, that I
can understand.

Maybe these thoughts were at the forefront of my mind
as I left the hospital because I knew that my mother's
birthday was coming up, and that I would have to return
to Blumenau to celebrate with her as I did every year. And
not just with her, but with all her friends too. Even as a
small child I did not enjoy these events – there was always
too much attention on me. Adults standing round, staring
at me, commenting on me... I used to hate it. I never knew
what was expected of me.

Things haven't improved all that much now that I'm
officially an adult. I still always have the feeling that I'm

being wheeled out as a showpiece, and that something's expected of me but I'm not sure what. In fact, maybe it was better when Gorka and my mother still lived together. There was plenty of bickering and he could be very insensitive, but at least he always kept things pretty real. For all his faults, there's never any bullshit. In fact, maybe he goes a bit too far in the other direction. Everything is about money and who's screwing who over, and how important it is not to be the one being screwed over. My mother is more of a dreamer I guess, and that's fine so long as those dreams aren't all about you.

So, this was my mother's forty-fifth birthday, and I was right to be apprehensive about it. It turned out to be quite an ordeal. The ordeal actually started the night before, when I had a row with Marina. Nothing serious, just a disagreement about what film we should watch, which led to her saying that if I really loved her I would compromise about the film and watch what she wanted to watch for a change. Well, I said that wasn't fair because at least when I chose a film I looked for something which we could both enjoy, whereas there is no way I could enjoy the sappy crap which she liked. Anyway, it escalated a bit and maybe she was annoyed that I was leaving for Blumenau the next day without her. I think that was it because when, in an effort to make up, I asked her to come with me, she immediately forgot all about the film. And in fact we didn't argue again all evening, quite the opposite.

I hadn't been opposed to her coming to Blumenau as such. I just thought it would be boring for her. Also, I didn't want to give my family the impression that we were going to get married or anything like that. And I didn't want Marina to start thinking along those lines either. Plus I didn't really want her to witness me in that awkward family situation.

We left early the following morning and arrived in Blumenau shortly before midday. Marina had never been in Blumenau before and she loved the half-timbered Germanic houses with their pointed roofs. I used to love Blumenau's architecture too, though on this occasion it seemed precious and inauthentic. The houses were too quaint, the walls too bright and too recently painted. Also, the town was full of tourists, many more than I remember seeing when I was growing up, perhaps because the Oktoberfest was coming up. But Marina was enchanted by it. In fact, she leant so far across me when we passed the *Castelinho Moellman* that I nearly knocked a bicyclist off his bike.

'Wow, what is that? That building,' she said, blocking my line of vision with her arm.

'That? That's the castle Moellman. It's a copy of the city hall of Michelstadt, in the south of Germany.' I'd had to learn all that in school.

'It looks so old.'

'But it's not. It was built in 1978. First it was a department store, now it's the tourist information office.'

'Huh, that's not so romantic.'

'I know. I guess Blumenau is a bit like that. Everything looks great on the outside, but it's all a bit of an act.'

'Like everything, then,' said Marina.

'What do you mean?'

'Oh, nothing really,' she smiled back. 'Forget it.'

Was Marina referring to me? To my family? To our

country? She refused to say anymore, but that didn't stop me wondering. I like it when she makes me think.

*

My mother lives in a small house on a well kept street near the river, ten minutes or so from the *castelinho*. The river is only a short walk away. As a child I was not fond of the river: it is brown and sluggish and the kind of place in which I imagined piranhas to lurk, or those big primeval catfish with their ugly whiskers.

Blumenau gets more rain than the coastal regions and, sure enough, by the time we had pulled up in front of my mother's house it had started to drizzle. The door was open and I could see a number of people inside.

'Pietro, I really need the bathroom,' Marina whispered in my ear on the doorstep.

'I'll show you,' I said, and I was about to lead her upstairs to my mother's bathroom when I heard someone shout my name:

'Pietro!' bellowed Jorge, a colossal man who had been one of my grandfather's best friends. The summer my parents split up, Jorge had spent a lot of time with me. He'd shown me how to put up a tent, and he'd told me about the tribes he had lived with in the jungle – he was a professor of anthropology at the university. He also gave me my first penknife. He was older now, but his voice had lost none of its resonance.

'How was the journey? Did you take the 101?'

'Jorge, leave him alone,' interrupted my mother. Jorge has a thing about road directions – he can go on for ever. '*Caro*, come here. Where is Marina?'

'She had to go to the bathroom,' I said, embracing my

mother. Then my mother led me through into the living room where a number of her friends were gathered on the sofas and armchairs, all holding glasses of champagne.

'My son Pietro,' announced my mother. 'He is studying journalism in Florianópolis. In a few years we'll be seeing him on the television. He has recently been interviewing Senhor Otto Eisinger, the gentleman who tried to fight the robbers in the shop.'

'I saw that on the news!' exclaimed Kika. Kika is an estate agent in Florianópolis and probably my mother's oldest friend. 'In fact, I sold him the house he now lives in. A beautiful house with a perfect lawn, in Sambaqui. He was a very polite man. Beautiful manners.'

'Isn't that the man your mother works for?' asked a lady whose face always reminded me of a horse and whose name I can never remember.

'Yes,' said my mother. 'She's worked for him ever since my father died. He's still in hospital so she couldn't come.'

I felt bad for Vovó - she loves anything that resembles a family get-together. That must be her Italian side. We are not a big family, not even remotely, but there are certain people who have been friends for so long, they practically count as family. Jorge was one of them, as was Kika. Vovó would have enjoyed being here. In the past I have driven her up myself, but that has often been quite exhausting. She wants to know everything and she asks sneaky questions. Last year I think she drank too much wine; she became quite emotional when I said I had to go back to Florianópolis. As I said goodbye to her she said, 'Sometimes I really think you don't love me anymore.' There is probably no better way of driving someone away. I remember feeling quite relieved when I left the house last year. At least I won't have to go through the same thing again this year.

I looked around the room and noticed that my mother's friends were all staring expectantly at me. I realised that I hadn't heard a word they'd said.

'Young people today have so many options,' said Kika. 'With a degree I am sure you can do anything you want.'

'Well, I'd like to go into the media,' I said, 'but it's very competitive.'

'I'm sure it's very corrupt,' said my mother. 'People only give jobs to the people they know. If you are young and talented they will try to keep you down.'

There was an element of truth in what she was saying. In the media, a lot does depend on your contacts. But everything my mother thinks is based on the conviction that I am brilliant and that everything is predisposed against me because of that. I know she's just proud of me, but I do find it annoying.

'It has very little to do with being talented or not being talented. There are just a lot of people who want to work in this industry, and not a lot of jobs,' I said.

'One day you'll see,' said my mother. I felt a small surge of irritation but before it could grow any bigger I heard Jorge's voice booming in the kitchen. Thinking that he had probably cornered Marina, I went to look for him.

*

When I entered the kitchen, Jorge and Marina were examining my mother's shelf of old family photos. Marina turned round and smiled at me.

'I was just showing your girlfriend some family pictures,' said Jorge.

'You used to be so handsome. What happened?' asked Marina. Her hand sought mine and squeezed it. I looked at the photo they were staring at – it was one of me as a small child, my hair cut evenly around my head so that I looked like a mushroom.

'It's awful what parents do to their children before they can defend themselves,' I said.

Marina pointed to another photo. 'Isn't that your Seu Otto?' she asked.

'Yes, that's right,' I said. It was a faded photo of my grandmother and Seu Otto on the patio of the house in São Paulo. He was sitting on a garden chair with a pipe in his hand; she was standing rather formally behind him. I wondered how and why the photo had been taken, and why my mother had it on her shelf. 'She's worked for him for a long time,' I said. 'I used to go and stay for a week every summer in that house. It was very quiet and dark inside – I always preferred being out on the patio, although the stones cut my knees.'

'Here's your grandmother again. Who's that with her? He looks like you.' She indicated a black and white photo of my grandparents sitting at a seaside café, I have no idea where.

'That's Horst,' said Jorge, 'Pietro's grandfather, and my best friend. He died very young – that's when Anna-Maria went to work for Senhor Eisinger.'

'I'm sorry,' said Marina. Jorge continued to stare at the picture. After a pause Marina asked me, 'What was he like?'

'He died before I was born,' I said. 'I don't really know. Jorge was his best friend.'

'He was a wonderful man, but his life was not easy,' said

Jorge. 'He was born in this country because his mother, Freya, had been sent here from Germany when her parents found out she was pregnant. That was a big disgrace at the time, at least in a Catholic family. She died in childbirth – she was only sixteen. So Horst never knew his mother, and he had no idea who his father was. He was raised by his mother's relatives in Blumenau. But despite that, he had a wonderful sense of humour. Dark humour, it's true, but we used to laugh a lot. What else can you do?'

I did not know that Horst's mother was so young when she gave birth to him. I suppose I never asked. But maybe it's not so surprising. From what Seu Otto has been telling me these last couple of days, it seems that everything used to happen much earlier.

'What about Horst's grandparents back in Germany?' asked Marina.

'They didn't want to have anything to do with him. I think they were very hard-hearted. After all, they sent his pregnant teenage mother to Brazil pretty much to fend for herself. Poor Freya, dying so young and so far from home.'

'That is a sad story,' said Marina.

Jorge continued to stare at the photo for a few moments more. Then he turned towards us and said: 'It is sad, but the future is with you. When will you two young people start producing some grandchildren to liven things up?'

Marina was still holding my hand. I could feel my own palm grow hot and a little sweaty. I was about to reply that it was too early to start thinking about things like that when Jorge steered us back into the living room. Fresh glasses of champagne were being passed around and my mother and her friend Kika fell upon Marina as we entered.

'*Caro,*' my mother said to me, 'please can you see what is wrong with the hi-fi, I would like some music.' Then, to Marina: 'Pietro is wonderful when it comes to fixing things.'

Marina nodded but I could see she was just being polite. That's probably because it sometimes takes me a while to get around to fixing things in the apartment. She finds that annoying. Anyway, when my mother says 'fixing things', she really just means being able to use them. I went over to the hi-fi and, predictably, all I had to do was switch the setting from AUX to CD. I pressed play. Toquinho's tender voice introduced his *Samba para Vinicius*:

... eu queria agradecer a presença das pessoas que estão aqui no palco comigo; essas pessoas vocês não podem ver não, mas eles estão aqui, nas sombras, nas cores, nas luzes, do meu lado, estão em mim, em cada nota que eu toco, em cada intervalo de melodia, en cada acorde que eu faço, em cada musica que eu canto...[1]

'Ah, *o poetinha,*' said Jorge wistfully. I looked around the room. No one was speaking; everyone was straining to hear the words of Toquinho's lyrical recollection of his friend, the poet and musician Vinicius de Moraes.

... uma pessoa, uma pessoa especial, que está mais perto de mim que todas as outras, ele que foi meu filho e pai, irmão e amigo, aí onde você estiver, um beijo pra você, Vinicius de Moraes...[2]

'Pietro, change the song, it's too sad,' said Kika.

---

1 I would like to thank the people who are on this stage with me. You can't see them but they are here in the shadows, in the colours, in the lights; they are here beside me and within me, in every note and every chord I play, in every break in the music, in every song I sing...

2 There is one person, one special person, who is closer to me than all the rest; he was my father and my son, my brother and my friend. Vinicius de Moraes, wherever you are, I blow you a kiss...

'No, no, leave it,' said my mother. She had reclined on the sofa and closed her eyes. 'This is a sad country. We have all come from somewhere else; we have all lost someone. We should not hide from that.'

Maybe she is right. Maybe this is a country of loss. Is that why we have samba and bossa nova, why we love *saudade* so much? Is it to combat this sense of loss that we throw ourselves so passionately into dancing and lovemaking? Does the fanatic support of our football team seduce us into believing in some form of togetherness? And who is my mother thinking of? Is it her estranged husband, my father Gorka, shrewdly squeezing the last penny out of his clients? Is it her own mother Anna-Maria, my avó, tending to Seu Otto in the hospital? Is it her father Horst who died when my mother was still a young girl? Or is it her own grandmother Freya, poor Freya, sent here in disgrace with a baby in her womb, never to see her homeland again? If my family's history is representative, then this is a sad country indeed.

*

We stayed to watch my mother cut the birthday cake which Kika had brought for her, then we made our excuses. I had the impression that my mother's initial enthusiasm for Marina had cooled a little. Marina had grown quiet – she doesn't take pleasure in sadness the way my mother does. We said goodbye to Jorge who used the opportunity to explain to me his recommended route back to Santa Catarina, avoiding various diversions and roadworks. Then he asked me whether I had ever visited Pomerode, a small town half an hour north of Blumenau.

'No,' I replied truthfully.

'I go there once a year with Anna-Maria to visit your grandfather's grave,' said Jorge.

'That's where he is buried?' I asked. I had no idea; I had always assumed he was buried in Blumenau.

'Yes,' replied Jorge. 'And if you ever feel like coming with me, well, just tell me. You may find it interesting; there are many in Pomerode like your friend Seu Otto.'

'Thank you Jorge, I would like to go with you.'

Jorge squeezed my shoulder with his bearlike paw. 'I haven't been yet this year. I'll probably go in a month or two, when it's not so hot. There is a bit of a climb to the cemetery. If you'd like to come, then just tell your grandmother and she will get a message to me, ok?'

'I'll do that,' I said. Jorge squeezed my shoulder again, then Marina and I left the house.

Marina slept for most of the drive back to Santa Catarina. I thought about this sad country of ours, and whether it really is characterised by a sense of loss. Then I thought about Seu Otto and how he too may be representative. It seems that the loss that has affected him most is neither the loss of his homeland nor of his parents, but rather the loss of his friend Siggi. That is something I would like to know more about, though I shall have to tread carefully. I do not want to upset an old man.

Chapter 14

THE MORNING of the operation was busy. Fernanda took my blood pressure, pulse and temperature. Anna-Maria arrived halfway through and unloaded a mountain of fresh fruit which she had just bought and which Fernanda told her I was not allowed to eat. Anna-Maria took this personally, as is her way. I explained to her that it was part of the protocol for a general anaesthetic but she kept repeating, 'But fruit is so healthy.' Once Fernanda had left, Dr. da Silva passed by to warn me that I would probably feel disorientated when I woke up. He also said that I would be on a stronger concentration of intravenous morphine for the first 24 hours after the operation and that we'd see how things went after that.

Pietro arrived in the middle of the morning, once the nurses had left. I was happy to see him; talking to him would take my mind off the operation. I prepared myself for more inquiries about my family. I have nothing to hide, but they are not the happiest memories. Pietro, however, had other ideas. His first question was:

'How did you meet Siggi?'

Meeting Siggi... now that, on the other hand, is a happy memory. I closed my eyes and thought back to the *Jungvolk,* and to the Hitler Youth *Mutprobe.*

*

I was 13 years old and still a member of the *Jungvolk*. In order to graduate into the *Hitler Jugend* I knew I would have to pass the *Mutprobe* – the test of courage. We were all very nervous about it – we didn't know what to expect. It was up to the senior HJ leader to devise the *Mutprobe* and it differed from place to place. Making boys jump off a five-metre diving board was popular in summer, even for boys who couldn't swim. There had been a time when boys were made to jump wearing a helmet. When you hit the water, the helmet strap would jerk your head back. One boy broke his neck that way; after that, jumping with helmets was banned.

I was initiated in the winter of 1943. We had been told to wear our summer sports gear, but we had still not been told what the initiation would entail. We were standing around the stove in our old wooden *Heim,* nervously chatting to each other and trying to warm our shaking hands with the little heat that the stove gave out. The two supervisors who were also our schoolteachers had left us. They said that a more senior HJ leader would be conducting the initiation. The minutes dragged interminably as we stood there shivering. I thought to myself how different things had been back on that warm summer afternoon when I had sat by the open window, observing the honeysuckle tapping agaist the window frame and drinking in its intoxicating fragrance.

Although we were, for once, left to our own devices, I don't think that any of us felt like playing the usual pranks. Now that I think back to that cold January afternoon, I realise that the waiting and the nervousness were part of the *Mutprobe*. At the time I just thought that the HJ leader had been delayed by the blizzard which was blowing outside the frosty windows.

Despite our vigil, we were caught off guard when the door was flung open by a tall, thin figure wrapped in an ankle length black leather overcoat. He strode purposefully into our wooden *Heim,* admitting a flurry of snow particles. He looked slowly around; I remember being struck by the pale blue of his eyes, almost like a husky's. Then he announced: '*So, Jungs, jetzt geht's los!*' before striding back out of the room and indicating to us to follow.

Outside the *Heim,* standing shivering in the snow, was another *Kameradschaft* of boys, also in summer sports gear. I recognised a few of them from my school, but they were members of a different *Heim.* The HJ leader in the leather coat paired us off – myself with a thin blond boy. We were told to stand in two lines, then the HJ leader marched us to the boating lake in the park. In summer I often used to swim in that lake, but now the ice was frozen thick and the cafés and boating houses – always so busy in summer – were boarded up and covered with a thin layer of snow.

We marched onto the lake and stopped more or less in the centre where a number of pick axes were lying. It was evident that there had been a couple of holes in the ice about ten metres apart but that they had recently refrozen. We were instructed to open them again and took it in turns to hack away at the ice with the pick axes. As we hacked, shards of ice flew up and stung our faces. Meanwhile the HJ leader walked up and down between the holes, dragging his foot and clearing a little gully between the two holes in the ankle deep snow that covered the ice.

Once the holes had been reopened to a width of a metre or

so, we were made to line up facing the HJ leader. He explained the *Mutprobe* to us: we had to swim under the ice from one hole to the other by following the line of light that we would see through the ice where he had cleared the gully. When we got to the hole on the other side we should pull ourselves out with the help of the rope which would be in the water and whose other end he would be holding. If anyone couldn't swim, he said, they should go home now and wait until the summer to undertake the *Mutprobe*. At this a couple of boys left. I knew that one of them at least could swim but I was not surprised that he left. I was also feeling nervous and I was the best swimmer in our *Heim*. In fact, I had won a number of races in the boating lake over the summer, including a prize for swimming underwater. If I was afraid, I imagined that the others would be a lot more afraid.

The HJ leader made me go first – perhaps he knew about my swimming success of the summer. I was aware of the anxious faces of my friends as they watched me take off my clothes. I was standing naked and barefoot in the snow but my heart was beating so fast that I did not feel the cold. The HJ leader told me to jump into the hole rather than climb in since I would probably cut myself on the jagged edge of the ice. *'So, hinein mit Dir!'* he shouted.

I took a couple of deep breaths and thought back to the sunny summer evenings I had spent splashing around with my friends in that same lake. Though the lake looked very different now, I tried to think of it as a friend. I imagined those cold dark waters welcoming me as an old acquaintance now making a surprise visit out of season. Then I closed my eyes and jumped.

As soon as I came up to the surface, I was forced to blow

out all the air in my lungs. The temperature of the water took my breath away. I was panting violently and treading water as best I could. I saw a faint fog hanging before my eyes; the fog cleared and I wondered briefly whether it had in fact been there at all. The HJ leader observed me with a look of detached amusement. I knew the direction I had to swim and, as soon as my breathing had stabilised, I ducked under the ice.

The line of the light above me was not hard to see; from below it was a beautiful sapphire blue dividing the murky darkness on either side. I followed the line swimming a sort of breaststroke on my back so as not to lose sight of it for a moment. Occasionally I reached out to touch the ice above me; it felt jagged and rough. I also remember thinking how strangely peaceful it was beneath the ice. Then, almost before I knew it and long before my breath would have run out, the murkiness faded and I found myself surfacing in the second hole, surrounded by applauding boys. The HJ leader threw the end of the rope to me. I tried to seize it but my limbs were so cold that my movements were like those of a drunk. Finally I got a grip and, with the help of two other boys, I was dragged over the lip of the ice. My body was shaking but internally I felt a suffusion of warmth. I was reminded of the way my feet had felt when I first walked in the cold water of the Baltic, back at Zoppot, on the day of my initiation into the Jungvolk. And now I had passed the initiation into the Hitler Youth.

Someone threw me a towel with which to rub myself down. While I was putting my clothes back on, another boy completed the swim, and then another after him. I stayed by the exit hole to help others get out of the water –

that was the hardest part. After I had thrown the third boy the towel, I saw that the blond boy with whom I had been paired off was about to go. However, there was something different about his manner. We had all been terrified but it looked as if he was just pretending, just going through the motions. In any case, he jumped in just as we all had and then ducked down under the ice without waiting for his breathing to stabilize. The HJ leader and the other boys were still making their way towards the exit hole when I suddenly saw the boy swim straight past. He was swimming much faster than the rest of us had, possibly because he was doing a normal breaststroke with his belly to the ground and only looking up at intervals.

The HJ leader arrived just in time to see the boy's legs disappear under the ice on the other side of the hole. I was standing closest to him; he looked at me and barked, '*Schnell!*' I suppose we had been trained to respond to just this sort of situation. I didn't hesitate: I jumped into the water fully clothed and, without coming up for air, I took two strokes in the direction the boy had been swimming. Almost immediately I saw his legs in front of me and I grabbed one of his ankles. This must have terrified him because he lashed out and spun round at the same time. Once he had seen me, I swam back towards the exit hole which was no more than a couple of metres behind us. As soon as I had emerged, the other boy's head appeared beside me. This time the cheering was a good deal louder and even the HJ leader looked relieved. We climbed out and I was introduced to Siegfried – that was the blond boy's name. He was ordered to accompany me back to the *Heim* since I no longer had any dry clothes. The *Mutprobe* continued but only once the HJ leader had instructed the remaining boys to swim on their backs and not to lose sight of the line of light above them.

As we ran back to the *Heim*, Siegfried told me that he had deliberately swum past the hole just to scare us. Later, when I got to know him better, I realised that was just the kind of thing he would do. Siggi had no fear, you only had to watch him climb to know that. At the time I just thought he was too proud to admit that I had saved his life.

*

I opened my eyes and saw that Pietro was chewing the end of his pen and looking thoughtfully at me. Then he said, 'Do you think Siggi was telling the truth? Was it just a trick to scare you?'

'I don't know,' I replied. 'Siggi was different to the rest of us.'

'In what way?' asked Pietro.

'Well, he was a phenomenal athlete, a natural sportsman. If I was a better swimmer, it was only because I trained whenever I could. Siggi was a runner and a climber. Throughout our time in the HJ he helped and encouraged me. When we started learning to climb at the summer camp in the mountains, he would show me where to place my hands and feet if I got stuck. In winter we used to run barefoot cross-country races around Bochum; they were supposed to toughen us up.'

'That's crazy,' said Pietro.

'When Siggi saw that I was tiring he would run next to me for a while, making jokes and chatting away. At the beginning I thought that he did all this out of gratitude because I had saved his life. Later I came to realise that it was just the way he was and that, in any case, it would not have mattered to him whether I actually did or didn't save his life under the ice; what mattered was that I had been prepared to, and for that he granted me his friendship unreservedly.'

'How did he feel about water?'

'I'm sorry?'

'After that incident, was he afraid of the water? If he really had nearly drowned, then he might have been afraid of swimming after that. That's what happened to one of my surfing friends. He almost drowned and now he's stopped surfing,' said Pietro.

'No, that didn't happen to Siggi,' I said. 'Far from it. He once swam with me across a big mountain lake at night, to the girls' camp on the other side. It was a long way; we had to swim for almost an hour. It was also severely prohibited.'

Pietro sat forward in his chair. 'Did the girls know you were going to swim over?' he asked.

'They knew we were going to try,' I said. 'It was forbidden for girls to be in the boys' camp, and for boys to be in the girls' camp, but on some days boys and girls were allowed to hike together. We also used to have lessons together once a week – we were at the camp for six weeks, after all. Christiane was in the BDM camp, on the other side of the lake.'

'Christiane, the one you were telling me about, the girl from the Nuremberg rally?'

'Yes, exactly,' I nodded. 'She was a couple of years older than me. When I went to the camp she was already a junior BDM leader. That was in the summer of '44. And, although we were young, there were not many HJ boys who were older than us. The older ones had already been conscripted.'

'Was Christiane also from Bochum?'

'Yes, from the same *Heim* in fact. I had seen her at *Dienst,* but the first time I actually spoke to her was on the march to Nuremberg. Later, I got to know her better at the summer camp. When the BDM and the HJ hiked together, the boys had to walk in front of the girls. But sometimes, at the end of the day, we were allowed to walk side by side. Christiane and I walked together whenever we could.

'Christiane was friends with a younger girl whom Siggi liked. I suggested to Christiane that Siggi and I could swim across the lake in the night and visit them in the girls' camp. Of course, I didn't know when we would be able to swim across, and there were sentries who guarded our camp every night. If we got caught, not only would we be in a lot of trouble but so would the sentries who had failed to stop us.'

'What kind of trouble?' asked Pietro.

'Well, punishments could be quite brutal. One boy who fell asleep on sentry duty was made to run around the perimeter of the camp wearing all the clothes he had while the HJ leaders stood round and booted him in the bottom. It was a very hot day and he eventually collapsed. But the worst punishment would have been the shame of being kicked out of the HJ. That could also happen, but usually only for the most serious crimes.'

'Like?'

'Like unnatural acts, for instance. Boys who were caught engaging in acts of a homosexual nature were expelled.

That was the law.'

'I see. So, you didn't want to swim across because you knew that whoever was on sentry duty would also be punished if they failed to stop you?' said Pietro.

'That's right. It was Siggi's idea to swim across on the night on which we were both on sentry duty ourselves. Also, Siggi knew that there would be a full moon that night. That worried me even more; it would be much easier to see us in the water. However, Siggi thought it was a good omen. He liked things like that – full moons and summer solstices and so on.'

I paused for a moment, thinking to myself how strange it was that in the Hitler Youth we were encouraged to think in terms of pre-Christian rites and rituals in the same way that the hippy people do today, and yet it was in the context of a completely opposite ideology.

'So, Siggi knew there would be a full moon,' prompted Pietro.

'Yes,' I said. 'And that was the night we were due to be on sentry duty, so I asked a girl in my class to pass on a message to Christiane that we would try to swim across the lake.'

'You really liked Christiane,' said Pietro. Was it a question? I couldn't tell. I said:

'Yes. Yes I did. I used to think of her a lot. I often thought of her as I had seen her on the Zeppelin field – eyes shining in the reflected glow of the searchlights.'

Christiane had meant a lot to me. Well, I can't pretend that I knew her all that well, but she had certainly fueled my fantasies. The thought of seeing her alone and in the dark at the girls' camp, on the other side of the lake, had been almost unbearably exciting.

'Siggi and I were both very excited,' I said. 'The lake was bigger than anything we had swum across before. Also, those glacial Alpine lakes are extremely deep, deeper than anyone knows. I was frightened by the thought of prehistoric creatures lurking in the depths, ascending to the surface once a month to graze on Hitler Youth boys by the light of a full moon.'

I saw Pietro smile.

'And that was also the day of the climbing competition,' I said. 'A great day.'

'Tell me,' said Pietro.

Chapter 15

THE MORNING of the climbing competition dawned brightly. We checked our equipment in the early light. There were two other teams of climbers in the final; each pair had to climb the three new routes marked out on the *Drachenwand* – the fifty metre rock face behind our camp. The climbing instructors had marked out the new routes and secured the pitons the evening before. We had not yet seen them, but we were to be timed on each route and at the end all the times would be added together to determine the winning pair.

Siggi and I both climbed well. Siggi led, going up ahead of me and clipping the rope to the pitons while I belayed him from below. It was a pleasure to watch him climb. He was so smooth and graceful on the rock face – no scratching or scrabbling. I remember the way his hands moved over the stone, both curious and reverential. At times they seemed to stroke the rock. When Siggi neared the end of the rope, he would find a ledge from which to belay me while I climbed the same route, unclipping the rope and the carabiners from the pitons as I went. I did not climb as naturally as he did; it was more of a fight for me. However, having watched him closely, I knew where the hand holds and foot holds were, and I was able to climb the pitch almost as fast as he had.

We climbed the first two routes effortlessly and posted the fastest times on each. It was almost midday by the time we started on the third route. By now the other HJ boys and the Jungvolk who had spent the morning exercising outside the camp had returned. There was quite a crowd at the base of the *Drachenwand*. Siggi was well known for his climbing exploits – he had climbed certain routes by himself that even the instructors could not scale. The only exception was Kurt Gruber, the eighteen-year-old Bavarian climber in charge of our company. However, since he was a native of those mountains, he was thought to have an unfair advantage.

Gruber was widely respected. He was only eighteen but he had already seen action and been promoted to the role of HJ leader. We all hero-worshipped him to some extent. But I wouldn't say he was popular; people were too afraid of him, especially the younger boys. Siggi, on the other hand, was extremely popular. He was friendly and easy-going. That might have been a problem for some boys; after all, the HJ was founded on principles of strict obedience and discipline. However, Siggi's charm and his reputation as a fearless climber and gifted all-round athlete meant that he managed to avoid confrontation with the more authoritarian figures – even Kurt Gruber treated him with indulgence. It also meant that the crowd that had gathered at the base of the rockface at the start of our third climb wanted us to win.

The third climb was probably the hardest although Siggi, with the crowd cheering below, made light work of the first pitch. When he had reached a ledge where he could secure himself and the rope, he called down to me to follow. I couldn't see him because the ledge was above a slight overhang; nor could he see me. Nevertheless, I was confident that I would be able to follow his exact route.

It was midday by the time I started to climb. I could feel the sun vertically above me, burning my shoulders. The *Drachenswand* was in shade for most of the day and I was not used to climbing in direct sunlight. The glare of the light on the rock made me wince and after just a few minutes sweat began to drip into my eyes. The beginning of the climb had still been in shade and I had not thought to remove my jumper; my skin against the rough woollen material now began to itch.

Somehow I must have deviated from the route Siggi had taken since I found myself having to make use of a narrow crack, wedging my forearms between the two rock slabs in a technique I had rarely used. The crack became so narrow that soon I could only insert my hands, and then just my fingers. The rock around me was completely smooth; there were no hand holds or foot holds, only the crack. I saw that the crack came to an end a few metres in front of me – the two sides of the crack fused seamlessly back together. My arms were starting to tire; I had been climbing too aggressively, fighting the rock. I realised I would have to climb down in order to climb up again. I began to feel anxious – climbing down is never pleasant. However, once I was in a stable position with my weight on my legs, I leant my forehead against the rockface for a few seconds to compose myself. I took a few deep breaths and blinked the sweat from my eyes. Then I closed my eyes and tried to imagine being somewhere completely different; I imagined swimming in the cool waters of the lake, my limbs suspended in its liquid embrace. When I opened my eyes again I felt much calmer.

The overhang of Siggi's ledge was directly above me. I called up to Siggi to give me some slack, then I retreated back along the crack. I recognised the route he had taken and followed it, catching up with him on the ledge. We both climbed the next pitch fluidly and I lifted the flag at the top of the climb to indicate to the timekeeper below to stop the clock. We jogged down the walk off though the woods and around the back of the cliff for the third time that morning. I knew that my error in following the crevice had cost us valuable minutes but as we approached the group of spectators at the bottom of the cliff their cheering grew louder. They clapped us on the back as we jogged to the timekeeper's desk. The timekeeper confirmed that all the results were in. We had won the competition. Then Kurt Gruber shook our hands and said that the results would be officially announced at roll call the following morning. We went to get the lunch that the Hungarian cooks had been keeping back for us, but neither of us was hungry. We both felt euphoric.

After winning that climbing competition, I felt as though nothing could ever go wrong. That, I suppose, is the confidence of youth. I never considered the possibility of any outcome other than success. After lunch we attended our afternoon classes. We were excused training in the early evening because we had won the competition and because we would have to be on sentry duty that night. We tried to rest but we were both too excited by the prospect of the night swim to the girls' camp; we only dozed fitfully. After the evening meal we sat around the campfire whilst Kurt Gruber told the story of Siegfried slaying the dragon. This was a tribute to Siggi and we both felt honoured by it, although I don't think that any of the other boys realised why it was significant. When Kurt Gruber finished telling the story and the songs were starting, we made our way to the perimeter fence to begin our sentry duty. Even from where we were positioned, we could hear the singing in the distance. As we sat and listened, the full moon rose above the *Drachenswand*; it bathed the rockface in pale silver light and reflected off the black waters of the lake in front of us.

At our summer camp, sentry duty was very dull. I had heard of other places closer to Bochum where it was not uncommon for camps to attack each other at night. That would have been exciting. However, we were the only HJ camp for miles around in these mountains and, since the girls would never attack us, there was really nothing to fear. It was often a struggle to stay awake. But that was not a problem on this occasion – Siggi and I were both nervous.

We waited until after the singing had ended and the campfire had died out. Then, when we thought that everyone had gone to bed, we left the sentry post and made our way down to the shore of the lake. The water's edge was fringed with trees. Usually we swam naked in the HJ. However, we did not want to arrive totally naked in the girls' camp – that would have been too much. So we didn't take off our underpants, even though I thought Siggi's looked ridiculous on him – so bright and white in the moonlight against his sunburnt skin.

We entered the water and stumbled a little on the slippery stones. A few metres in, we were already out of our depth; we started to swim. The two or three centimetres of water on the very surface of the lake were much warmer than the water just a little further down. We struck out towards the opposite shore, a dark band in the distance.

*

I slow my stroke to match Siggi's. The first few minutes of a swim are always the hardest, until you establish a rhythm. I move as stealthily as possible, stroking the backs of my fingers against the surface of the water on the return stroke to minimise splashing. Siggi, beside me, does the same. After a few minutes I feel myself settling into the stroke. My body is very light in the water; my hands feel like they are pulling me forward along an invisible rope. I am aware of the water and the moonlight and of Siggi's body, never more than a couple of metres away from my own. The future and the past fall away; I feel that I inhabit a perfect present in which all the significant threads of my life come together like strands in a climber's rope. Winning the climbing competition is the same as dedicating myself to the Hitler Youth, and that is the same as daring to swim the lake. Loving Christiane is the same as loving the Führer, which is the same as loving Germany and the old myths and the Hitler Youth.

I know that we will get into trouble if we are caught. However, I am not anxious. Deep down, I know that this is the right thing to do. It is what a mythic German hero would have done, what the Führer would have wanted, even if the rules forbid it. I continue swimming, my breathing cyclical and calm, my strokes regular and effortless. When I turn my head to breathe, I catch sight of a flash of moonlit skin – Siggi is still beside me. This is what my world has contracted to: the dark water, my friend, and Christiane waiting for me. I begin to feel that my mind and my body are only very tenuously connected; it is a strange sensation. Then, stranger still, I see us both from above, myself swimming beside Siggi, my body paler than his. There is moonlight on the water, swirls and eddies behind us. I see us from further and further away. We become very small, two pale dots in the darkness of interstellar space.

I never again experienced anything quite like that.

*

There is a wooden jetty sticking out into the water ahead of us. Sitting at the end of the jetty, wrapped in blankets, are two small figures. We swim towards them. As we approach, both figures shrug the blankets off their heads and onto their shoulders. I immediately recognise Christiane. The other girl has long blond hair; I have seen her on the hikes, and of course Siggi has talked about her, but we have never met.

Siggi and I swim towards the wooden ladder at the end of the jetty. The girls whisper to each other as we climb out, then they hand us their blankets to dry ourselves with. I am shivering. Christiane rubs me through the blanket. The blond girl does the same with Siggi. She has a brown, sunburnt nose and a dusting of freckles. Siggi introduces us. I have forgotten her name, but I remember that her hand in mine felt as small and frail as a young bird.

We follow the girls through the camp and climb up to a point from which we can see the lake below us. We sit on the damp earth and, well, we talk for a while. And we watch the moonlight sparkle on the surface of the water.

But the moon is already high in the sky, and Siggi and I both know what that means.

'We have to go,' I say. 'We've got to be back at our posts when the relief arrives.'

We walk back down through the forest, to the water's edge. We kiss the girls goodbye, then we hand them the blankets and wade back into the cold water. We strike out for our own camp once again.

Swimming back to the camp is much harder. We are both tired and we feel the cold more. Siggi is slowing noticeably. We start to swim breaststroke – that way we can talk to each other. We see our camp in the distance and stare intently at it but all appears quiet – there is no sign that our absence has been noticed.

After what seems like hours, we are finally able to stand up in the water. We embrace there and then, in the shallows; it has been an exceptional day and, exhausted as we now are, we both want to enjoy the moment. But as we embrace I hear a voice:

'*Ach so!*'

We both jump. On the pebble beach I see the looming figure of Kurt Gruber.

'*Kommt sofort her,*' he says.

As I said earlier, we admired Kurt Gruber a lot, but he was not known for his kindness. Quite the opposite. However, I knew that he liked us both, and that he would certainly have respected our success in the climbing earlier that day. I thought I might be able to appeal to his clemency. However, before I could say anything I felt his heavy, calloused climber's hand on the back of my neck, yanking me out of the water and thrusting me towards the pile of clothes.

'So, *Du verschwinde* – get lost,' he said. I picked up my bundle of clothes and saw out of the corner of my eye that Siggi also made a movement in my direction.

'*Du bleibst hier* – you stay here,' Kurt said to Siggi. For a brief moment, Siggi's face appeared frozen in a mask of fear. I had never seen him like that before – Siggi was fearless. But in the next moment he looked at me and nodded, and I imagined that he too was thinking that he could appeal to Kurt's clemency. In fact, thinking back to Kurt's fireside rendition of the story of Siegfried and the dragon, I was sure that Siggi's chances of success were greater than mine. Kurt had always treated Siggi indulgently. But if Siggi were to succeed in persuading Kurt to turn a blind eye to our transgression, it would be best if no one else were there to witness it. So I grabbed my clothes and ran through the woods towards the campsite. I got under my blanket and resolved to wait until Siggi reappeared and I knew what our punishment would be. However, despite my anxiety, I was overwhelmed by tiredness and I fell asleep after a short while.

*

I was woken by the bugle call at six the following morning. My heart sank when I saw that Siggi's sleeping bag was empty; I thought that he had probably been made to leave during the night and that I would be following very soon.

I lined up for roll call that morning full of foreboding. The presence of a large shiny BMW motorbike by the entrance to the camp was another worrying sign; only the SS drove those bikes. Instead of the announcement of our victory in the climbing competition, I now expected a public humiliation, perhaps even an immediate expulsion at the hands of an SS officer. However, I was just lining up in front of the *Tingstätte* – the meeting place – when I heard Siggi's voice whisper in my ear, *'Alles klar'*. I looked round to see him standing in the row behind me. He didn't smile in his usual, easy fashion. In fact, there was something blank and distant in his manner, but before I had a chance to ask him where he had been and what was going to happen to us, Kurt Gruber climbed the small wooden stage at the front of the *Tingstätte*. He made the usual formal announcements about the programme for the day – eating times, sentry duty and so on. Then he introduced SS Brigadeführer Wolfgang Raue.

Herr Raue mounted the stage. He was of average height with drawn features and an eye patch; his appearance was at odds with his relative youth. Kurt Gruber announced that before the war Herr Raue had been one of the most famous climbers in Germany, that he had been awarded the Knight's Cross with oak leaves at Stalingrad, and that he was on sick leave recovering from the injuries he had sustained. Herr Raue strode to the front of the stage, brought his heels together and saluted as if he were springloaded. He smiled and was silent for a long moment. Eventually he spoke:

'Boys,' he said, 'I have not come here today to speak of wounds nor of decorations. I am here today because this was the last place I was happy. Some of you will find that hard to believe, but it is true. Five years ago I was the age that some of you are now; I was in my last summer with the HJ. As a child I grew up in these mountains - they are my home. When I think back to that summer, I remember climbing with dear friends, none of whom are alive today. Since that time I have shivered through the long Russian nights; during those nights I often thought of this place, of the songs and the stories, the *Drachenwand* and the lake. I tell you this because I want you to enjoy it to the full while you still can.

'When I think back, I also remember our impatience. I wanted action and the chance to test my courage, the chance to win glory. Many of you will no doubt feel that way. It is right that you should feel that way. But do not lose sight of what you already have because you think only of what is to come.

'I have been asked here today to award the Hitler Youth dagger to two of your comrades. These two *Hitlerjungen* have distinguished themselves by their courage, their physical prowess and their pursuit of excellence. They have not yet had to spill their blood for Germany, but what they have achieved here would make the Führer just as proud. Many of you will have watched them climb to victory yesterday. Otto Eisinger and Siegfried Rackus, please step forward to receive the blade.'

I was dumfounded but I had little time to wonder. Boys had started cheering and Siggi and I were pushed forward as hand after hand clapped us on the back. This was extremely unusual; the dagger was almost always presented upon graduation from the HJ, hardly ever before that. Occasionally in recognition of acts of great bravery, but rarely simply for winning a sports competition.

Siggi and I mounted the steps that led up to the wooden stage. The cheering died down as we shook hands with SS Brigadeführer Raue. He indicated to us that we should kneel on the wooden floor. As we did so, two younger boys appeared before us. Each boy held in his hands a red velvet cushion. On each cushion lay the silver Hitler Youth dagger with the small swastika embossed on the handle. Engraved in the middle of the blade were the words *Blut und Ehre*. Brigadeführer Raue took my right hand in his right and Siggi's right hand in his left, then he placed our right hands over the daggers on the two cushions. He started to recite the oath of allegiance to the Führer and we repeated it after him. When we had finished repeating it, he pressed the daggers into our hands and our friends again began to cheer.

Chapter 16

ONCE PIETRO had left, Fernanda exchanged my white gown for a pale green one, then she gave me an elasticated plastic cap for my head. The anaesthetist arrived as I was putting it on. He was a large man with big, rough hands – quite out of keeping with his occupation and with the polka dot bow tie he was wearing. He explained that I would shortly be taken through to the operating theatre where he would give me a small injection – a 'scratch', as he called it – and I would not feel anything until I woke up later in the day with an artificial hip. The pain might be considerable, he said, and I should not be afraid to use the morphine drip to which I would once again be attached. He then looked at his checklist and ran through a few final questions – Did I have any allergies? Was I currently taking medication? – before asking for my signature at the bottom of the list. I signed, he nodded and assured me that I had nothing to worry about, then I was by myself.

I felt ill at ease. In part, this was because I was nervous about the operation. But I also felt that I had not been entirely honest with Pietro. I hadn't lied to him, but I had not told him everything that had happened during the hour we spent at the girls' camp. There are some things I am not comfortable sharing with him. Yet in my own mind those events loom large, especially now that I have begun to wonder whether the similarity between Siggi and Pietro could be more than a mere coincidence.

*

The girls offer to show us the camp. We follow them along the path which slopes up into the woods from the shore of the lake. When it becomes steep, I go ahead and take Christiane's hand. When the path evens out again, I do not release her hand and nor does she remove it from mine. So we walk hand in hand through a glade of silver birch and alder. The white trunks of birch gleam in the moonlight and I can hear the tinkling of water to our right where a small brook runs into the lake, now a little way below us.

'On some nights we come here to tell stories,' Christiane whispers into my ear. And I can see why – it feels like an enchanted place.

Christiane tugs my hand. *'Komm, gehen wir zum Ausichtspunkt,'* she says, then she releases my hand and strikes away from the path. I look round but by now Siggi and Freya are some way behind us.

Siggi and Freya – that's it. The blond girl was called Freya.

I turn to follow Christiane. The slope grows steeper and we climb over buried roots and between rocks. The trees thin out and I can see the light of the moon reflected off the surface of the lake. Christiane's hand seeks mine and I hold it for a moment, then I pull her towards me and kiss her on the lips. And it was there, in that opening between the trees, overlooking the lake, that I made love to a woman for the first and, perhaps, the last time.

I have not slept with many women since Christiane, and it never felt as right as it did on that first occasion. That is not usually the way, I know. Over the years I have come to realise that I do not love women the way that other men do. On that first occasion I believed I did, but I also loved a great deal more besides. I loved the sparkling lake below me and the cold water swirling about me and the hot sun on the *Drachenwand*. I loved my friends, and my country, and bravery, and honour, and the Führer who had brought all these things together. So when I made love it was not just about Christiane; indeed, it was not even primarily about Christiane.

Afterwards we sat for a while on a rock looking out over the lake. We talked about the first time we met, during the long march to Nuremberg, just after I had joined the Jungvolk. I reminded her how she often took our side in arguments with older boys. She smiled at that and said, 'Yes, I always liked you.' Then she ran her hand through my hair, which was still damp from the swim. I lay down so that my head was resting on her lap. When I looked away from her, I could see the lake glittering below us.

After a while, I broke the silence. 'We are very lucky,' I said. Christiane didn't reply, so I went on, 'I mean, our parents were never part of anything like this.' Still Christiane did not respond. 'They never got to experience anything like this,' I said as I gestured to the lake below us. Then I looked up at Christiane and saw that her brow was furrowed. 'Don't you think we are lucky?' I asked.

'Yes,' she replied, 'but I'm scared too.'

'What's there to be scared of?' I asked, surprised.

Christiane looked gravely down at me.

'Promise you won't tell anyone what I'm about to tell you,' she said.

'I promise.'

'I have an older brother who is a painter,' she said. 'My father sent him away to live in Hamburg. He wanted to send him to South America but my mother begged him not to.'

'Why did your father send him away?'

'My brother doesn't believe in the Führer. He says the party is evil.'

'What?' I asked, astonished.

Christiane pressed her finger to my lips and whispered 'Shhhh'. Of course, I knew that the party had its critics, but I never imagined that they would come from good families like Christiane's. Jews and traitors might hate the Führer, but not pillars of the community. At that moment, on that particular day, the thought that the Führer could be evil struck me as absurd.

'Christiane, if it weren't for the Führer and the party, none of this would be possible. Don't you see that?'

Christiane didn't reply. After a while, she said, 'Please Otto, you must never tell anyone.'

I wanted to convince Christiane that her brother was wrong, but then I heard Siggi's voice calling my name.

Christiane pulled away from me abruptly. I called back, 'Here. We're coming.'

We stood up and dusted the earth and the twigs from the blanket, then we followed the path back down through the trees. From a distance I could see Siggi and Freya standing pressed together. They pulled apart when they saw us. Siggi indicated the height of the moon in the sky, then we returned to the wooden jetty where Siggi and I dove into the lake to swim back to our camp.

*

I have never been happier than I was in the days following the climb and the hour by the lake with Christiane and the award of the HJ dagger. I felt I could do anything. Siggi felt it too, I am sure of that, but he expressed it through a surfeit of energy that verged on mania. I suppose it was his nature to push the boundaries; that is what makes a great adventurer. Every night he planned some sort of mischief and I felt it was my duty to accompany him. Mostly they were just harmless pranks – letting down tents or hiding people's clothes whilst they were asleep; the punishment for any of these would not have been severe. But one night Siggi woke me in order to raid the storage tent - he had seen our Hungarian cooks sneak out of the camp, leaving the tent unguarded.

Siggi and I crept into the tent. We found piles of tinned food and enormous bags of sugar and flour. I am not sure what we were hoping for, but it wasn't this. We carried on searching and our thoroughness was eventually rewarded with a bottle of unopened Hungarian *slivovitz*. We took the bottle and ran up through the woods to a small clearing on raised ground; from there it was easy to see if anyone was approaching. Then we sat down and passed the bottle of lukewarm *slivovitz* between the two of us in the way that only determined adolescents and drunks can.

We were young, entirely unaccustomed to alcohol and we were in very good shape. It did not take long for this potent homemade spirit to take effect. At first we became very talkative. As our excitement grew, so our voices were in danger of becoming too loud and one of us constantly had to shush the other. We were soon giggling uncontrollably. There are few things more likely to induce uncontrollable laughter than the combination of alcohol, high spirits and the danger of giving oneself away. We kept passing the bottle to and fro and soon the edges of my perception began to blur and everything that mattered seemed concentrated in the figure of my friend.

'Siggi,' I said, 'I am so grateful to you.'

'What?' he said.

'No, I'm serious. I am so grateful to you. I know what a great climber you are. I know you could climb with anyone.'

'That's nonsense.'

'It's true. You know it's true. And I want to give you something...'

I put my hand in my pocket and took out the small piece of amber with the insect's wing trapped inside. I always carried it in my pocket.

'I want you to have this,' I said. 'It's a talisman.'

Then I lit a match and held the amber in front of it. Siggi had already started to protest but he was immediately captivated by the light of the dancing flame glimpsed through the ancient resin and through the delicate insect's wings. He stared intently at it.

'The fly got stuck to a drop of *Harz* on a prehistoric tree,' I said, then I pressed the piece of amber into his hand.

'You really want me to have it?'

'Yes.'

We passed the bottle back and forth a few more times, then Siggi said, 'Otto, the climbing is nothing. I know this sounds *Schmalzig,* but I feel like you are the brother I never had.'

'Really?'

'Yes, really.'

'I feel like that too.' I took another swig. I could feel the beating of my heart. 'I had an older brother. He died before I was born.' Maybe, I thought to myself, maybe it is his soul in your body.

Siggi was again staring at the match through the amber. He looked across at me. His eyes appeared slightly glazed in the light of the flame.

'Then we will make a pact,' he said. 'As blood brothers.'

Siggi gave me the matches, then he unsheathed his Hitler Youth dagger. He held it in his right hand. My vision had become so blurred that I could barely make out the words engraved on the blade. Then Siggi held out his left hand and laid the shiny metal against the heel of his palm on the inside, a little above the wrist. He pushed the blade down until the skin was depressed, then he pulled it smoothly a few centimetres across. There was a second during which the wound appeared pale and surprised, then a trickle of blood began to flow, very bright and very red even by the flickering light of the match.

Siggi took my left hand in his left hand. My heart was thumping in my chest and I could hear a rushing noise inside my head. He touched the cool metal to my palm. '*Keine Angst,*' he said, then he pulled the blade across. I felt no pain. Again there was a brief moment before the blood began to flow. Siggi wiped the blade on the grass then put it back in its sheath. He extended his left hand towards me and we pressed our palms together and clamped them with our right hands.

In the silence that followed I felt that the world was spinning around me. Then I heard Siggi's voice:

'Otto, do you know why we weren't punished?'

'What?' I said.

'We weren't punished because Kurt made me… makes me do things I don't want to do.'

'Like what?' I asked. 'Like sentry duty? I also hate sentry duty.'

'No Otto, disgusting things.'

Siggi's words came out slurred. I wasn't sure that I had heard him correctly. The world was spinning and I felt nauseous. What was he saying? That Kurt made him do things he didn't want to do? Maybe climb faces he didn't think he could climb? But Siggi was drunk too. He didn't know what he was saying. The world was spinning faster and faster and the rushing sound was getting louder. I tried to focus on Siggi's face – something solid and familiar – but it was just a blur. My mouth was filling with salty saliva. I swallowed again and again. Then in the next instant I was being sick, violently.

*

I felt nauseous in the hospital too, but not because of the memory of the *slivovitz*. No, it was the fact that I hadn't been allowed to eat all day. However, I was spared the sight of the other patients wolfing their lunch by the arrival of the two nurses who were going to wheel me into the operating theatre.

The nurses both congratulated me on the attempt to apprehend the gunman in the shop. It seems that everyone knows about me in this hospital. However, I was not given any time to bask in pride. The nurses undid the wheel locks and wheeled me out of the ward, along a spearmint green corridor, into a lift and up to the fourth floor.

The anaesthetist with the bow tie was waiting for me in the ante-room of the theatre. Now he was wearing a white gown. The nurses attached a little clip to the end of my middle finger, then they took my blood pressure with an inflatable black armband around my elbow. I warned them that those devices make me nervous and that the reading might not be accurate but the anaesthetist dismissed my concern with a breezy '*tudo bom*'. He took hold of my left hand and told me that I would feel nothing more than a little scratch. I looked away and dug the nails of my right hand into my palm to distract myself. The precautions were unnecessary; there was no pain. The last thought I remember was wondering what would happen if the anaesthetic didn't work.

Chapter 17

S EU OTTO will be in the operating theatre by now. I am not worried about him. Fernanda, his nurse, told me that these operations are routine. And he's a tough old man, no doubt about that.

It's a beautiful afternoon. I decide to go for a surf – there are things on my mind, things I need to think about. I drive home to get my board. Marina is at home. I suggest to her that she come surfing with me. We haven't surfed together for ages.

'I have to work tonight,' she says.

'So do I,' I say. 'And I have to see Seu Otto after the operation. Let's just go for a few waves before dark, then we'll come straight back.' Usually we'd also have a few beers at one of the restaurants by the beach after surfing. When we first got together, that's what we'd do most evenings – surf, have a few beers, smoke a joint. But that was before I was sponsored by Kauai, and before I'd started promoting nights at *Divino*.

We drive to Moçambique. It's a few miles north of Joaquina and you get a lot of posers on the beach. However, I don't want to see anyone from Kauai. They'd want to know about which contests I was planning to compete in and so on, and that's not a conversation I want to have. At least, not right now.

Marina is in good spirits. I realise that it's been a while since we have done something fun together, something other than shopping for groceries or running errands. She rests her arm against the back of my seat and strokes my neck. I put my hand on her knee but I can't leave it there for long because I have to keep changing gear. Then my phone rings. Marina opens it and holds it to my ear. It is avó.

'Pietro!' she shouts down the phone. Even when their hearing is fine, old people always seem to shout into phones. 'Pietro! Seu Otto is out of the operating theatre. He's fine, but he's very tired. He would like you to visit but he'd prefer you to come tomorrow morning.'

'Sure, no problem,' I say. The phone cuts out before I can say goodbye. Avó has still not mastered the mobile phone.

'Your grandmother?' asks Marina.

'Yes,' I say. 'The operation went well but Seu Otto is tired. I'm going to see him tomorrow morning. That means we have the whole afternoon to surf.' I squeeze Marina's knee.

'This story about Senhor Eisinger is a great opportunity, Pietro. You have to make the most of it.'

'I know, I know,' I say. I don't like the insistence of her tone. I squeeze her knee harder, digging my thumb and index finger in at just those two points where the sensation teeters between pain and pleasure.

'Ouch, Pietro, stop it.' Marina pulls the hair at the back of my head and I let go. We look at each other crossly, but only for a second. Neither of us can keep a straight face for long.

*

I park the combi on the side of the sandy track that leads down to the beach. We pull out the two surfboards. Marina's is a longboard. The sky is clear but there is a strong breeze which catches the board as she walks and sends her zigzagging across the road. I take her board under one arm and carry my own shorter board under the other.

Moçambique is a right and left beach break. It's not a hard wave, so the water is often crowded here. But today there are surprisingly few surfers out. Marina and I paddle out next to each other. The water is not cold and there is no need for a wetsuit. I duck under a couple of waves and soon find myself out in the ocean, beyond the break. Marina catches a wave on the inside, taking it all the way to the beach. I am alone.

I sit on my board. My feet dangle in the water. The sun is high in the sky. In front of me, Moçambique is a strip of bright white sand offset by the greenery at either end of the beach. There are no white apartment blocks here. This is how the island would have looked to the first Portuguese settlers, five hundred years ago.

I allow the first three waves of a set to pass me by. I was anticipating a four, but the fourth doesn't come. It doesn't matter. I feel at peace. I notice my breathing, now slow and even after the exertion of paddling out. My breath rises and falls like the swells of the set that just passed.

If I hadn't grown up here, would I still love surfing? If I had grown up in the mountains, would I be a climber? If I had grown up in war-time, would I be a soldier? To what extent is one predisposed towards a certain way of life, and to what extent is it something you learn? What would Seu

Otto be like if he had been born on this island in place of me?

The wind has dropped and the ocean is smooth, almost glassy. These are optimal surfing conditions, and yet I always feel a slight apprehension when it's like this. It was on a day like this that João's younger brother Miguel almost drowned. One moment he was surfing with us, alongside us, the next his limp body was washed up on the beach. I didn't notice until the lifeguards came running down to carry him further up the beach. By the time we were with him, they had already resuscitated him. His face was pale and oddly green and there was a yoyo of drool hanging from the side of his mouth. He was shaking pretty violently too. The strange thing was, he could never tell us what had happened. He didn't remember it at all. The waves weren't particularly big and there were no hidden rocks. He was probably hit on the head by a surfboard. There were a lot of surfers in the water that day. If someone did hit him, they never admitted it. In fact, they left him to drown. Bastards. On the other hand, maybe they didn't know they'd hit him. I hope that was the case. Poor Miguel, he never surfed again after that.

When something happens suddenly, I guess you don't know how you'll react. I mean, maybe it was another surfer who hit Miguel that day, and maybe that surfer had never thought of himself as the kind of person who would pretend it hadn't happened. It seems to me that we really don't have all that much control over our split-second decisions. How do you know how you'll react until something like that actually happens?

But then, with some people you can be pretty sure that

they'll react the right way. Take Seu Otto. I'd trust him to make the right split-second decision, like he did when he jumped into the frozen lake to save Siggi. So maybe the way you respond in those split seconds is not entirely due to chance. Maybe you can cultivate your character to make it more likely that you'll react in a certain way? Isn't that what Seu Otto's Hitler Youth training set out to achieve? It encouraged him to take risks, to challenge himself, so really it should be no surprise that he attacked the gunman in the shop.

I suddenly feel worried that I'm not cultivating my character in the right way. I'd like to think that if I accidentally hit someone with my board, I'd dive in to check that they were ok. But it has never happened, so how can I be sure? There are aspects of my life that I am not proud of, and I wonder whether, if they started to pile up, they might influence my ability to make the right split-second decision.

When Seu Otto was young, he tested himself by climbing. Maybe that's where he learnt to overcome fear. You can do the same thing with surfing. I mean, you can really challenge yourself – bigger waves, shallower breaks. You can always push your limits.

But it's about more than just surfing or climbing. It's about finding a life that challenges you, that enables you to be the best person you can be. That's what Marina wants for me. Sometimes she can be a bit pushy, and then I get irritable. But really she just wants the best for me, and I love her for that.

I know I could stay on this island, and surf, and, with a bit of luck, I could start making some money from promoting. But there must be more to life than this. If Seu Otto were my age, I'm sure he'd have bigger plans. He'd want to get off Santa Catarina and make a name for himself. Lead a life to be proud of, even if it meant starting again on the other side of the world, which is what he did. I don't think there are many people here who would understand that, but I do.

I think I am onto something with Seu Otto's story. I hope I'll be able to sell it to a newspaper, maybe even to a TV channel. That's where the big money is. I'll have to decide on an angle. But first I have to ask him about Siggi's death. I sense his reluctance to talk about it. It must be painful. Or perhaps Seu Otto is even hiding something? But I don't think he'd do that.

I should ask him about the holocaust too. Perhaps he is afraid I will think he is a Jew hater and a racist because he knew what was being done in the concentration camps. But he was a young boy – what could he possibly have done to stop any of it?

There is one professor at my university with whom I have a good relationship. He is called Paulo Monteiro, Doutor Paulo Monteiro. He is one of the few professors I really respect. He teaches journalism but he's adjunct faculty – he's still active in the field. I'm always suspicious of the professors who teach but don't practise. If they are so knowledgeable, then why don't they put that knowledge to use in the real world, at least some of the time? Often, I suspect it's because they couldn't make it in the real world. But Paulo Monteiro is not like that. In fact, he's pretty well known for his journalism. He may be able to help me.

*

I see another set approaching. My anticipation mounts. This time I pick a wave and start to paddle. Dropping in, the lip of the wave pitches in front of me, allowing me to pull right into the tube on take-off. I drop in and stand up at the same time. I am immediately inside the hollow of the wave; the cylinder of water is barrelling all around me. I drag my hand in the wall of water. I am deep in the tube but I can see the daylight ahead, as if through a telescope. I drive towards the light, pumping for speed. And then I am out of the barrel, back in the light and the sun. I feel reborn.

The sets come in smooth and regular for the rest of the afternoon. I haven't enjoyed surfing so much for years. Occasionally I see Marina, but she prefers the smaller inside waves. I lose track of time. It is only when the setting sun begins to blind me that I realise how late it is.

When I come out of the water, I see Marina sitting on her surfboard on the beach in front of the dunes, where the sand is dry and warm. I go to join her.

'Looks like you were having fun out there,' she says, smiling.

Marina is an attractive girl, but it's still amazing what a few hours in the sun and the ocean can do. Her hair is lighter. The little freckles on her nose are more pronounced. Her green-grey sun-strained eyes are clearer than usual. I can even see a hint of brown around the pupil. I sit on the surfboard beside her and we kiss. Her lips are salty but her mouth tastes sweet and I spy the can of coke in the sand beside her.

We sit and watch other couples walk along the beach. The men here are gym bunnies who mostly look as if they'd pop if you pricked them. Their girlfriends are used to being stared at. Their tiny *tangas* are often invisible between their bronzed butt cheeks. I am sure many of them have had surgery, though I don't always find it easy to tell. And yet, for once, I am not interested in any of them. I am happy to be with Marina.

Chapter 18

I HEAR the sound of my own voice. I open my eyes and see that I am still in the ante-room of the operating theatre. A puzzled, dark skinned nurse is looking at me.

'*Ó Senhor Eisinger, fala muito,*' she says.

'But when are they going to operate on me?'

'*Já o fizeram,* they've already done it.'

'Already?'

'*Sim senhor.* How do you feel?'

'I feel fine. My hip is throbbing a bit. And I'm hungry.'

'*O Senhor* has the morphine drip on his right. Now we will return you to the ward. Dr. da Silva will visit shortly.'

I feel very sleepy, very dreamy. The world is soft and fluid. A second nurse enters the room and positions herself behind my head. Together the two nurses wheel me back down the corridor and into the lift. I barely register the jolt as we pass over the metal threshold. The dark-skinned nurse apologises. I reach up and press the button for the morphine drip. The effect is almost instantaneous. As I am wheeled along the pastel green corridor, I feel like a boat drifting on a spearmint sea. My eyes keep closing but I do not fall asleep. I am back in that twilight world between waking and sleeping, a world in which I can consciously steer my dreams. If only ordinary life were more like this.

My bed is wheeled back into the ward where Anna-

Maria is patiently waiting for me. At first I keep my eyes closed and pretend to be asleep; I do not yet have the energy to face her. Then, out of curiosity, I open one eye a tiny amount so that I can observe her. She is a woman of robust good health. There is also something of the Italian peasant about her. She has that stolid, bovine quality which centuries of unquestioning faith breeds in womenfolk. As I watch her, she releases hold of the little package on her lap and begins to toy instead with the crucifix around her neck. Then she leans across to smooth the sheet that covers me. The little package slips off her lap and spills its contents onto the floor. I see a number of Polaroid photographs of a lawn, of my lawn in Sambaqui. Very green in the sunlight.

'Anna-Maria, *tudo bom?*' I say.

'*Seu Otto, graças a Deus! Como se sente?* How do you feel? How is your hip? Does it hurt? I was so worried!' Her brow is furroughed with concern.

'*Com calma Anna-Maria, com calma...* I feel fine, just tired.'

'I did not know what to bring you, so I bought a photo camera and took these photos of the lawn. It was looking so beautiful today.' She passes me the photos.

Anna-Maria is right, the lawn looks more beautiful than I have ever seen it. Its greenness is so fresh and so intense that it appears to pulsate with energy, with life-force. When I stare at the picture, it seems as if I can smell the grass and hear the whisper of the brave little shoots pushing their way up through the soil.

In one of the photos, Valdemar is leaning on a rake and beaming at the camera with his thumb raised.

'Valdemar is very proud,' says Anna-Maria.

'He should be. The lawn looks wonderful.'

'Not of the lawn. Of you, Seu Otto.'

I continue to look at the photos but my thoughts are elsewhere. I realise that I do not pay sufficient attention to the feelings of others. Anna-Maria had bought a photo camera and taken pictures of my garden as a present for me and I almost hadn't opened my eyes because I find her matronly solicitations a little straining. In fact, all I am conscious of at such times is her resemblance to a peasant woman. And when I think of Valdemar, I think of nothing but his indolence, yet here he is grinning from ear to ear because he is proud to work for me. Truly I am an ingrate. How does that sad song go? *No peito dos desafinados tambem bate um coração*[3].

'Seu Otto, are you alright?' asks Anna-Maria.

'Yes. I'm tired, that's all,' I reply.

'You should sleep. I can call Pietro to tell him not to come. I know he was planning to pass by later this evening.'

'Well, I would like to see him, but maybe you could ask him to come first thing tomorrow morning?'

Tomorrow morning will be a fresh start, fresh like the young green shoots in my lawn.

'And Anna-Maria, thank you for the photos. Thank you very much.'

When I say that she looks genuinely happy. And I feel happier too.

*

I spend the next few hours drifting in and out of pleasant morphine dreams. Dr. da Silva materialises at my bedside.

---

3 'A heart also beats in the breasts of those who sing out of tune.' From *Desafinado*, by Tom Jobim.

How funny, I think to myself, he has silver hair and is called da Silva. I try to explain this to him but he looks confused. Then I realise that it is only humorous if you also understand English. It is strange how languages are getting confused in my mind.

Dr. da Silva tells me to rest. He looks at the bag of i.v. morphine above my head and warns me not to take more than I need, but I am too old to worry about addiction. Then he says that tomorrow I will have to try to move my hip with the help of a physiotherapist.

Depsite my tiredness, or perhaps because of it, I cannot sleep. The pain in my hip becomes a crescendoing throb which can only be alleviated with repeated presses on the morphine button. The night is long and slow and painful. When I press for more morphine, I feel my body relax but the images of the past crowd in on me and I cannot fight them off. Some are frightening, and these are the most insistent. I see the faces of the past - beautiful faces, battered faces, faceless faces. But eventually the cold grey light of dawn insinuates itself around the edges of the window blind. Thereafter, there is some respite as I drift out of consciousness.

*

When I wake, there is the bustle of activity in the ward. Pietro is sitting in the chair beside my bed, reading. On the bedside table there are two green coconuts with straws in them.

'For breakfast?' I ask.

This time Pietro is not startled.

'Yes, if you feel like it.'

Coconut water is a popular drink on the island – in

summer the roads are lined with vendors. If you buy a coconut they will make two holes in the green husk, one for the straw and one for the air to escape. In the past I have not particularly enjoyed the salty sweet taste, but on this occasion I found it surprisingly pleasing.

I think Pietro could see that I was tired since he settled himself into his chair and we both sipped our coconuts in companionable silence. The coconut water had a vivifying effect – I soon began to feel less tired, although with greater wakefulness came greater pain in my hip. I disregarded Dr. da Silva's advice and gave myself a couple of generous presses on the morphine button.

'So…' I say.

'Um, well, I just thought you might be tired and want to rest,' replies Pietro.

'I shall rest when I am dead.'

Pietro smiles. 'Are you sure?' he asks. I nod in reply. 'Well, I'd really like to know about Siggi. What happened to him? You said he had an accident.'

I have known from the beginning that Pietro would eventually want to find out what happened to Siggi. Nevertheless, I feel ill prepared to answer. Siggi's battered face has haunted the night from which I have just emerged. His death feels more recent than at any other time during the last half century. It also signified the end of my own childhood, and for that reason it is doubly painful. I have managed to banish it from my mind for the best part of my adult life, but in the last few days, since the incident in the shop, I have felt myself moving inexorably closer to it. Well, perhaps now is the time to bring it into the open. Didn't Fernanda say that the patients who talk the most get better the fastest? What's more, my body is full of a chemical whose purpose is to combat pain. I should take advantage of that.

'Siggi's accident...' I took a deep breath. 'It is not something I like to speak about. I have tried not to think about it.'

'Well, if it is very hard for you –'

'No Pietro, I think that would not be fair to you. I have told you so much about him already. And then you also remind me of him.'

'I do?'

'Yes, very much. Ever since you were a young boy you have looked similar to him. You have many of the same characteristics. If Siggi were here now, and if he were your age, he would be doing exactly what you are doing. He also liked to ask questions.'

'Really?' asked Pietro. He looked like he was about to break into a grin.

'Yes, I swear it,' I said. 'And I will tell you everything that happened. But first will you pass me the water?'

Siggi leant across to pick up my glass and I gave the morphine another squeeze.

'So,' I said, 'I told you that Siggi and I were chosen to climb the Matterhorn as part of an HJ expedition?'

'Yes. When was that?' asked Pietro, his pen once again poised.

And I start to prise open the lid.

*

Autumn 1944. Two weeks after the climbing competition, after being awarded the dagger, the announcement is made public: Siggi and I have been chosen to join an elite team of HJ climbers on the Matterhorn. We are excused duties so that we can train. While the others have to spend their days packing up the camp and filling in the latrines, we climb with Kurt Gruber. We range far from the usual routes. In the mornings we walk through the woods to an untouched face that Kurt knows; after all, these are the mountains in which he grew up. Then we climb for an hour or two, until our forearms feel like lead and we cannot continue. We stop to eat a sandwich on a ledge or at the top of the face before finding a walk off and returning to camp. Often Siggi and Kurt go off together because they both climb faster than I do.

The idea that a Hitler Youth team should climb the Matterhorn originated the year before, as a propaganda exercise said to have been dreamt up by Goebbels himself. The ministry hopes that photos and news reports of the next generation of HJ boys achieving such feats for the Fatherland will raise the morale of German soldiers everywhere; this is especially necessary following the disaster of the Russian campaign, though of course we never refer to it as such. That's also why it is important to climb a mountain like the Matterhorn – it is iconic, perhaps the most famous peak in the Alps.

The easiest route is via the northeastern Hörnli ridge, on the Swiss side. That was where the first HJ expedition was supposed to climb in the summer of 1943, but that expedition had to be postponed owing to delays in getting permission from the neutral Swiss authorities. Now the war is going much worse but permission has finally been granted.

*

We are astonished by the send-off we get when we leave the

camp. Our friends and the younger Jungvolk boys whistle and wave as we are driven away in a staff car. We are taken to Munich where there are a number of photographers waiting for us. Flash bulbs go off in our faces and limping or otherwise disabled journalists – the fit ones have been conscripted – stand by with notebooks on the platform as we board our carriage. Eventually the train pulls out of Munich station, though only after a considerable wait during which most of the well-wishers transfer their interest from us to a newly arrived train carrying wounded soldiers from the Eastern Front. Through the carriage windows we see gray, haunted men peering out at us.

The other climbers are already in the carriage. There are four Bavarian pairs and one Austrian pair. Siggi and I have never heard such absurd accents before; at first, we can barely keep a straight face in their presence. Later, in Zermatt, I share a room with them while we wait for the weather to improve. We become friends and I learn to appreciate their sense of humour. Kurt Gruber is also part of the team, and there are two guides from the *Gebirgsjäger,* the mountain infantry. They are on leave from Crete, where they have been fighting the partisans. Despite being on leave, they never remove their grey military caps with the *Edelweiss* insignia. They are both superb climbers.

*

The journey to Zermatt is interminable. It is a wonder we get there at all – the train timetables seem to change almost hourly. It is the first time in two months that Siggi and I have had to sit beneath a roof for more than an hour, so it is hardly surprising that we get twitchy long before we reach our destination. From Munich we go to Karlsruhe, then we board a military lorry which is also carrying our climbing equipment. The lorry takes us to the Swiss border, which we have to cross on foot before taking a bus to Basel. In Basel we spend the night in the dormitory of a youth hostel. The following morning we continue to Zermatt by train.

We arrive in the early evening, just as ominous, low-hanging clouds are moving in. From time to time we catch glimpses of the mountain. It is a truly awe-inspiring sight, a towering pyramid of rock that stands alone and serene, with no other peak anywhere near it. The mountain dominates the skyline from every angle. I feel a healthy trepidation.

Before dinner we go for a walk along the river. As if the atmosphere were not subdued enough already, the guides take us to see a graveyard where there are a number of graves of climbers who have died on the Matterhorn. Four of the seven who made the first successful attempt back in 1865 did not survive the descent. We all offer a silent prayer that there will be no plaques bearing our names on that wall, beside the other fallen climbers.

The following morning the rain is falling heavily, and it is cold. The clouds do not lift all day and we pass the time playing cards in the hostel. I am sharing a room with the two Austrian boys while Siggi shares with Kurt. He spends most of his time in our room and only returns to his own to sleep.

I wake at dawn and look out of the window. It is still raining, so I return to the warmth and safety of my bed. However, when I wake again the sun has burnt the clouds away and is flooding our small wooden room with light.

The Matterhorn rises before us with a light dusting of snow against a blue sky. After lunch we go for an acclimatising hike and test our equipment. The sun improves our collective mood and we leave the village of Zermatt gustily singing a number of HJ songs, to the bemusement of the local Swiss farmers in front of their dark wooden hay silos.

The air is still humid on the wooded hillside because of the morning's rain. The scent of pine needles is overwhelming; it is truly the smell of the mountains. Insects buzz about, glorying in the sunshine. Clouds of butterflies take to the air in alarm at our approach, as do the thousands of flies which cover the steaming cowpats on the path. But we soon climb above the tree line, where there is a slight breeze and the air is less humid. We snake our way up the well-trodden path between bright blue cornflowers towards Schwarzsee. Looking back, I see Zermatt growing ever smaller on the valley floor. I want to continue singing but the route is steep and I am out of breath.

In the late afternoon, we test our climbing equipment on a small rockface just outside the village. Although the newspapers carry frequent reports of equipment shortages on all three fronts, we have been well looked after. Everything we need has been included – ropes, pitons, carabiners, crampons, ice-axes; the full arsenal. We go to bed shortly after dusk, praying that the weather will hold.

We are lucky; the following day dawns clear and windstill. We leave the hostel and head for the Hörnli hut, just above Schwarzsee and at the foot of the Matterhorn. We will spend the first night there and then climb the northeast ridge to the much smaller Solvay hut on the following morning. We will attempt the summit on the day after that. If all goes well, we will be back in the Hörnli hut that same night.

We arrive at the Hörnli hut in the middle of the afternoon. The hut is situated on a rocky outcrop at the beginning of the Hörnli ridge. From the terrace of the hut you can see the summit rising to the sky; it's an intimidating sight. We hide our nerves by making jokes and playing pranks. We are more boisterous than usual. Only Siggi is subdued. That is hardly surprising – he is the best climber amongst us and therefore, obviously, the least nervous. That is why he can afford to stare calmly into the distance while the rest of us are joking and laughing.

Later that evening I go to get snow from the shaded area behind the hut to boil in order to make tea. We eat as the sun is setting; the shadows chase the orange glow up the Matterhorn. While we eat, one of the *Gebirgsjäger* explains to us the route to the summit. We will climb roped together in teams of two. The only exception is my own group – I will climb in a three with both Siggi and Kurt. We will leave around seven the next morning and hope to get to the tiny Solvay hut by midday.

We retire to the large dormitory shortly after our evening bread. Some people fall asleep immediately but a combination of nerves and the thin air keep me awake until long after midnight. Even when sleep does come it is intermittent and punctuated by vivid dreams in which I am running through tunnels. Siggi, lying next to me, appears to be suffering from similar difficulties; he tosses and turns throughout the night. At one stage I hear him rummaging in his rucksack. Then I hear the rustle of his clothes.

'It's not time yet,' I whisper to him.

'I know,' he says.

The rustling continues. I feel the change in weight as he gets off his mattress, which is pushed up against my own. A few seconds later I hear the creaking of door hinges. I open my eyes and see Siggi framed in the doorway. Behind him I catch a glimpse of snow-covered rocks reflecting the moonlight. I am surprised by the brightness and I think to myself that the moon must be full. Siggi appears to hesitate for a second in the doorway; I have the impression that the world darkens for a moment, perhaps from a passing cloud. I see that Siggi is staring at me and I am struck by the strangeness of his expression – a look of sadness combined with something else, something I don't recognise.

I assume that Siggi is going outside to pee – I have already been a couple of times myself. But something about his expression prompts me to ask: 'Where are you going?'

He doesn't reply. He continues to look at me. The moonlight grows brighter again and I think to myself that his expression is one of pity. Then he says:

'*Wir Jungen schreiten gläubig der Sonne zugewandt.*'

I recognise the line from one of the Hitler Youth songs. It means 'We young step out in faith to greet the sun.' It is Siggi's favourite song. Then he slips out the door.

When I next open my eyes, the first grey light of dawn is creeping into the room. I roll over and feel something small and hard against my temple. It feels like a pebble. I pick it up and hold it towards the light. It is the piece of amber which I gave Siggi the night we got drunk on the *slivovitz*. I sit up and see that Siggi's bed is empty and his clothes and rucksack are gone. I roll the piece of amber between my thumb and forefinger. I have a sense of foreboding.

Is Siggi in the latrine again? Or did he never come back to the hut? Maybe he slipped on the ice outside?

I jump out of bed and approach the less austere of our two guides. He opens his eyes as I get close.

'Siggi is not in his bed,' I say.

'He's probably in the latrine,' the guide replies, his voice husky with sleep and with the dryness of the air.

I want to say that perhaps Siggi has had an accident, but I do not want to cause alarm.

Now the others are stirring. The guide tells Kurt that Siggi is missing. Kurt immediately orders us to go out and look for him. We are dressed and outside within minutes. I check the small wooden hut of the latrine in case the door has jammed and Siggi is stuck inside, but the door is open and the hut is empty. We call out his name and climb a small distance up and down from the ridge. Our voices travel far in the cold morning air. I climb out of sight of the hut to where I collected the snow the evening before. The snow is frozen hard on top. I can hear from the direction of the voices that by now the others have fanned out over the ridge. I look closely at the frozen snow to see if there are any fresh tracks, but there are none.

I listen again to the voices of the others and I look around at the peaks which serrate the distant horizon. My eyes come to rest on the rocky flank of the Matterhorn and I follow it all the way up the northeast ridge. Then I see a tiny black dot already two thirds of the way up the ridge. Could it possibly be Siggi? Who else could it be? The dot is climbing with extraordinary speed. I shout to the others and run back to the Hörnli hut. By the time I arrive they have already spotted him. I observe the rare sight of two battle-hardened *Gebirgsjäger* staring in open-mouthed wonder.

We assemble on the terrace of the Hörnli hut. Everyone is talking about Siggi's egotism and selfishness. We have been trained to be competitive and to seek glory, but not at the expense of our comrades. Nevertheless, there is also a grudging respect for Siggi's courage. To climb without a rope at the speed he is going is far beyond the rest of us.

The guides confer briefly, then they announce that we will climb all the same, just as if Siggi were still with us. The only difference is that Kurt and I are now a team of two. As we leave the hut, one of the guides notices that Siggi has taken the HJ flag which we had intended to plant on the summit for the photo. This angers the others; they mutter obscenities. But I can tell that the two *Gebirgsjäger* are impressed – the flag will have added considerable weight to Siggi's rucksack.

We head further up the Hörnli ridge. The mass of the ridge blocks our view of Siggi. The air is thin and we are climbing fast. My lungs burn but I only register the sensation intermittently. I think back to Siggi's expression when he left the hut during the night. Was it a look of pity? Perhaps because he was leaving me behind? Did he feel sorry for me? He need not have done. I know that there is no way that I could have climbed the way he is doing right now. I would certainly have slowed him down. No, I am not hurt that he left me behind.

As we emerge from beneath the shoulder of the ridge, I am astonished to see that Siggi's progress has, if anything, speeded up. He cannot be more than half an hour from the summit. The early morning sunlight has only just climbed over the ridge of the Italian Alps that lie further south; the first rays brush the very top of the Matterhorn, turning it a delicate pink. Siggi continues to move steadily upwards until the warm glow embraces him. Then he stops. I imagine him up there, alone, facing the sun. And then I remember what he said as he slipped out of the door, that line from the Hitler Youth song – *We young step out in faith to greet the sun*. Suddenly everything falls into place; it all makes sense. This is not the crazed climb of an egomaniac. It is a private act of worship, a dedication to the Führer and to Germany. He has climbed alone not to beat the rest of us but because the harder a task is, the greater its value as an offering and a dedication.

Soon Siggi starts to climb again. He continues to move steadily upwards, between rocks bathed in sunlight. I wonder whether he has seen us while he was resting. It is unlikely; we are still in the shade. I see him inch closer and closer to the summit and then, all of a sudden, he disappears. I feel a sudden panic until one of the guides announces that the summit is flat. I am reassured. The guides are unable to disguise their admiration for Siggi's climb. I overhear one say to the other: '*So ein kleiner Bursche, so ein grosser Berg*[4].

I am happy for Siggi. I know he is a much better climber than I will ever be, but he was my climbing partner and, although I am not there with him now, in some way I feel that his success reflects on me too. It is a pleasant feeling to

---

4 Such a small boy, such a big mountain.

be happy for another person, to share their success without jealousy or resentment. But as I am thinking this, I hear a gasp from the boy next to me. He is staring at the summit. I look up and see a tiny black dot plummeting through the air, a black dot with something red trailing behind it. The black dot grows larger as it falls – it is a human body. A human body with arms extended, holding the Hitler Youth flag like an oversize cape, and it falls with the stillness of a diving bird. Then the body hits the steep rock slope two hundred metres below the summit. It bounces and cartwheels before sliding like a rag doll, limbs jiggling in an inhuman way, down the long, snow-dusted triangle of the east face. Finally it comes to rest at the top of the glacier that meets the bottom of that face, some distance below the Hörnli hut.

Silence. The sound of one boy vomiting, then another and another. I cannot accept what I have just seen. Siggi cannot have fallen after reaching the summit. It is impossible. The summit is flat. There must have been someone else up there. An old man of the mountain. An ogre. Siggi has thrown the ogre off the mountain before he could be thrown off himself. I begin to believe this passionately.

The guides are also shaken. They tell us to wait while they confer out of earshot. Then they instruct Kurt to take us back to the Hörnli hut. We are all trembling. There is nothing to harden you to the sight of a body being broken like that. The others start to climb back down the way we have come but I refuse. I still cannot believe that Siggi fell. I insist again and again that it wasn't him, that it must have been someone else. In the end the guides agree to take me with them to where the body lies. The route is long but not hard – we drop below the height of the Hörnli hut then traverse the top of the glacier.

We pick our way sideways across the rocky flank of the mountain. My movements are robotic. The slope where the body has come to rest is not particularly steep but we have to rope up because of crevasses. We can see the body from a distance but I am the first to get close enough to identify it. It is Siggi. In the first moments I am filled with hope; his body is lying there so peacefully, almost as if he were asleep. The guide kneels with his cheek to Siggi's mouth to feel his breath, but there is no breath. And only then do I register that one side of Siggi's head has been indented like the concave face of a deflated football. I feel the bile begin to rise. I get to the end of the length of rope that connects me to the guides before the retching starts. It lasts a long time and when I have finished the hard granular snow all around me is stained green and yellow.

One of the guides is climbing up the gentle incline of the snow face to retrieve the Hitler Youth flag, which is a bright red dot in the distance. The other guide is standing just behind me.

'*So gings mir auch beim ersten mal,*' he says. That's what my first time was like.

I turn around. His face is stony. Expressionless.

'*Aber man gewöhnt sich daran. Vielleicht ist das noch schlimmer.*' But you get used to it. Maybe that's the worst part.

When the second guide returns, they spread the flag on the snow next to Siggi, then they lift him onto it. That is how we return to the Hörnli hut, with Siggi's body slung in the flag and carried by the two silent *Gebirgsjäger.*

The next few days are a blur. A rescue team is called to carry Siggi's corpse back to Zermatt. A number of party officials arrive the following day and lecture us repeatedly on the necessity of keeping the accident a secret. The officials are polite, but underlying their words are hidden threats. Lowering morale at this critical time is equivalent to treason, they say. They remind us of the punishments for cowardice, for desertion, for treason. They say that it is hard to keep a secret, but it is precisely that difficulty which makes it meaningful. We are instructed to say that the attempt had to be postponed due to inclement weather and that Siggi died of pneumonia caught in Zermatt.

We return quietly to our homes. Siggi's funeral in Bochum is a rushed affair and there is no viewing of the body. By the time his coffin is lowered into the ground, I too have learnt to assume the stony, expressionless visage of the two *Gebirgsjäger.* In the days following the funeral, I scan the newspapers for mention of Siggi's death. I only come across it once, in the *Völkischer Beobachter.* The newspaper repeats, word for word, the line that the party officials insisted upon: the attempt had to be postponed due to inclement weather and Hitlerjunge Siegfried Rackus (15) died of pneumonia caught in Zermatt.

Two weeks after Siggi's funeral, I volunteer for the Volkssturm. I am now serving alongside Herr Weiss, my old maths teacher. I accompany him to the Flak installations where I see Max and Sepp. I am not permitted to discuss Siggi's accident with anyone – that is indeed the hardest part. I could perhaps have spoken to Kurt Gruber, but he is sent to join an SS regiment in the East. We correspond once or twice by letter but we do not mention Siggi. Gruber does not survive the war.

The first time I visit Max and Sepp at the installations, they want to know about the expedition. I respond monosyllabically. It seems to me that Max is envious of Siggi's sudden illness and death: Siggi didn't have to go through night after night of terror. I want to tell Max that Siggi's death was a tragedy of a different sort, but that it was preceded by a virtuoso display of skill and courage. But I also realise that, if I tried to tell people that Siggi climbed the Matterhorn all by himself, no one would believe me. It saddens me to think how the truth can be distorted, how a few party officials and an article in a newspaper can shape the beliefs of a nation. However, when I look around at the sunken faces of the other Volkssturm recruits, I also understand the importance of morale. In the autumn of 1944, it was still possible to believe that Germany was not yet doomed. If the distortion of the truth was the price of keeping that hope alive, then I decided that I could live with it.

Chapter 19

I HAVE run out of blank sheets in my notebook, and the last few pages are covered in scrawls. Seu Otto has just finished telling me what happened to Siggi. I feel contrary emotions. On the one hand, I am saddened by the tragedy of a death which seems so unnecessary. And I am moved by Seu Otto's own reaction. He was clearly affected – once or twice during his narrative, his voice grew husky with emotion. I have never heard him speak like that before. What is more, these are apparently feelings and memories that he has kept in check his entire life. I cannot even begin to imagine what it must be like to dredge them up now.

On the other hand, I am also delighted. I am delighted because the narrative which Seu Otto has just unfolded exceeds my most optimistic expectations. I do not need to comb through the material, trimming here and padding there, in order to extract a story. On the contrary, two angles clearly present themselves. Firstly, the HJ attempt on the Matterhorn had been a propaganda exercise dreamt up by Goebbels; when it went wrong, the truth was suppressed. Even the newspapers did not report the correct version of events. In these days of Rede Globo's stranglehold on our own media, Seu Otto's account of Siggi's death is highly topical.

Secondly, it seems to me that Seu Otto himself is

unaware of one central aspect of the events. Did Siggi really fall? Might he not have jumped? And might there not be a very good reason why he jumped? These are the questions I must put to Seu Otto now. I do not want to distress him, but it seems he is willing to talk. And, although this may be hard for him, are we not together pursuing the truth? Is there a more noble goal? Seu Otto is not one to flinch from things because they are hard.

Seu Otto's eyes are closed but I do not think he is sleeping.

'Seu Otto?' I say. 'How do you feel?'

He does not respond for a full minute, maybe two. Then, like an old sea turtle, he slowly opens his eyes. 'I feel well,' he says. 'Surprisingly well.' He reaches up for the morphine button. Given how much morphine he must have in his blood, I am not surprised he feels well.

'Maybe it is good to talk,' he says.

'Seu Otto, there's something else I would like to ask you.'

'So ask.'

His lips are dry and I pass him the water. He drinks very cautiously, as if the water were poisioned. Just wetting his lips.

'Seu Otto,' I say, 'can I be honest with you?'

'Of course, Pietro. I only ever want you to be honest with me.'

'I don't want to offend you.'

'Pietro, speak.'

'Well, the thing is, I've been wondering... from what you have been saying, it sounds to me like there was something strange, something... unnatural, about Siggi's relationship with Kurt Gruber.'

'Kurt and Siggi were friends. We were all friends.'

'But there are certain, well, irregularities. Like the fact that you shared with the Austrians while Kurt shared with Siggi. Or that, after you swum across the lake, you didn't see Siggi again and the next day you were awarded the dagger instead of being punished.'

'We were awarded the dagger for the climbing, not the swimming,' corrected Seu Otto.

'Yes. But in an environment like that, with only boys and no real accountability, it just seems the sort of place where it would have been easy for an older boy to abuse a younger boy and to get away with it.'

After a pause, Seu Otto asks, 'Are you suggesting that Kurt was abusing Siggi?'

'I'm just wondering what kind of a person Kurt Gruber was, that's all.'

'We all looked up to him. I told you before, he was stern but we admired him.'

I said nothing, but I had the impression that Seu Otto was holding something back.

'You said that you wrote to him when he was sent to the east?'

'Yes, just two letters. He was attached to one of the *Totenkopfverbände*.'

'The what?'

'The *Totenkopfverbände*. The Death's Head Regiments. They guarded the concentration camps.'

I feel a twinge of excitement, the sense of excitement that arises when there is total honesty. I musn't let this opportunity pass. I hadn't planned how to broach this topic but Seu Otto appears to have done so of his own accord.

'So you knew about the concentration camps?' I say.

Seu Otto takes a deep breath. 'We knew that they existed,' he replies. 'We thought they were for enemies of the state – anarchists, Bolsheviks, Jews who wanted to destroy Germany. We thought they were prison camps and labour camps. We didn't know they were extermination camps. I didn't find that out until the end of the war, when the Americans denazified us. They forced us to watch footage of the camps. At first we didn't believe it was real.'

'But you already knew about the Death's Head Regiments.'

'We knew they guarded the camps, that's all.'

'Did you know about the Final Solution?'

'Not at the beginning. We knew that the Führer had a plan to remove the Jews from Germany. We thought they were being forced to emigrate.'

'How did you feel about that?'

'To be honest, I didn't care very much. We used to have endless lessons about race and eugenics in the Hitler Youth; it was very boring. How to recognise the semitic skull from the curvature of the cranium, that sort of thing. But we were brought up to believe that Jews were the enemies of the state, that it was because of them that the First World War had been lost. In fact, I was taught to read from a storybook called *Der Giftpilz,* The Poisonous Mushroom. In the story a mother goes out to pick mushrooms in the forest with her young son Franz. There are lots of good, healthy looking mushrooms. Then Franz points to a dark, malevolent, leering mushroom with a Jew's hooked nose. The drawing used to scare me a lot. Franz's mother warns him that one such mushroom is enough to poison a whole family. She teaches him that there are good and bad people just as there are good and bad mushrooms, and that just as one bad mushroom can poison a whole family, so too one Jew can poison a whole village, a whole city, even "*das Ganze Volk*". When you are young and everybody tells you the same thing, you don't question it.'

I can understand how that might be the case. If you are eleven years old and the teacher who teaches you about courage and honour and loyalty is also teaching you about eugenics and the evil of Jewry, it must be very hard to know how to separate the two. An eleven-year-old probably doesn't possess the critical faculties to make up their own mind. Or maybe there is a very small percentage who do. But they would be the outsiders, the dissidents who would one day end up in the camps themselves.

'Yes, I can see how difficult that must have been,' I say. 'But what about when you found out that the Final Solution meant extermination? How did you feel then?'

'It was only at the very end that people started talking about that. At first we didn't believe it. When the Americans forced us to watch footage from the camps, we thought it had all been staged; we thought it was Allied propaganda. But, a week or so after the armistice, the Americans who were denazifying us took us to a railway siding outside Borken. They made us open the sliding doors of a freight train that had been on its way to Bergen-Belsen. The carriages were full of rotting human bodies, Jews who had starved to death. We had to bury them. We were continually sick all day. That's when I realised what had really been going on.'

'*Nossa.*'

Seu Otto stares blankly at the ceiling, but I sense that

there is turmoil behind that blankness. Once or twice his eyes open wide and a look of fear ghosts across his face. I wonder whether I have already pushed him too hard. But I also suspect that what he is telling me now may never be repeated. I must use this opportunity.

'But when you realised that's what was happening in the east, how did you feel about Kurt Gruber?'

'Well, that is something that the world will perhaps never understand. Kurt Gruber was a good man. Of course there were bad men too, but Kurt Gruber was a good man. For a good man to do things against which his conscience balks, that is the supreme test. Anyone can fight bravely when he is defending his wife or his daughters from the Russians. The real test is when a soldier is given orders that he does not wish to carry out.'

'What does that test?'

'It tests his loyalty, his devotion, his love for the Führer. The harder a task is, the greater it's value as an offering and a dedication.'

'Even when that task involves killing innocent people?'

'*Particularly* when that task involves killing innocent people. Kurt would never have wanted to kill women and children. And therefore that is the greatest sacrifice he could have made.'

I can see a sort of twisted logic in what Seu Otto is saying. The Hitler Youth trained boys to believe in the absolute value of discipline. What can be more disciplined than carrying out an order which appalls you? If the value of action is measured by how difficult it is, then carrying out such an order would be of the greatest value.

And yet, I cannot understand Seu Otto's insistence that

Kurt Gruber was a good man. That, surely, is his blindspot.

'But Seu Otto, don't you think there may have been something unhealthy about Kurt Gruber's relationship with Siggi?'

Seu Otto does not reply immediately. His expression is no longer blank; quite the opposite – he stares intently at me. Then he says, 'Well, there was one thing. One night Siggi and I got drunk on a bottle of *slivovitz* which we found in the cooks' storage tent. That was not long after we swam across the lake. Siggi told me that Kurt had been making him do things he didn't want to do. "Disgusting things," he said.'

'So what did you do?' I prompt.

'I didn't believe him. We were both blind drunk. And Siggi never mentioned it again.' After a pause, Seu Otto says, 'And maybe I didn't want to think about it.'

'But perhaps it was the truth?' I say. 'Wouldn't that explain why you weren't punished for the swim, and why Kurt shared the room with Siggi? And might it not also explain Siggi's death? Maybe Siggi didn't fall. Maybe he jumped.'

Seu Otto says nothing. But I am more and more certain that I am right.

'Siggi had no one to turn to, no one who would believe him. He tried to tell you, and he couldn't bring himself to try anyone else. Killing himself was the only escape he could think of. If his death was deliberate, that explains why he left the piece of amber on your pillow; he knew he would never see you again. And it explains why he chose to jump with the flag. His death was the solution to a personal problem and not an indictment of the Hitler Youth. He probably hoped that his body would be carried back wrapped in the flag.'

I realise I have been speaking very fast. My face feels hot.

'It is possible, I suppose,' says Seu Otto after a long pause. 'But there are so many possibilities.'

'That's just what I was thinking. And there are so many stories here. The censored account of the Matterhorn expedition. Sexual abuse in the Hitler Youth. Siggi's suicide. Seu Otto, when I've finished writing this investigative piece, I'd like to try to sell it to a paper. There's enough here to capture people's attention, even sixty-five years after it all happened. If it's alright with you, I'd like to speak to my professor as soon as possible.'

'Pietro, I only said it was a possibility.'

'I know,' I said. 'But the possibility is enough. It's not like it will go to court.'

'No, I suppose not.'

Seu Otto looks drained. I should let him rest now. I check my watch. It is not yet midday. I have the whole afternoon to chase down Doutor Monteiro.

Chapter 20

Pietro has left and I feel exhausted. I close my eyes but once again, just like during the night, sleep will not come. But this time it is memories of Max which insist on rising to the surface.

Max, the *flakhelfer* who helped me dig the foxhole. Max, who died a hero's death.

After destroying the tank and running back to the headquarters at Heiden, I was interviewed by Hauptmann Brandhoff. Hauptmann Brandhoff shook my hand and said he was honoured to have met me. I knew that if I tried to tell that to my friends, they would never believe me. But that is what he said – '*Es war mir eine Ehre*'. Those were his exact words. Even now I find it hard to believe. And it was Hauptmann Brandhoff who then arranged for me to be driven by sidecar back to the Volkssturm headquarters at Wulfen.

Hauptmann Brandhoff's orderly hands me a piece of *Fliegerschokolade* wrapped in foil – the chocolate containing methamphetamine which is usually only given to airmen flying night missions. Then I am introduced to the motorbike driver who helps me into the sidecar. The bike is one of the new military green BMW R75's. I have seen a few over the past year, but I never dreamt that I would ride in one. The driver kicks the starter a number of times then adjusts a valve before the engine finally splutters and catches.

I lean back in the sidecar and rest my head against the spare tyre behind me. It is uncomfortable but I am too tired to care. There are tall pines either side of the road. I follow the strip of blue sky between the pines. After a quarter of an hour I see a number of Allied bombers returning home. The driver tersely assures me that there is no danger for us. The road is well hidden by the tall trees.

The last stretch towards Wulfen is across open ground. The driver pauses for a moment to scan the horizon. There are no planes to be seen. The 5th Armoured Division were advancing south while Wulfen lies directly east. We will not meet them again, at least not today. The driver guns the bike out into the open. The snowfields either side of the road are so white that it hurts my eyes. I can see each tiny crystal reflecting the light, or is it the effect of the *Fliegerschokolade*?

In the distance, one of the Flak installations is smoking. I cannot see the installation itself since it is in a hollow whose contours have been softened by the snow. But this is where Max and Sepp both work.

The road passes next to the hollow. As we get closer, I can see the top half of one of the anti-aircraft guns. The body of the gunner is slumped forward in his chair. The driver stops the bike in the middle of the road, level with the installation. He kicks the gearshift lever a few times but the lever refuses to go into neutral. The driver scans the sky then turns off the engine. He strides towards the slumped body. In the absence of the noise of the spluttering engine, I become aware of a quiet whimpering. The driver has heard it too; he remains motionless on the lip of the hollow. His attention is caught by something within the hollow. The driver has his back towards me and so I cannot see his expression.

I am afraid to look. However, after a short while my curiosity gets the better of me and I stand up in the sidecar. In the centre of the hollow there is a child on hands and knees, whimpering pitifully. He is wearing the regulation issue overcoat which drags behind him in the snow. He has left a trail of concentric circles, very red against the white, spiralling inwards towards the centre of the hollow. As he turns towards us I see why he has left this trail: where his face should have been, there is just a bloody mess. His face has literally been shot off. The dark hole of his mouth is still there but nothing else; no eyes, no nose. The boy with no face continues to crawl in ever decreasing circles and to whimper. As he turns away from us I notice his curly blond hair, still pristine at the back. And only then do I realise that this poor dying creature is Max.

The motorbike driver pulls his pistol from his holster. He walks in a straight line through the concentric spirals of blood to the centre of the circle, smudging the spirals as he goes. Max must have heard something because for a moment he stops crawling. The driver stops a metre away from him and points his pistol at the back of Max's head. The report cracks like a whip across the hollow. Max's body collapses in the snow. The driver remains immobile for a long moment, his pistol hand outstretched.

After the shot there is silence. I see the driver's breath in the cold air and pick up the faint whiff of gunpowder. The driver returns to the bike; his skin is ashen and the muscles of his jaw clench and unclench. None of this seems real. It is a great cosmic joke. I have to fight the impulse to give in to the waves of hilarity which are building inside me.

I concentrate on the sensation of the cold wind on my face. I realise that I have been crying, but the tears have dried by the time we arrive at the Volkssturm HQ at Wulfen. The driver stops the bike in front of the main gate. I am about to get out when I feel his heavy hand on my shoulder.

'Mach Dir keine Sorgen,' he says. 'Er war auch ein Held.' He was a hero too.

He squeezes my shoulder and I clamber out of the sidecar, then he roars off. But I draw comfort from his words. Max died a hero's death.

And now? Do I still believe that? What would Pietro think?

Max died like a poor animal. He was defending his country, that's true, but there was nothing brave or glorious about it. He would never have chosen to die that way. One moment he had a face, the next he didn't. In the end he was killed by a German soldier. His death achieved nothing.

The whole thing was madness, madness from beginning to end. Children against airplanes and tanks. The soft, pale flesh of children against hard, cold steel. Sacrifice on an unimaginable scale to sate the ambition of a nation. Yes, truly a form of madness. And yet, and yet, might there not still have been something heroic about it? Heroic not despite the madness, but because of it?

Chapter 21

'YOU CERTAINLY have a story here. You must decide what you want to do with it; that will determine your angle.'

I am sitting in Doutor Monteiro's office in the University's Media Studies faculty. There are no windows but the office is spacious. The walls are lined with bookshelves. Propped on top of the bookshelves are a number of Doutor Monteiro's awards. Some are plaques with his name on them, others are small sculptures. One is an amazingly kitsch pink porcelain unicorn, or maybe it's a joke. Monteiro himself is a small man with leathery skin and crows' feet. His hair is grey but thick and his blue eyes are bright and energetic.

'If you want to use this for your dissertation, then I suggest that you focus on the mechanics of the Hitler Youth – the initiation, the selection process, that sort of thing. Keep it factual, back up the interview with research and plenty of references, and you'll get a good grade. However, if you want to get something published in a newspaper, then you will have to tie it in more directly to Senhor Eisinger's own life and pitch it in relation to the incident in the shop. But if you want to make some money from this, well, then you really have to look to television. I could put you in touch with someone in television.'

I feel my pulse begin to quicken. 'Really?' I ask.

'Yes, I know Doutor Raposo well. He owes me a favour. Well, more than one.' Monteiro frowns as he says this.

'Doutor Raposo? From *Histórias Humanas*?'

'Yes. But you will want to be very careful in your dealings with him.' I expect Doutor Moneiro to continue, but he appears to think better of it and remains silent.

'Why?' I prompt.

Monteiro's silence lengthens. He seems lost in thought. Eventually he says, 'Doutor Raposo is a shark. Don't be fooled by his show – he is only out for himself.'

I have seen Doutor Raposo's show. It airs on the History Channel. Dr. Raposo conducts an in-depth television interview that sheds light on some little known or controversial aspect of the past. There is always a scandal uncovered, a sense of righting past wrongs. I have seen him interview elderly *indios* from the jungle who describe how their land was taken from them by the government in the 50s, before the rights of natives were properly protected. I also saw a more recent show in which he interviewed a senior politician who is also one of Brazil's biggest landowners. Dr. Raposo accused him of using slave labour on his plantations. It caused quite a stir.

'I know you want this to be about the Hitler Youth and Siegfried and the freedom of the press in Germany, and those are all interesting subjects. Maybe Dr. Raposo will go for it – he is an intelligent man, after all. However, when Brazilians think about the Hitler Youth, they think of the war criminals who escaped here. They think of Dr. Mengele, Adolf Eichmann, Klaus Barbie. Dr. Raposo, and the mass media in general, is not in the business of correcting misconceptions; he gives the viewers what they want. If he scents blood with your Seu Otto, then he will be ruthless. Don't think that you will be able to protect him.'

'But Seu Otto is being celebrated as a hero,' I say. 'Did you see him attack the gunman in the shop?'

'I did see that. And you are right, if the viewers want a hero, that is what Dr. Raposo will give them. But he will require Senhor Eisinger to comply absolutely. If he doesn't, it could get unpleasant for him.'

I cannot see why anyone would want to cast Seu Otto in a bad light, why anyone would want to bully him. Everyone has seen how brave he is. And, with a little patience, he has been willing to share his deepest secrets Even if Dr. Raposo lacks that patience, I feel sure that I will be able to provide it.

'You could make a tidy sum with this interview, I don't deny that,' says Monteiro. 'And it could certainly open up some doors for you once you graduate.'

'And you would be willing to put me in touch with Dr. Raposo?'

'Yes. But shouldn't you speak to Senhor Eisinger first, just to make sure he knows what he is letting himself in for?'

'I don't need to do that,' I say. 'Senhor Eisinger wants his story to be told – the truth behind his best friend's death and the censorship of the expedition.'

I hear my own fine-sounding words. But am I telling the truth? Is that really what Seu Otto wants? Or is it just what I want him to want? Doutor Monteiro looks searchingly at me. He allows the silence to build. The silence makes me feel uncomfortable. Eventually he says, 'Well, Pietro, you must know how things stand with Senhor Eisinger. I will leave all that to you. No journalist ever got anywhere without ambition. I would be happy to arrange a meeting between you and Dr. Raposo.'

*

I leave Doutor Monteiro's office and make my way to the campus carpark. The sun is shining and I walk past a group of girls in short skirts who smell like mint tic-tacs. Usually this would make me feel happy to be alive, but for some reason it doesn't.

Doutor Monteiro says that I could make up to ten thousand *reais* for this interview, so long as Dr. Raposo accepts my role as a co-producer. Even splitting that 50/50 with Seu Otto, it would solve all my current financial difficulties. And yet I feel no joy. Maybe I am apprehensive because I still need to get Seu Otto's consent. Of course, the money will not mean as much to him as it does to me. He may not wish to offer up his own past in exchange for financial gain; he has enough as it is. Maybe I shouldn't mention the money at all. But then how do I get him to agree to be interviewed?

Didn't Seu Otto say that the hardest part was not being able to tell people what really happened on the Matterhorn? He was forced to lie to his friends, to let them believe that Siggi died of pneumonia when in fact he had climbed solo to the summit. But isn't this interview the perfect platform for Seu Otto to announce the truth to the world? Even though there's probably no one left alive who knew Siggi, it is the principle that matters. The truth will be out there, and it will be thanks to Seu Otto.

Chapter 22

I WOKE up late the following morning. Sunlight fanned across the floor of the ward. I had slept very deeply. I didn't remember falling asleep but it must have been some time during the afternoon. I certainly did not remember being awake at dinner. Nor did I even remember saying goodbye to Pietro, or how we had left things. Then I caught sight of the intravenous morphine drip still hanging above my head. It was empty. I must have finished it all during Pietro's visit. No wonder the details were hazy in my mind.

'*E finalmente*,' came a voice from across the room. 'You sleep like a baby.'

I looked around. The patient who had been on my side of the room had gone; the bed was empty. However, the gaunt man opposite – the one who had devoured the tasteless *feijão* – was staring at me with interest.

'*Bom dia*,' I said.

'*Boa tarde*,' he replied with the smugness of those who have woken long before you.

I looked at my watch. The man was right, it was indeed past midday. It was many years since I'd slept past midday. And even now I did not feel fully awake. My limbs were very heavy. At the same time it dawned on me that the pain in my hip was no more than a dull ache. Really it had been a most beneficent night's sleep.

The long conversation with Pietro must have tired me. Although the details were hazy, I knew that I had now told him more about my life than I had ever told anyone. I began to feel a little uncomfortable about this.

My sense of uneasiness was cut short by the arrival in rapid succession of Fernanda, Anna-Maria and Dr. da Silva. Within moments there was a little crowd around my bed. Dr. da Silva informed me that the bandage would now have to be removed from my head since my first hour of physiotherapy was scheduled for that afternoon and I would need my other eye to help me balance. Fernanda immediately began untying the bandage with the result that my head was within dangerous proximity to her voluminous bust and I feared for the access to my airways. Anna-Maria busied herself straightening the bed sheets and piling even more cards and letters on the table beside my bed. I didn't notice the arrival of the physiotherapist until Dr. da Silva introduced her to me – she was a small, mousy woman called Linda Pereira.

The removal of the head bandage did not live up to my expectations. My eye was still so swollen that I was unable to see any more than a faint luminous blur through it. However, I was aware that Dr. da Silva, Fernanda, Anna-Maria and Linda Pereira had all taken a step back to evaluate my damaged physiognomy. Anna-Maria appeared a little shocked – I could see that with my good eye – but in general the consensus appeared to be that the swelling was going down and the injury healing satisfactorily.

Fernanda and Linda Pereira together lifted me into a wheelchair that had been brought to my bed. I was astonished at how strong Linda Pereira was, despite her slim frame. She began to wheel me out of the ward and told Anna-Maria that a nurse would bring me back from my first session in an hour. She wheeled me along the corridor, into the lift and out again, through the lobby and the crowded waiting room.

As we entered the waiting room I had the distinct impression that a hush descended. There was a television mounted in the far corner of the room showing a football match. Most people's attention was fixed on this. There was one young family right at the back who seemed particularly interested in the game. However, when one of their boys caught sight of me, he started tugging on his father's shirt and whispered something in his ear. The man pretended to scan the room; his eyes alighted briefly on me, then he whispered in his wife's ear. A few seconds later she turned round, also pretending to scan the room. Their attention soon returned to the football match and only the youngest of their children stole another furtive glance in my direction. This time I nodded my head ever so slightly towards him, a gesture that he seemed to appreciate. He beamed delightedly at me and I realised that, within the walls of this hospital at least, people knew who I was.

I also had the impression that Linda Pereira was pushing the wheelchair very slowly through the waiting room, in what was almost a stately manner. Once we were outside she sped up considerably. I had not been outside since the fight. I found myself enjoying the warm sunshine and the sight of green bushes and palm trees, which cast a pleasant shade on the gravel paths along which I was now hurtling. I asked Linda Pereira to slow down.

'Of course Seu Otto.' Then she added, '*O seu nome*, your name – Otto Eisinger – what does it mean?'

'What do you mean, what does it mean?' I asked.

'Well, what do the words mean? My name, for example, means *beautiful pear tree*.'

'Yes, yes, I suppose it does.' This suddenly struck me as very amusing. I did not want to offend the poor beautiful pear tree who was still whisking me along the gravel path at breakneck speed, but at the same time I found it hard to restrain my laughter. It was a sensation I had not had for, well, for a very long time. In the end I was unable to stifle the sound, but it came out in so contorted a fashion that Linda Pereira thought I was choking and slapped me forcefully on the back. This distracted me sufficiently for my phlegmatic nature to re-establish itself.

'I'm afraid my name doesn't mean anything,' I said. 'It's just a name, that's all.'

'Ah, but a famous name,' replied Linda Pereira.

'Yes, perhaps. Famous once again.'

*

During my first hour of physiotherapy, I realised that I would have to learn to walk all over again. The healthy do not realise the true complexity of the most mundane actions. But Linda Pereira turned out to be a very patient, gentle and encouraging physiotherapist. The even, dignified stride I now possess is in no small part due to her. Despite the difficulties and challenges of the rehabilitation programme, I never dreaded the sessions in the way that, I have heard, other patients do.

*

Anna-Maria was waiting for me back in the ward. In her

hand she was holding her portable telephone, cradling it as if it were a Fabergé egg.

'I have just spoken to Pietro,' she said. 'He would like to talk to you. I told him to call back in half an hour.'

'Ah,' I said.

'Will you speak to him?' pursued Anna-Maria.

'If I'm not asleep by then.'

'But it is only 3 o'clock.'

'My sleep patterns have become very irregular.'

'You need to come home,' pronounced Anna-Maria.

I was about to point out to her the impracticalities of her suggestion, but then I remembered my study with its books and the perfect grass just outside the window and beyond that the fishermen wading out to the oyster nets in the bay, and I suddenly felt a great desire to return to Sambaqui.

'Yes, maybe I do,' I said.

'Dr. da Silva says you can leave tomorrow if you wish, so long as you come to the hospital daily for your therapy.'

'Anna Maria, I think you are right. I think it is time to go.'

'Really?'

'Yes, really. Please make the necessary preparations, and inform Valdemar that I shall be examining the lawn the day after tomorrow. I believe he ought to be fertilising at the end of this week.'

At that moment Anna-Maria's portable telephone shattered the peace with its strident ring.

She took one look at the phone and announced, 'It's Pietro.' I have always believed in woman's superior intuition; nevertheless, the confidence with which she proclaimed this amazed me.

'Pietro, *um momento,* here is Seu Otto,' she said, opening the phone and passing it to me.

'Seu Otto,' said Pietro, 'please allow me to apologise. I must have exhausted you yesterday morning. Avó said you slept all yesterday afternoon and up until midday today.'

'*Não tem problema,*' I said. 'I slept extremely well and tomorrow I shall be going home. I feel much better.'

'That is wonderful.'

'Pietro, I have enjoyed our conversations, or what I remember of them. My memories are a little hazy, I must confess. Nevertheless, when I am back home and fully recovered you must come by and we can discuss more cheerful things.'

'That's what I wanted to ask you about. Do you remember I told you I was going to speak to my professor? Well, he thinks this is a great story. He said that the suppression of the truth behind Siggi's death and the strangling of free speech is a theme full of contemporary resonance. And my professor is friends with Doutor Raposo, the producer of *Histórias Humanas* on the History Channel. He's going to put me in touch with Doutor Raposo; if we sell him your story then maybe he'll give me a job when I graduate. And he would pay well for an interview with you. History Channel is owned by *Rede Globo* so money is—'

'*Basta Pietro,* that is enough.' I had begun to feel increasingly uncomfortable as I listened to Pietro's little speech. 'I do not wish to make money from Siggi's death,' I said.

Pietro was silent for a moment. Then he said: 'Of course, I understand that. But Seu Otto, you would be letting the world know the truth. Didn't you say that the worst thing about it was that you weren't allowed to talk about what really happened? Well, now you can tell the world: Siggi didn't die of pneumonia. He climbed the Matterhorn all by himself.'

Pietro did have a point.

'Don't you think this is what Siggi would have wanted?'

Again, I couldn't deny that there was truth in what Pietro was saying. But still, the idea of talking about Siggi's death on public television didn't feel right.

'And you would be helping me,' said Pietro. 'It's a very competitive industry. This could be my big break.'

Again I didn't reply. Pietro went on:

'Please, Seu Otto, just think it over. But I was phoning for another reason too – I would like to invite you to judge a surfing competition next Sunday at Praia Joaquina. My friends are organising it and the hero of Sambaqui would be the guest of honour.'

'Well, thank you Pietro, I am flattered. But I know nothing about surfing.'

'*Não se preocupe*, Seu Otto. I'll explain everything to you. Please do come. I have discussed it with the organisers and they were delighted that you might be there. It's great if we can get someone famous to judge the event – it means more publicity and more spectators. So please, at least think about it.'

'I'll think about it,' I said. 'Thank you, Pietro.'

Chapter 23

THE FOLLOWING day I went home with Anna-Maria. She wheeled me carefully out of the hospital to a waiting van. The driver opened the sliding door and pushed a button which caused a small platform to be lowered to the ground, rather like the lifts on the back of removal lorries. I was wheeled onto the platform that then raised me to the floor of the van – an ingenious system.

Once back at home I spent the rest of the day in my study, dozing intermittently. With Anna-Maria's help I was able to climb the stairs to my bedroom. I do not think I cut an elegant figure, wedged between the banister and her ample behind, but her own sturdy legs inspired confidence and those first few days back in my own home passed without mishap.

I was surprised that my daily routines failed to provide the welcoming sense of familiarity which I had been anticipating. My sleeping patterns continued to be irregular and I had to supplement my sporadic nightly rest with naps throughout the day. At times, when waking from a nap in my armchair, the objects in my house, the same objects that I have collected over the course of my lifetime, seemed strange and new, as if I had never seen them before. Even the lawn was no longer familiar; it seemed even brighter and greener than I remembered, just as it had looked in

Anna-Maria's Polaroid photo. I was disconcerted to note how profoundly I had been affected by the incident in the shop, and the operation, and the long conversations with Pietro.

By the day of the surfing contest, I was able to move around autonomously. After a week in a wheelchair, this was a source of considerable satisfaction. Of course, I still needed crutches, and my palms were sore from practising with them up and down the path that runs around garden. However, this was a price I was happy to pay; I did not want to appear pitiable at the contest.

The lack of movement in my hip meant that even simple tasks like getting dressed took much longer. Consequently I had allowed myself a full hour in which to prepare myself on the morning of the competition. This was fortunate since I became entrapped in my suit trousers. Anna-Maria was out so I had to shout out of the window for Valdemar's assistance. Once Valdemar had liberated me, I finished dressing and sparingly applied the pomade which is sent to me once a year from London's Bond Street. I slipped a white handkerchief into my top pocket. Anna-Maria irons beautifully, and also starches and folds my handkerchiefs to perfection. I patted the white triangle in the top pocket of my suit jacket and manoeuvred myself in front of the long mirror.

The elegant cut of my suit disguised the fact that I had lost weight during my stay in the hospital. Yes, I thought to myself, truly that is the skill of a good tailor – to make clothing which will compensate for physical fluctuations. The swelling around my eye had subsided, leaving just a dark smudge beneath the eye itself. I thought I looked quite rakish. What is more, with the bright light reflecting off the sea behind me and my back to the window, my appearance in the mirror was wholly satisfactory – not only well dressed and lean, but also remarkably upright for a man of my years.

Pietro had offered to send a friend of his to come and pick me up in the combi. I had politely declined the offer and instead asked Anna-Maria to book me the taxi that was now sounding its horn outside the house. I feared for a moment that the taxi might leave before I made it to the front door, but Valdemar had already engaged the driver in friendly conversation.

The drive to Joaquina beach took me right across the island, past Lagoa with its hordes of *mate*-sipping Argentine tourists and alongside the calm waters of the saltwater lagoon, Lagoa da Conceição. Here I often see couples my own age sitting in deckchairs on the shady grass by the water's edge; their grandchildren splash around in the shallows or hang from the large, swan-shaped white pedalos that can be rented from the rickety wooden pier. Sometimes the parents do the pedalling. The shiny brown bodies being towed along behind the swans are like so many grinning little Lohengrins.

The grandparents rarely move from their deckchairs. In fact, they often appear to be asleep. But then their grandchildren come with toys to be inflated or pebbles to be admired, and I think that the old couples are probably happy. It is at moments like these that I sometimes experience a sense of regret that family life was never vouchsafed me. I have led a full life, there is no doubt about that, but on occasion I do wonder whether an essential part is not perhaps missing. There have been certain moments and certain experiences that I would have liked to share. Equally, there have been moments when I have been grateful not to be beholden to anyone. And, frankly, my feelings for another person have never been sufficiently strong as to outweigh the inevitable ennervations. What's more, living with a woman would have necessitated the carnal act, and my adult desires have rarely led in that direction. Although now, at my age, perhaps it is permissible to live in a union for the sake of companionship alone? It is an appealing thought: to live with someone who is not an employee, not to have to observe the barriers required by that relationship, but to have someone with whom to share the remaining joys and sorrows of life. Perhaps it is not out of the question.

The world has changed so much. I am not referring to the technological and medical advances, impressive as they are. No, I am thinking of the social norms, of the behaviours that are considered acceptable in today's world. For instance, it is not unusual to see young men walking hand in hand through the streets of Florianópolis. In the Hitler Youth, such behavior would have earned you a fearsome beating, immediate expulsion, probably some time in a correctional facility and, in extreme cases, chemical castration. Even in my adult life in Brazil, such predilections were secrets to be guarded at all costs. And now the politicians are debating whether to raise the status of the union of man and man to that of a traditional marriage. Truly, the world has changed. Since the operation, I have not been able to still that small voice which wonders how different my life might have been had I been born half a century later.

After a couple of miles the road parts from the lagoon and climbs gently towards the enormous dunes that tower above Joaquina beach. The road ends shortly before the beach; there are a couple of hotels, two or three white kiosks, and a rundown seafood restaurant. The beach is wide and empty and sweeps for many miles down to the south of the island, which on this occasion was clouded by a slight haze. The taxi driver helped me out of the vehicle and I hobbled towards the concrete steps leading down to the beach.

In the far distance I could make out the red-tented constructions which Pietro had told me to look for. I hesitated. There was no road that ran parallel to the dunes and it would have taken me the best part of the afternoon to stagger with my crutches across half a mile of soft sand. I was considering getting straight back into the taxi to return home when I spotted a small vehicle, like a motorbike with four oversize wheels, racing towards me from the direction of the red tents. The driver seemed to be waving at me. I leant against the railing by the top step and waited. The vehicle travelled fast over the sand and soon pulled up level with me. Then the driver released the controls – they were more like handlebars than a steering wheel – and vaulted onto the sand. He was an extremely handsome young man, his brown eyes almost gold in the bright light. As he stroked his tousled hair out of his eyes, I noticed the perfection of his boy's body – shoulders tapering to almost impossibly thin hips and low-slung shorts revealing the subtle undulation of abdominal muslces.

'*O Senhor Eisinger?*' he asked.

I nodded.

'It is a great honour to meet you. My name is João. Pietro sent me to pick you up. Unless, of course, you wish to drive?'

'To drive that?' I asked, pointing at the four-wheeled motorcycle.

'Yes, *o Senhor*. It is the only vehicle allowed onto the beach. But don't worry, it can easily take two people. We will put your crutches in the surfboard holder and you can hold onto me if you feel unsafe.'

I made my way over to the vehicle. João took my crutches and loaded them between the two metal struts that stuck out from the side. Then he helped me into a side-saddle position on the cushioned seat before supporting my shoulders from behind as I rocked back and drew my good leg over the seat. I was being very cautious; Linda Pereira had instructed me that on no account was my knee to be raised above my hip. João pressed a button on the handlebars and the motor sprang to life. Then he nimbly jumped onto the cushion in front of me.

'You can hold onto me,' said João.

I placed my hands around his waist like the pillion rider on a real motorbike. João turned the handlebars to the side and described a large arc in the sand. I felt his muscles tighten as he accelerated in the direction of the red tents.

I looked down at the sand rushing by beneath the footrests. Then I looked back and was surprised to see how far we had already come from the dunes.

'*Tudo bom?*' he shouted over his shoulder.

'*Tudo bem,*' I replied, the air rushing into my mouth and throat.

João stopped the vehicle in the shade behind the small wooden scaffold next to the tents. With his help I was able to dismount – clumsily, it must be said, but without drawing undue attention to myself. João handed me my crutches and I straightened the handkerchief in my pocket and smoothed the creases in my suit. I was about to walk round to the front of the scaffold when I heard a familiar voice:

'Seu Otto!' Pietro sounded jubilant. I turned round to see him striding towards me in his swimming trunks.

'Seu Otto, I am so happy you came. I'm sorry about the quad bike, we were denied permission to bring a car onto the beach. Was it alright?'

'It was invigorating,' I said.

'When I saw you through the binoculars I sent João to pick you up. I hope you didn't mind.' Pietro smiled at me.

'Not at all, not at all. A charming boy.'

'He's a very good surfer too, as you will see. Now let me introduce you to the other judges.'

'But Pietro, I already told you, I don't know the first thing about surfing,' I said.

'I'll explain it all to you. This afternoon is just an air competition. It's not difficult to score.'

As he was saying this, Pietro mounted the steps onto the wooden scaffold. There were already five people sitting there. They were the other judges and they each had a small desk in front of them. On each of the desks a few sheets of paper were pinned down by a pair of binoculars. Pietro introduced me to each judge in turn. Despite their long, unkempt hair, each one of them stood up and shook me firmly by the hand.

'They all look very young,' I remarked quietly to Pietro.

'Perhaps, but they are some of the island's best surfers.'

Pietro indicated the last, empty desk. I was about to sit down when he said, 'I am afraid you may get too hot. I should have told you that these events are quite casual.' It was true, everyone else was just wearing swimming trunks.

'It would have made no difference,' I said. 'I always wear a suit when I leave the house.'

At that moment a tall, attractive girl gleaming with coconut-scented tanning oil appeared at Pietro's side. Her white dental floss bikini was indecently skimpy. She was slim but her breasts were not insignificant. I wondered if they were made of plastic.

'Seu Otto, may I introduce my girlfriend, Marina.'

Marina shook my hand – limply – and flashed a very white smile. She must have had her teeth whitened; there are dentists who will do that.

'Seu Otto,' she lisped, 'I have heard so much about you – the Hero of Sambaqui. I saw you on the television. It is a great honour to meet you.'

'Marina works in the Jungle bar in Barra, where they have the best caipirinhas,' interrupted Pietro. 'She's agreed to serve them here, you know, to keep the judges happy. And to sway them into scoring me favourably.' Pietro winked at me and affectionately put his arm around Marina's waist. She pushed him away.

'Seu Otto, will you have a caipirinha?' asked Marina.

'No thank you. I am still taking antibiotics,' I replied.

'Come Seu Otto, just one. It will help you get into the spirit,' said Pietro.

I am no great admirer of that sickly lime based cocktail.

Nevertheless, the young couple appeared so keen for me to accept the offer, and were waiting so expectantly, that I did not have the heart to disappoint them.

'Well, why not?' I said.

Pietro pulled the chair out from the desk and I sat down carefully while Marina returned to the makeshift bar beside the scaffold, surrounded by customers sipping their drinks. I could not help noticing that the other two bargirls were wearing similarly insubstantial dental floss bikinis that disappeared between their bottom cheeks. Really, I had thought Pietro would have better taste.

Pietro shuffled the papers on my desk. 'So, Seu Otto, this is the air competition,' he said. 'You are looking for the surfer who performs the most radical air in the most critical section of the wave. The score ranges vary for different types of air. An ollie, for example, can be awarded anything between 2.0 and 5.0, and a stale fish or an air 360 can get anything from 7.0 to 9.0. The greater the air, the higher the score. Here is a sheet for you with the different types of air and the maximum and minimum scores. There are some drawings so you can see what they look like.' Pietro was interrupted by the sounding of a horn directly above us. 'I have to go now, I'm in the next heat. If there's anything you don't understand just ask the other judges, ok?'

'How do I know who is who?' I asked.

'It'll be announced over the loudspeaker,' said Pietro over his shoulder; he was already halfway down the wooden stairs. Then he called out, 'Seu Otto, thank you so much for coming,' before running off to join a cluster of surfers who were standing around with their boards.

I began to read the scoring guidelines but I could make little sense of them. There were a lot of drawings of stick men with arrows pointing in different directions. I was just thinking that it really was very hot on the judges' scaffold when I once again caught the strong scent of coconut oil. Looking round, I saw Marina's glistening form bearing down on me. She placed a large, poison green caipirinha on the desk in front of me. I took a tentative sip and was pleasantly surprised to find it less sickly and more refreshing than I had anticipated. I took another sip while waiting for Marina to leave. However, the miasma of coconut persisted and when I turned around I saw that she was still standing behind me.

'There he is,' she said, pointing out to sea. And it was true, Pietro's blond shock of hair could be seen heading out into the waves alongside the other surfers.

'He really admires you, Seu Otto,' she said.

'He is a very sympathetic boy. And a handsome one too, as I am sure you are aware.'

'He is handsome, but so are lots of boys here,' said Marina. I could not fault her on that. 'But Pietro is different.'

She looked at me expectantly. When I didn't reply she continued, 'Most of these *surfistas*, they're happy so long as they can surf and have a couple of beers in the evening and…' she paused momentarily, '… and get laid regularly. I'm sorry Seu Otto, but it is important that you know this. You see, Pietro isn't like that. He wouldn't be happy just surfing and living in one of these beach shacks.' Marina gestured dismissively towards the dunes. 'Pietro really wants to do something with his life, you know, to make a difference. He has a big heart. That's why I think he admires you so much. He knows that you also have a big heart.'

'He does?' I asked, surprised.

'Of course. He told me the story about your best friend, the one that you said looked like him. It's so sad. I'm so sorry.'

Marina seemed genuinely downcast, saddened by something that had happened over half a century ago on the other side of the world. Once again I realised that I had judged too hastily, that beneath the shiny coconut oil and the indecent dental floss this was a girl with a kind heart.

'That's what I love about Pietro,' she said. 'He really cares; he wants to make a difference. But it is so hard to get started.'

'He is intelligent and well-mannered. I am sure he will do well,' I said.

'But that's not enough. He needs to get his toe in the door.'

'Well, if he gets a good degree…'

'You know how much he admires you,' interrupted Marina. 'Don't you want him to do well?'

'Of course I want him to do well,' I said.

'Then why don't you want to do the television interview? It would be so easy for you, and you would be helping him so much.'

Ah ha, so this was what the caipirinha and the flattery and the attention was all about. 'It's not that simple,' I said. 'I don't want to profit from the death of a dear friend. That feels like a betrayal.'

'Then do it for free, just for Pietro's sake,' she said, imploringly.

I didn't reply. I did not like the idea of telling Siggi's story on film. It felt too personal. What's more, when I thought back to my conversations with Pietro in the hospital, I was no longer so sure what Siggi's story was. Pietro thought that Siggi's desperation had driven him to commit suicide, and I had to admit that this was a possibility. But what did that mean? That the Hitler Youth was an organisation in which the abuse of a young boy could go unchecked? An organisation in which such abuse might even be encouraged? Had I buried my head in the sand all those years ago? And was I therefore complicit? But when I think back to the person I was in those days, wasn't that the best, the bravest, the most heroic that I have ever been? And wasn't it the Hitler Youth that made me what I was?

So many questions. But there is one thing I know for sure: Siggi reached the top of the Matterhorn all by himself. The rest is conjecture. So couldn't I avoid these difficulties by just sticking to what I know? No conjecture, no hypothesis, just facts. How hard can that be?

'It would help Pietro so much,' said Marina.

I did not know whether the interview would be as useful to Pietro as Marina seemed to think. On the other hand, if I stuck to the facts, then what harm could come of it? And I did want to help Pietro if I could.

'Alright, I will do it,' I said.

'Really? Seu Otto, you will do the interview?'

'Yes,' I affirmed. 'Tell Pietro to arrange it with Anna-Maria.'

'I knew Pietro wasn't wrong about you. Thank you so, so much.' Marina flashed her white teeth at me.

'Now please, Marina, it is time for me to judge the radical air.'

I turned back round to face the sea where the *surfistas* were already leaping off their boards into the foam. Then I felt Marina kiss me lightly on the cheek. From up close the scent of coconut oil was not at all unpleasant.

*

It was very hot in the sun but the caipirinha was ice cold and surprisingly refreshing. Also, I found myself enjoying the surf competition. Through my binoculars the wet bodies glistened in the sunlight. There appeared to be an almost inexhaustible variety of ways to fall off a surfboard. I was struggling to match what I saw before me to the drawings on the paper that Pietro had given me, but with the caipirinha taking effect this did not trouble me greatly.

After a while, however, my eyelids began to feel heavy and I was aware that my posture was deteriorating – I was slouching over my desk. The glass beside me contained just lime skins and a few remaining cubes of ice. I put the glass in front of my face and rested my chin on the table and tried to force my eyes to stay open by focussing on the ice cubes. They sparkled in the sunlight, almost melted now yet still retaining something of their cool blue transparency; a pleasing antidote to the heat of the day. My eyes closed a little more and I was aware that my mind was starting to wander. Cool blue ice, a shade like that sapphire line above me, the freezing waters holding me. Siggi's foot kicking in front of me, seizing it in my hand, my hand bleeding from the cut in the flesh of the palm, bleeding into the snow in concentric spiralling circles, spiralling like a whirlpool, sucking down the surfers, sucking down Pietro on his board...

*

'*O Senhor Eisinger!*'

I opened my eyes. There were faces all around me. Concern in the faces.

'Is *O Senhor* alright?'

The light was bright. I did not recognise the faces.

'*Seu Otto?*'

I looked to the voice. The coconut girl. Pietro's girlfriend. 'Marina,' I said.

The concern was still in the faces surrounding me. Young faces. There was some movement now, one face disappeared and was replaced by another. The bodies moved very carefully.

'What happened?' I asked.

A hesitant cough.

'*O Senhor* fell asleep,' said one of the other judges. You were talking in your sleep, then shouting, then thrashing about. The empty glass was knocked off the table, then *O Senhor* woke up. It is nothing to worry about. It is easily cleaned up.'

I looked down. It was true, the wooden planks of the scaffold were covered with hundreds of tiny shards of broken glass. The judges were all barefoot; that was why they were moving so carefully. Then I saw a small pile of lime skins and lime pulp nestling in my lap. I started to brush the sticky mess onto the floor but small flecks of pulp stuck obstinately to the dark material of my trousers.

'Here, let me help,' said Marina. She began to brush my trousers with a damp towel.

'Are you alright?' asked one of the judges.

'I'm fine,' I replied.

'We thought you might be having an attack.'

'What sort of attack?'

The judge shrugged and said, 'I don't know. Any sort.'

The loudspeaker announced that the contest would recommence shortly. One of the other bikini-clad girls mounted the scaffold with a small broom to brush the bits of broken glass into a pile. Marina pawed at my trousers where tiny particles of lime pulp continued to resist her efforts.

'I am going home,' I announced.

Marina looked up, surprised. 'Do you not feel well?' she asked.

'Not very well, no.'

That was not entirely true. I did not feel ill. However, with moisture seeping through my trousers and the prickly sweat of embarrassment beginning to trickle down my back, I had a great desire to be elsewhere. What is more, I felt I had caused a scene that was beginning to verge on the grotesque.

I stood up and stabilised myself against the desk.

'But Seu Otto, wait until Pietro returns. You might hurt yourself,' said Marina.

'I will be fine. Please pass me my crutches.'

Marina passed the crutches and I began to make my way over to the steps, occasionally feeling a tiny shard of glass crunch underfoot. I felt Marina's hand on my elbow.

'Please, leave me now,' I said, shaking it off. 'It is enough.'

I descended the steps, lowering myself from one to the next with some difficulty. Of course, there was now no one to help me onto the four-wheeled motorbike, or to drive it, so I decided to walk back to the steps in front of the restaurant where João had picked me up. It was a long way but I had the whole afternoon ahead of me. In any case, making the journey on foot, no matter how long it took, was preferable to begging for a lift.

I started to make my way across the wide expanse of the beach. I had to pause every few minutes to rest my hands; the handles of the crutches had made them quite sore. But each time I paused I turned around and looked back with pride at my lengthening tracks in the sand – one footprint with a small indentation either side, like some peculiar three-legged animal.

After a while the wind began to pick up. I could see the currents of sand grains snaking over the beach. My more distant footprints were no longer visible; they had been smoothed over by the wind, the memory of my passing entirely erased. I looked down at my feet and at the grey rubber tips on the ends of my crutches. The wind whipped at my ankles with increasing ferocity and at times the ground was obscured by the swirl of tiny particles. I was reminded of the first beach I ever saw – the beach at Zoppot on the windy Baltic coast where I found the piece of amber with the insect wing frozen inside. I could never have imagined that seventy years later I would be the acclaimed hero of Sambaqui, battling resolutely forward on my crutches between the Atlantic breakers and the great dunes. No one can deny that I have come a long way.

Chapter 24

A WEEK after the surf contest, I take a flight to São Paulo to meet Dr. Raposo. He only has time to see me over breakfast, so I have to spend the night in a cheap hotel and take a taxi to his office the following morning. Fortunately I am able to pay for this with my winnings from the surf contest.

The Rede Globo offices are housed in a tall building whose mirrored windows reflect the early morning clouds that are scudding by. As I enter the building, I cannot help thinking to myself how lucky I am. Of all the thousands of students graduating in media studies and journalism this year, only a tiny proportion will have the opportunity to set foot inside the headquarters of the most powerful television and media company in Brazil, and the fourth largest in the world.

Since the day I went surfing with Marina, I have had a sense that the tide has been turning. This was confirmed by my victory in the surf contest. It was only low-level pro, but still, it was a good win considering how little I have practised. And now I am about to enter the offices of Rede Globo; I feel I am standing on the threshold to my future, and all really thanks to Seu Otto.

The long reception desk stretches from one side of the entrance hall to the other. The desk itself is made of glass and inside the glass bright tropical fish are swimming around. The desk is staffed by cold, sleek young women with erect postures, all of whom are wearing the sorts of handsfree headsets which you usually see on fighter pilots. I choose a receptionist who looks less glacial than the others and inform her that I have a breakfast appointment with Dr. Raposo. Her hands dance over the keyboard, she puts through a call and then asks me to take the elevator to Dr. Raposo's offices on the 4th floor.

When I get out of the elevator, I am confronted by another icy receptionist. She checks my name on a list and asks me to take a seat. I am about to sit down when I notice that the photographs and awards which hang on the walls all depict Dr. Raposo. There is a framed magazine clipping showing him with the dispossessed Indians from the *Histórias Humanas* episode. Raposo has his arms around the Indians and is grinning from ear to ear, although they look less cheerful. The caption reads: 'Doutor Raposo, presenter of *Historias Humanas*, is awarded the Roberto Mourinho prize for his exposé of government greed.'

Another photo shows Raposo in black tie at a gala awards ceremony. He is triumphantly brandishing a golden figurine in his hand. I move around the room looking at more pictures. Most of them depict Raposo at different gala events. He usually has his arm around some model or reality TV star.

'O Doutor Raposo,' the receptionist announces.

I look up to see Raposo himself. He looks just as he does in the photos – grey hair tied back in a pony tail, an earring in one ear, and gaunt, pointed features. Standing beside him is a girl in her twenties, his assistant, obligatory clipboard in hand.

'Have you eaten?' he asks.

'No.'

'Good. The breakfast in our roof-top café is excellent. Come.'

We take the lift up to the 11th floor and are shown to a table outside, on the corner of the terrace. The view is spectacular: the grey metropolis stretches away from us in every direction, as far as the eye can see. The scudding early morning clouds have also disappeared and the sky is an unadulterated blue. Only where the sky meets the horizon is the blueness smudged by a faint line of smog.

'Pietro, I hate to waste time. Let's get straight to the point. I have spoken to Professor Monteiro and he assures me that you can deliver this Senhor Eisinger.'

Doutor Raposo stares at me. There is no warmth in his eyes.

'I can arrange the interview,' I say.

'So tell me,' he says, 'why should I go through you? Why don't I get my own people to set it up?'

'Because Senhor Eisinger has agreed to do this interview as a personal favour to me. He won't do it otherwise.'

'Ah ha. I see. Perhaps I underestimated you. If we are to pay you for the privilege of this interview, I would like to know, what can you guarantee?'

'Well, Senhor Eisinger will tell you about the attempt to climb the Matterhorn, about the –'

'Yes yes, I have read the treatment. I know his story. But I need something with meat. Something which will cause a stir. Can you guarantee me that?'

'I can guarantee that Senhor Eisinger will tell you the truth, the truth about a number of things which, until his recent hospitalization, he had never spoken to anyone about. Human stories that have been repressed for half a century, buried in an old man's subconscious –'

'Pietro, I hold a doctorate in psychology, you will not impress me with jargon.'

Professor Monteiro had warned me about Dr. Raposo's manner. Even though I had been prepared, I feel under attack.

'Dr. Raposo, Senhor Eisinger will tell you the truth about his past. I can promise you no more than that. But I also believe that the truth should be enough, especially when the story is as interesting as Senhor Eisinger's.'

Dr. Raposo is about to reply, then he thinks better of it. He leans back in his chair and surveys the cityscape.

'Pietro, I was an idealist once. But ideals are not enough, not in this business. You need a nose too, a nose for a story, a nose for scandal, and a nose for what the public wants. And, maybe most importantly, you need to be ambitious. That's something you cannot teach. But the fact that you are here, offering me this story, confident that only you can make it happen, well, that shows me you have ambition. And you have your ideals too, otherwise Senhor Eisinger would not trust you the way he does. Do you have a nose? I'm not sure. But I am prepared to take a chance. You say you can guarantee that Senhor Eisinger will speak to me openly and freely? Well, let us hope that will be sufficient. As you say, the truth is a very marketable commodity. But it must be the whole truth. On that understanding, I am willing to proceed. What do you say?'

Dr. Raposo has made his position clear. He wants complete openness, complete honesty from Seu Otto. It seems like a fair demand. To the best of my knowledge, Seu Otto has been open and honest about everything. Perhaps it has not always been easy for him – it has run counter to fifty years of defences. But, since the accident, he has been willing to look candidly at the past. And he has agreed to do the same in an interview, in front of a television camera. Surely this is a guarantee I can give? Surely I can deliver what Dr. Raposo wants? I have complete faith in Seu Otto's honesty. And yet, for some reason, I find myself hesitating. Something is making me feel uncomfortable.

'Is there a problem? If there's a problem, it would be best to tell me now,' says Dr. Raposo.

'There's just one thing,' I hear myself say.

'Yes?'

'Well, Senhor Eisinger will only do the interview if it takes place in his own home.'

For the first time, Dr. Raposo smiles. That is to say, one side of his mouth is drawn upwards. A tiny tweak.

'I prefer to conduct interviews in my interviewees' homes. It helps me understand them,' he says. Then he leans forward and extends his hand.

'I'll have my lawyers prepare the rest,' he says. 'Sacha will take care of everything else,' he indicates his assistant with the clipboard. 'But remember: complete honesty.' Then he shakes my hand and leaves me to breakfast by myself.

Chapter 25

In the days following the surfing competition, I made a particular effort to focus on my old routines. I read the papers, listened to the news and discussed the day's gardening with Valdemar. Anna-Maria prepared my favourite food and I whiled away the twilight hours watching the fishermen wade out into the bay. For a small fee, I arranged for Linda Pereira, the physiotherapist, to visit my house. By staying away from the hospital I was able to avoid reminders of the last few weeks.

I also avoided speaking to Pietro directly. Most of the time Anna-Maria acted as an intermediary. If I am honest, this was partly because I was feeling guilty about Pietro. I was afraid that I had made him look foolish for inviting me to judge the surf competition. After falling asleep at my judge's desk and smashing my glass, I had attempted to make my way back across the beach unaided. The Coastguard subsequently found me lying on the sand where I had collapsed, exhausted.

When Pietro and I eventually did speak directly, he mentioned neither the incident with the Coastguard, nor my falling asleep and breaking the glass. Quite the opposite; he was effusive in his expression of gratitude for the fact that I had attended the competition and that I had agreed to be interviewed by him on film. So I was in fact quite pleased to have the opportunity of the interview in order to prove myself worthy of the generosity of his feelings.

Upon his return from São Paulo, Pietro called to tell me that the producer of the show had agreed to film the interview in my library in Sambaqui. This was the one stipulation I had made. I thought that I would at least feel at ease in my own home. However, I could not have predicted that things would turn out as they did.

Having informed me that Dr. Raposo was happy to film in the library, Pietro asked, 'Seu Otto, you will answer the questions just as you did in the hospital, yes?'

'Pietro, I don't remember exactly what I said in the hospital, but I shall stick to the facts, that I can promise you.'

'And if, say, someone else were to ask the questions?'

'Facts are facts, Pietro. It doesn't depend on who's asking the question. But I only agreed to be interviewed by you. Who else will be asking the questions?'

'It is possible that Dr. Raposo may ask one or two questions himself. But they will be my questions. Just like in the hospital.'

But it was nothing like in the hospital.

*

I rose early on the morning of the interview and went for a swim in the bay, something I have only recently started to do again. I am no longer able to swim as far as before, and I am very conscious of not kicking too hard with my new hip, but it is a great pleasure to be able to start each new day in this way. It makes me feel that things have more or less returned to normal.

I decided to wear my best dark suit, the one I usually only wear to funerals. I knew Pietro was planning to ask me once again about Siggi's death and I thought the suit would set the right tone. I was dressed and ready half an hour before Pietro, Dr. Raposo and the film crew were due to arrive, so I went down to my study and occupied myself with the *Folha de São Paulo*. It was of course my visit to Florianópolis in order to buy that very publication that had set in motion this whole sorry cycle of events. But if I am honest, I also have to admit that, despite everything, I have enjoyed the acclaim that the incident has brought me. What is more, if things had not happened the way they did, I would never have become friends with Pietro. Despite what had happened at the surfing competition, I found myself looking forward to Pietro's arrival with considerable anticipation.

The doorbell rang punctually at 11 o'clock and I went to open the door myself. Pietro was standing on the doorstep. I had never seen him so presentable. His hair was brushed in a side parting and he wore an elegant navy blue suit. There was an unmistakeable warmth in his handshake. For one brief moment I was tempted to cast decorum to the winds and to embrace him, but I checked the impulse.

'Seu Otto, may I introduce to you Dr. Raposo, the presenter and producer of *Histórias Humanas,'* said Pietro, indicating the slender man just behind him.

'A pleasure to meet you, *Sr Doutor,'* I said.

'Please,' he said, 'call me Ruben.'

Ruben Raposo must have been in his fifties, although his grey hair was tied in a ponytail and he wore an earring. His pointed features reminded me of an animal; I was not sure exactly which.

I led Pietro and Ruben Raposo into the house. As they stepped forward I caught a brief glimpse of the circus behind them. There were two large vans parked in the road and people rushing about everywhere – unloading boxes, checking lists, shouting down portable telephones.

'Please, do sit down,' I said, indicating the small leather sofa in my study. 'Would you like tea? I can ask Anna-Maria to prepare tea.'

'Do not trouble yourself, Senhor Eisinger,' said Dr. Raposo. 'We have a catering lorry outside. They will provide us with everything we require.'

'I see,' I said.

The silence was broken by Pietro: 'Seu Otto, how much do you know about Senhor Raposo's show?'

'Which show?'

'*Histórias Humanas* – have you seen it?'

'No, I am afraid not,' I replied truthfully.

Ruben Raposo shifted his weight forward on the sofa and addressed me:

'*Histórias Humanas* has been running for eight years. We have a million viewers nationwide and the concept has been exported to Chile, Argentina, Peru and Bolivia. The show consists of an extended interview with an individual whose life is of special interest – that would be you, Senhor Eisinger. I conduct the in-depth interview, which is our point of departure. The interview will later be edited together with other relevant scenes, in this case old footage of the Hitler Youth and of early Alpinists, as well as newsreel from the Second World War. We may even send a film crew of our own up to the Hörnli hut – it depends. In any case, it doesn't matter that you are unfamiliar with the programme. I often find that the most successful interviews are with people who have not seen my show; they do not know what to expect and do not try to pre-empt me.' Dr. Raposo brought his palms together and leant back against the sofa.

'You will be interviewing me yourself?' I asked.

'Of course,' replied Dr. Raposo.

'I thought Pietro was going to interview me,' I said.

'Pietro is helping me to produce the show. There is no question of him conducting the interview,' said Dr. Raposo.

I had expressly informed Pietro that I wanted him to interview me. I am not in the habit of divulging my life's story to anyone, let alone to strangers. I looked towards Pietro and for a moment I thought I saw a flicker of guilt cross his face.

'I am sorry, Seu Otto,' he said. 'I tried to call you but I was unable to reach you. It would be impossible for me to conduct the interview on Dr. Raposo's show. But I have spoken at length to Dr. Raposo and I can assure you that he will be asking you exactly the same questions that I asked you. Just tell him what you told me.'

'If the questions are the same, then why don't you ask them?' I asked.

'Because it is my show,' interrupted Dr. Raposo with an arrogant air of finality.

'I see,' I said.

I was not at all happy about being interviewed by Dr. Raposo. He made me feel ill at ease.

*

A few moments later a girl with a clipboard in her hands came into the room.

'The make-up artist has just arrived,' she announced.

Ruben Raposo turned to me:

'Do you have a quiet place to do your make-up? With all the lights and cameras it's going to get busy in here.'

'I never wear make-up,' I said.

'Please, Senhor Eisinger, we are professionals,' said Ruben Raposo.

I was not sure what he meant by this. I was about to point out to him that, whether Ruben Raposo was a professional or not, he would have to get used to the idea that Otto Eisinger does not wear make-up, but before I could state this Pietro said, 'With the lights they'll be using it's important. It's normal. No one will notice.'

The earnestness of Pietro's expression persuaded me. There are times when stubbornness is a virtue, and others when it is not. I pride myself on my ability to differentiate the two.

*

Once my face had been amply powdered, I returned downstairs to find that my study had been turned upside down. Two chairs had been moved so that they were almost opposite each other; there was a camera mounted on a tripod pointing at each chair. The heavy mahogany coffee table had been taken from the middle of the room and propped up against the wall. The bookshelves behind the desk had been cleared of my collection of antique snuff boxes. The boxes had been replaced with a selection of leather-bound books which were not my own. This, presumably, was to make me appear more learned.

Through the open front door I could see a number of people smoking. Beyond them, at the end of my drive, a group of local children were trying to see what was going on. A guard was holding them back. As I turned my back to the door I caught sight of Anna-Maria standing by herself in the corridor.

'Seu Otto,' she said, 'I tried to stop them. I told them to leave your things alone but they said you wouldn't mind and they would put them back. They even moved your snuff boxes.'

I had once become quite irate with Anna-Maria for moving things around in my study. In fact, as I recall, she had broken the hidden hinge on one of the snuff boxes by trying to clean it. On that occasion, I had sternly informed her never to touch anything in that room again. To have one's personal possessions moved about for whatever reason is very enervating. However, I was touched by Anna-Maria's distress on my behalf.

'Thank you, Anna-Maria,' I said. 'It is an irritation and I am grateful for your concern. However, I fear that matters are beyond our control. We shall have to wait until the circus has moved on.'

The girl with the clipboard appeared at my shoulder.

'Senhor Eisinger, are you ready?' she asked.

I nodded, whereupon she went outside and called to the group of technicians who were smoking. They shuffled into the house; they were bearded and dishevelled and reeked of cigarettes. While I settled into my seat opposite Ruben Raposo, the lights were switched on and trained on two large, white screens at the back of the study. Two more lights were angled towards Dr. Raposo and myself. A girl walked around taking readings on a lightmeter. White sheets were held up to the cameras which the cameramen then adjusted. I was introduced to the director. He was a tall man standing at the back of the room. He was studying two television screens and muttering occasional comments to the cameramen. Two other men wearing bulbous headphones angled a couple of furry microphones above our heads.

While all this was going on, Ruben Raposo opened a file of notes on his lap. He explained to me that I should take my time and answer his questions as fully as possible. I should try to include the question in the answer. Since the show was not live we could re-shoot any questions or answers as the director saw fit.

Now that the room was quiet, the tension was palpable. I looked around for Pietro. He was standing at the back of the room but I could barely make him out because of the strong lights trained on me. I would have liked to catch his eye. I was beginning to feel anxious.

My mind went back to the afternoon of the surfing competition. I remembered the hot sun, the sickly caipirinha, and Marina asking me to help Pietro by doing this interview. I also remembered my resolution of that afternoon – to stick to the facts. Nothing but the facts.

Chapter 26

THE TALL director walked into the middle of the room and snapped shut the film slate. Adopting a regal air, Ruben Raposo said:

'Senhor Otto Eisinger, the hero of Sambaqui, it is a pleasure to meet you,' then he leant forward to shake my hand.

'So, Senhor Eisinger, you are known to the Brazilian public as the man who attempted to apprehend two gunmen.'

'Not two. One. I tried to hit one of them,' I said.

'I'm sorry, you tried to hit one gunman,' said Dr. Raposo. 'How did you try to hit him?'

'I tried to hit him with my walking stick,' I replied.

'May I ask how old you now are?' asked Dr. Raposo.

'I am seventy-seven.'

Dr. Raposo held my gaze for a moment before asking, 'Isn't that a little old for such acts of heroism?'

'One is never too old for heroism,' I said.

'Cut! Cut!' called the director from the back of the room. 'Go tight on that.' The camera lens that was trained on me moved a few centimetres. 'Senhor Eisinger, please will you say that again,' said the director.

'Say what again?'

'What you just said.'

'That one is never too old for heroism?'

'Say it with conviction,' chimed in Ruben Raposo.

'One is never too old for heroism,' I said.

'More conviction,' repeated Raposo.

I said it again, louder.

'Good,' said the director, exchanging a brief look with Ruben Raposo.

'So, Senhor Eisinger, what made you hit the gunman with your stick?' asked Ruben Raposo.

I thought for a moment. 'I was angry,' I said.

'Why were you angry?'

'I was angry because he didn't think I was worth watching.'

Ruben Raposo gave me a searching look, then he said, 'Is that the only reason you were angry?'

'Yes,' I replied.

He paused for a moment. 'But is it not also true,' he said, 'that you had just seen photographs in a magazine that reminded you of your time in the Hitler Youth?'

'That is true,' I said, 'but that is not why I was angry.'

'But did those photos not remind you of the fact that you had been decorated as a war hero when you were in the Hitler Youth?'

'I was not decorated. I was told that I would be commended for a decoration which I never received. And by that time I was in the Volkssturm and only nominally the Hitler Youth.'

Ruben Raposo opened the file on his lap. After a moment he said: 'And in the Jungvolk before the Hitler Youth?'

'That is correct,' I replied.

'Can you tell me how you became a member of the Jungvolk?'

'There's not a lot to tell. The Jungvolk became mandatory in 1938. I was eight years old. That was deemed old enough.'

'But tell me about the initiation ceremony,' he said. 'That was surely a memorable day for you. What happened that day?'

'At Marienburg? Well, we were initiated in an enormous castle. Or at least, it seemed enormous to me then. It might not seem so big now.'

I noticed that Pietro had appeared just behind Ruben Raposo's chair and was whispering something to him. Dr. Raposo nodded and then Pietro said to me: 'Seu Otto, do you remember telling me about finding the amber? Will you tell Dr. Raposo about that?'

'The amber? On the beach?'

Pietro nodded and Ruben Raposo said, 'Tell me about the amber.'

'Well, that was the same day as the initiation,' I said. 'It was the first time I had ever seen the sea. There were about twenty of us, and two teachers from our school who were also leaders of our *Heim* – that was the name for the place where the Hitler Youth used to meet. We took the overnight train to Danzig and then on to Zoppot. The ceremony at Marienburg wasn't until the evening, so we had the whole afternoon in Zoppot. The teachers took us down to the beach. It was very wide and very windy. We weren't allowed to swim but we were allowed to get our feet wet. That was enough for most of us – the Baltic is very cold.

'After a while I left the others and started to walk along the beach by myself. It was all new to me – the wind and the spray and the sand beneath my feet. It was also the first time I had ever been away from home. Just as I was about to turn back towards the group I saw a small, brown, shiny stone lying on the sand. I picked it up; it was very light. I spat on it and polished it on my shorts, then I held it up towards the sun. In the middle of the stone I could see an insect's wing, very delicate and perfectly preserved. I could also smell a faint trace of pine. Later I found out that amber is the resin from the ancient pine forests of the north. The resin used to drip from prehistoric trees and trap the insects inside.'

'And what happened to that piece of amber?' asked Dr. Raposo.

'What happened to that piece? Well, I kept it as a sort of talisman. I kept it for a number of years. I had it with me in Hamburg, when I boarded the ship to Porto Alegre. That was in 1947. I left as soon as I got my papers. My father had relatives who lived in Blumenau and who had emigrated before the war. They were friends with the Hering family. They promised to look after me when I arrived, and to help me find work. I was only 17 but I was desperate to leave Germany – I wanted a new start, a fresh beginning. My mother didn't feel that way; she stayed in Germany, but she came with me to Hamburg to see me off. I said goodbye to her on the quay. She was very tearful but I wasn't upset at all. I couldn't wait to get to Brazil.'

While I was speaking, Ruben Raposo kept nodding ever so slightly with his head. When I paused, he raised his eyebrows and urged me on with a more significant nod. I found it quite enervating.

'The crossing took five weeks,' I said. 'I was very excited when Porto Alegre finally came into view, still shrouded by mist, on the morning of the last day at sea. I was standing on the deck; the other passengers had not yet woken. I could feel a faint breath of wind on my face and could see the green hills rolling back from the port. It was my first glimpse of the Americas, of the New World, and also of my future. I realised that in this new world I could shape my own destiny. It was a moment of great significance for me and I felt that somehow I had to mark it. That was when I decided to throw the piece of amber into the water at the entrance to Porto Alegre. I felt for it in my pocket. I held it up towards the sun one last time to see the fly's wing, then I threw it as far as I could into the water of the port.'

Ruben Raposo looked up. 'A symbolic moment,' he said.

'Yes, it was,' I replied.

Dr. Raposo had returned to the open file of notes on his lap.

'You did not tell Pietro about throwing the amber into the sea?' he asked.

'I don't remember.'

'But you did tell him that you gave the amber as a gift to your friend Siegfried. Is that true?'

'Yes,' I said.

'Tell me about Siegfried,' said Dr. Raposo.

'Siegfried was my best friend in the Hitler Youth. And he was my climbing partner.'

Ruben Raposo allowed a lengthy pause to develop. 'Please, Senhor Eisinger,' he said, 'it would be much better if you could answer my questions as fully as possible.'

I nodded.

'Thank you. So, can you tell me why you gave Siegfried

your talisman?'

'I gave Siegfried my talisman because we swore an oath of friendship. It seemed like the right thing to do.'

'And this oath of friendship was a blood oath?'

'Yes.'

'What does that mean?'

'It means that we both cut our hands and mingled our blood. We were drunk,' I said.

'How did you cut your hands?'

'With a knife.'

'With the Hitler Youth knife you had recently been awarded?'

'Yes,' I said.

'What was the knife like?'

'Just like a normal knife, maybe a bit longer.'

'Was it about this long?' Dr. Raposo held his hands about twenty centimetres apart. 'And did it not have a groove on one side of the blade?'

'Yes.'

'How did you feel when you held the knife?'

'Well, I suppose I felt proud. It was a great honour–'

'Did it make you feel powerful? Do you not think it was a fetish object designed to empower adolescent boys–'

'Ruben,' the tall man at the back interrupted. Ruben Raposo turned to the back of the room and said something I didn't catch, then he turned back to me.

'I'm sorry,' he said. 'Where were we? Yes, the blood oath. You were drunk. That was when Siegfried confessed to you that he was being abused by one of the older boys,' Dr. Raposo looked down at his notes once more, 'by Kurt Gruber, is that right?'

'No, I don't remember that.'

'Siegfried didn't tell you that Kurt Gruber was abusing him?'

'No,' I said.

Dr. Raposo fired a look towards Pietro at the back of the room. Then he said, 'But was it not Kurt Gruber who recommended that you should be awarded the knife when you ought really to have been punished? Did Kurt not sometimes climb just with Siegfried, leaving you behind? Did he not share a room with Siegfried in Zermatt, leaving you with the Austrians?'

'Kurt Gruber was older than us but he was also our friend,' I said.

Dr. Raposo paused again. 'Did Siegfried once tell you that Kurt made him do things he didn't want to do?'

I didn't reply. The back of my neck was beginning to prickle with heat. The room seemed to be contracting around me.

'Did Siegfried tell you that Kurt made him do things he didn't want to do?' repeated Dr. Raposo, speaking very deliberately.

'I don't remember. Maybe I told Pietro that. But none of us wanted to do things like sentry duty. It was very boring. You had to stay awake all night and—'

'Senhor Eisinger,' interrupted Ruben Raposo, 'Unless Pietro's account of what you told him in the hospital is inaccurate, I have the distinct impression that you are hiding the truth. I ask myself why you would do that?'

I leant back to rub my neck against my collar. 'I am not hiding the truth,' I said. 'I was confused in the hospital, that is all. I had been given a lot of morphine. I am sure

Pietro did not mean to mislead you; sometimes one hears what one wants to hear. You of all people must know that.'

There was movement at the back of the room where Pietro was standing but again the bright lights prevented me from seeing his face.

'Let us return to the piece of amber. You gave it to Siegfried when you swore the blood oath, but he later gave it back to you. Tell me about that.'

'Yes,' I said. 'That was on the morning of the day that Siegfried climbed to the summit of the Matterhorn. The day he died. We were sleeping in the Hörnli hut, which is built on the rocky shoulder at the foot of the northeast ridge. I was woken in the middle of the night by the sound of Siegfried getting ready. My bunk was nearest the door and I felt the cold night air when he opened it. I asked him where he was going and he repeated a line from his favourite Hitler Youth song. Then he closed the door and–'

'What exactly did he say?'

'He said: "*Wir Jungen schreiten gläubig der Sonne zugewandt.*" It means: "We young step out in faith to greet the sun."'

'And then?'

'Then I woke up a few hours later, just after dawn, and I found the piece of amber on the pillow beside my head.'

'So he left it as a gift to you before he went to his death.'

'Yes,' I said.

'Before he committed suicide on the mountain,' said Raposo.

'No, no, that is not correct. He must have slipped near the summit. It was an accident.'

'Then he did not go knowingly to his death?'

'No.'

Once again Ruben Raposo fixed me with his gaze. 'So why did he leave the piece of amber on your pillow, if not as a parting gift? Or perhaps as a symbol of rejection?' he said.

'He left it because he did not want me to be angry that he was climbing alone, that he was leaving me behind. I was his climbing partner. And his friend. His best friend.'

Ruben Raposo shuffled the pages in the file on his lap. 'Senhor Eisinger,' he said, 'let me put the facts to you. Your friend Siegfried confides in you that your leader, Kurt Gruber, is making him do things he doesn't want to do. Kurt Gruber sexually abused Siegfried – that is why they disappear off together leaving you behind, that is why Gruber insists on sharing a hotel room with Siegfried. Siegfried has no one to whom he can turn. His best friend has looked the other way. He refuses your gift of the talisman, and also your friendship. He sees only one way out of his predicament, but he does not wish to die a coward's death – they moulded your minds well when it came to questions of courage. Siegfried thinks that by climbing the mountain alone, and by throwing himself off the summit with the Hitler Youth banner unfurled behind him, he would be escaping the abuse and the loneliness while at the same time displaying his attachment to the Hitler Youth values you all held so dear.'

Dr. Raposo paused and looked at me. In that moment I realised what animal he reminded me of. He had the pointed features of a fox terrier.

'No,' I said, 'that's not how it was. He slipped and fell. It was early in the morning, the rocks were slippery with frost–'

Dr. Raposo leant further towards me. His pupils were tiny pinpricks.

'*Ruben, com calma,*' said the director who was studying the televisions at the back of the room. Next to him Pietro had taken a step forward and was shifting his weight from left to right.

'Senhor Eisinger,' said Dr. Raposo, 'you told Pietro that Kurt Gruber later joined one of the SS Death's Head regiments. Is that true?'

'Doutor Raposo, you agreed–' said Pietro.

Dr. Raposo turned around and hissed something at Pietro, then he turned back towards me. 'Did you tell Pietro that Kurt joined a Death's Head regiment?

'I may have told him that. I don't remember,' I said.

'Is it true?'

'That is what I heard at the time. I'm not sure–'

Dr. Raposo's tongue flicked out to moisten his upper lip. 'But you knew about the concentration camps?' he asked.

Again I saw Pietro shift his weight in the corner of the room.

'No. I mean, we didn't know what happened there,' I said. 'We knew that political prisoners were taken to different locations, that's all.'

'But you just admitted you knew about the Death's Head regiments that guarded the camps? So how could you not know about the camps?'

Dr. Raposo's eyes flashed at me. He continued:

'Perhaps you deliberately turned a blind eye to the massacre of millions? Perhaps you turned a blind eye in the same way you turned a blind eye to the abuse of your friend Siegfried? Despite your decorations and your much-vaunted heroism, perhaps you do not possess the courage to confront the truth? Perhaps, Senhor Eisinger, you are a criminal and a coward?'

I felt my pulse quicken. How had this happened? Why was I being personally attacked?

'Doutor Raposo, let me tell you the facts,' I said.

'Please,' replied Raposo.

'Siegfried climbed the Matterhorn by himself, that is a fact. He was an outstanding member of the Hitler Youth, that is also a fact. It is possible that he jumped from the summit, and it is possible that he was abused by Kurt Gruber. However, that is mere conjecture. It has no part in a discussion which attempts to uncover the truth.'

'Senhor Eisinger, just because something is conjecture, that does not mean that it cannot also be true. You seem unable, or unwilling, to distinguish between possibility and probability. It is not just *possible* that Siggi was being abused and that he committed suicide. It is highly *probable*. Do you accept that?'

I remembered Gruber by the campfire after the climbing competition, telling the story of Siegfried and the dragon. I remembered the times when the three of us had been climbing roped together, depending on each other for our lives.

'No,' I said.

'Do you accept that the Hitler Youth manipulated you, turning you into deranged young fanatics? Do you recognise that one of the ways it achieved this was by creating a culture of fear and secrecy in which sexual abuse was encouraged?'

'No, that is completely untrue.'

'Again, I must ask myself why you cannot see the truth. Is it perhaps because you too were taking advantage of the system? Because you too were taking advantage of your best friend Siegfried?'

'What?'

'Senhor Eisinger, you have never married. Indeed, it seems that the most significant relationship you have formed in recent years is with the handsome young journalist who has been interviewing you. A journalist who, I might add, reminds you of Siggi. An erotic transference, perhaps?'

I could not believe what I was hearing. My pulse began to race.

'As a homosexual, it is not surprising that you defend the Hitler Youth. The organisation provided you with the cover you needed to indulge your urges.'

I felt the blood course through my veins. If I'd had the mobility, I would have leapt out of my seat and struck Raposo. The frustration of not being able to do so just fuelled my rage.

'I have never indulged any urges,' I shouted. 'The idea that I might have abused Siggi is... is...' I couldn't think of a word strong enough.

'The truth?' said Raposo.

'No! You have no idea of the truth!' I was shouting now. 'You will never understand, because you don't want to understand. You want me to say that we were all sadistic, child-abusing little Nazis? Fine, we were sadistic, child-abusing little Nazis! We just wanted to abuse each other and kill all the Jews! Are you happy now?'

'Cut!'

Raposo sat back in his chair. He did look happy.

I wiped the spittle from my lips and tried to get up. Pietro stepped forward to help but I pushed him away with my stick. Then I left the room.

Chapter 27

IN THE kitchen, Anna-Maria is preparing my evening meal. I take a seat at the kitchen table and watch her dicing the vegetables. She pauses briefly to fill a glass of water for me. When I try to pick up the glass, I notice how much my hand is shaking. So much, in fact, that I spill a fair amount of water onto the table.

I am shocked at what happened in there. How did I get so angry? All I had wanted to do was to stick to the truth. Instead, I ended up stating a complete falsehood just to spite Raposo. Except it didn't spite him at all.

Also, I have the feeling that, on some level, Raposo may be right. He said that I fail to distinguish between possibility and probability. Maybe he has a point. If I take the facts as I know them and examine them carefully, is it not indeed probable that Kurt was abusing Siggi? For sixty years I have not allowed my thoughts to go in that direction because, well, because I chose to bury my head in the sand. I was happy in the Hitler Youth, happier than I have ever been. I wanted to believe that we were all happy. I had to believe that. But my wilful ignorance makes me complicit. Maybe that is true of us all.

At the time, I believed I was doing the right thing. But somehow I got it all wrong. What does that make me? Certainly not the hero of Sambaqui, as I have recently allowed myself to believe. At best, it makes me a deluded old fool. But if Raposo is right, then I am a sadistic little Nazi. I hope he is not right. But I am no longer sure about anything.

My hands are still shaking. I look up from my glass and see Anna-Maria. She is moving around the kitchen in the same solid, dependable way she always has. It calms me to watch her.

Anna-Maria is also getting on in years. There are little wrinkles around her mouth and her hands are the hands of an old woman. Often she irritates me with her constant attention and meddling. And yet sometimes, on certain rare occasions, I feel that she understands me. On these occasions she seems to know what I am feeling, no matter how hard I try to hide it, and once in a while she will say something that, for no reason at all, will bring tears to my eyes. This is one of those occasions.

'Seu Otto, you are not a bad man,' she says.

*

I stayed in the kitchen for a long time. At the other end of the house I could hear the sound of voices and of things being packed and carted and slid across floors. From the noise of the front door I could tell that people were still trampling their way in and out. After an hour or so the sounds of activity began to diminish until there was just the occasional human murmur.

I was staring out of the kitchen window and watching the sun sink behind the clouds that shrouded the mainland. I could see bright, triangular rays of light emerging from behind the cloud; they looked like the blocky sunrays in a child's drawing. The fisherman usually waded out to check the mussel beds at this time; sure enough, I spotted a bowed figure all by himself in the middle of the bay. I wondered if he had performed that very act since earliest childhood. What a blessing to be able to trace so pure a line to one's past.

As the sun sank lower, so the light gained in colour and intensity. Anna-Maria's hands, which had appeared so aged and pale, now seemed to glow with orange warmth.

There was a knock on the kitchen door and Pietro came in.

'Seu Otto, the crew have tidied everything and left. Do you want to have a look?'

'Yes,' I said, 'I do not trust them.'

I left the kitchen and followed Pietro in the direction of the study.

'Seu Otto, I am so sorry,' said Pietro. 'Doutor Raposo promised me that he just wanted to talk about Siggi. I didn't know he would–'

'He wasn't wrong about everything,' I said.

Pietro turned round with a look of surprise on his face.

'I mean it,' I said. 'I am not the man you think I am.'

Pietro was about to say something but I raised my hand to silence him. We were in the study now. The orange light filtered through the slatted blinds and held the mites of dust that still hung in the air. I looked around the room. It was very tidy; the crew had put everything back where it had been. It was eerily quiet, as if the room itself were withholding some secret.

Pietro walked towards the bookshelf behind my desk and pointed to the rows of antique snuff boxes that were lined up there.

'I wasn't sure about these snuff boxes,' he said. 'They are all here – I counted them – but perhaps you had them in a different order? This one, for instance...'

He leant over and picked up the smallest and most beautiful of the boxes. As he did so the base fell away and the tiny box spilled its contents onto the wooden floor. Pietro stooped to one knee to pick up the base and the object which had been spilt. He rose slowly holding a small piece of amber between thumb and forefinger. Then he turned towards the window and lifted the amber to his eye. From where I was standing I could just make out the delicate tracing of a fly's wing trapped in the resin.

I didn't say anything.

Pietro continued to hold the piece of amber up to the light. There was a long silence, then Pietro asked:

'Is this the piece you gave to Siggi? The piece you said you threw into the water at Porto Alegre when you first arrived in Brazil?'

I didn't reply. Pietro fixed me with his gaze. His eyes were glassy.

'Is it the same piece?' he asked again.

I nodded.

Pietro continued to hold the piece of amber up to the light, twirling it slowly between thumb and forefinger. Then he replaced it on the shelf and made his way to the door.

When he reached the door he turned back round.

'Goodbye, Seu Otto,' he said, and he looked at me with an expression I had never seen before. Or rather, I had seen it before, only not on Pietro. It was exactly the way that Siggi had looked at me when he told me he was going to greet the sun, just before he slipped out of the door of the Hörnli hut.

Chapter 28

RUBEN RAPOSO, that bastard, screened the show about Seu Otto under the subheading, 'Otto Eisinger: Heir of Eichmann?' It's a sensationalist title and the viewing figures were correspondingly high. I really hope Seu Otto didn't see it. It twists the truth beyond recognition. The bit of the interview which gets the most airtime is when Seu Otto shouts, 'Fine, we were sadistic, child-abusing little Nazis!' Then there's a bit about other famous Nazis who fled to South America – Eichmann, Mengele and Barbie. At least Raposo doesn't deny Seu Otto's bravery in striking the gunman in the shop. However, he does suggest that it was Seu Otto's attempt to atone for the crimes he committed in his youth.

I am sure that the episode made a lot of money for Raposo, but I didn't receive any of it. Raposo claimed that Seu Otto had broken off the interview. The contract, drawn up by Raposo's lawyers, stipulated that if Seu Otto broke off the interview, there would be no payment. I didn't read the contract carefully enough. But actually, I don't mind all that much. I feel pretty bad about the way things turned out, and I don't want to make money off the fact that Seu Otto was goaded into saying some things which he really didn't mean. I should have paid more attention to Dr. Monteiro's warning.

A month has now passed since the interview, and I'm

back to dj-ing. Tonight I have a gig at Inferno, the only club in Cancupe. The club is beside the road that runs next to the bay; it faces due west and is a great spot from which to watch the sun set over the mainland.

I have also had time to think about the interview, and I now realise that I must take some responsibility for what happened. Seu Otto had expressly asked for me to interview him. I had promised him that I would – even though, after the meeting in São Paulo, I knew Dr. Raposo would never allow it. However, I really didn't think it would be a big deal. I thought Dr. Raposo would ask the same questions; I couldn't see that it might matter who was doing the asking.

Doutor Raposo made Seu Otto feel nervous. As a result, Seu Otto did not want to tell him what he had told me in the hospital. He did not wish to share these intimacies with someone he barely knew, and also, at some future date, with a viewing public.

I also think that Hitlerjunge Otto Eisinger could not accept that Kurt Gruber, the Hitler Youth itself, and all those values with which he identified so fiercely, could possibly be wrong. Or could possibly lead to the abuse of his best friend or, further down the line, to the murder of millions of innocent people. And I can see the difficulty. Many of the Hitler Youth values were noble and admirable. Loyaly, courage, honour… who can argue with them? But Seu Otto is an extremist. Not in the activist sense – although his boyhood act of bravery would certainly qualify him for that category too – but rather in the sense that he cannot see shades of grey. It is all or nothing. Seu Otto did not want to admit that Siggi committed suicide because, in his eyes, that admission would require him to reject all the values of his childhood, the good as well as the bad.

After Raposo and his crew had left, I went to go and look for Seu Otto. I found him sitting hunched in the corner of the kitchen. His face was very pale and his hands were shaking. I felt sorry for him: he looked like a man who had lost all his confidence. But when the piece of amber fell out of the box, I felt as if the ground had been pulled from under my feet. It suddenly seemed possible that everything Seu Otto had told me was a lie. I remember holding the piece of amber up to the light, but really I was just trying to steady myself in the face of that frightening groundlessness. It seemed to me in that moment that Seu Otto lived in a fantasy world. I had allowed myself to be drawn into it, but now the spell was broken. As I left the room, Seu Otto looked very small. A sad, lonely, delusional old man.

I no longer see things quite the same way. Seu Otto did lie about the piece of amber, but he never lied to me about it. In fact, we never talked about what happened to it after he found it on his pillow in the Hörnli hut. He lied to Dr. Raposo, but the lie was really a sort of wish fulfilment: he wished he had thrown the piece of amber into the water. Or rather, he wishes he could have left the past behind and made a completely fresh start here in Brazil. He desperately wanted to make a fresh start. And yet maybe we always carry the past with us. We can try to put it into boxes, but it is still going to be there, awaiting the moment to spill out.

For my part, I only thought about how this interview could help my career, and how it could get me out of my difficulties. I was not just selling a story; I was selling Seu Otto himself. I was prepared to offer up his values, his history, his identity in exchange for money. I never thought about what it would be like for him, what his feelings might be. I now also understand that Seu Otto's time in the hospital was something entirely out of the ordinary: the shock of the accident, the hospital ward, the morphine... it is no wonder that things were shaken up inside him. When he returned home, maybe he felt that he had said too much, that he had opened the lid of the box too far. He wanted to press it back down again, but I wouldn't let him.

I haven't spoken to Seu Otto since the interview. Perhaps I should call him. Perhaps I should apologise. Jorge thinks it would be a good idea. He rung me the other day. He wants me to accompany him to visit my grandfather's grave in Pomerode. He drives up there once a year with Anna-Maria. He asked me whether I had spoken to Anna-Maria, and I had to tell him that no, that I had been avoiding both her and Seu Otto. Then the whole story came out. Jorge even suggested that I invite Seu Otto to visit Horst's grave with us. I said I would think about it.

Chapter 29

A MONTH after the interview, I was swimming almost as far as I used to before the accident. And yet, strangely, the further I was able to swim, the less enthusiasm I felt. Day by day, the pleasure seemed to seep out of an activity I had always enjoyed so much. And so, in an attempt to recapture that pleasure, I challenged myself to swim further than I had ever swum before, even in the days when I was fully healthy.

It was a sultry afternoon. I had already swum that morning and I had spent most of the day sitting in my library. I was struggling to concentrate on any of the books in front of me. It was Valdemar's day off so I could not go outside to give him instructions. Anna-Maria was out shopping. I was at home by myself. There was a fat fly buzzing against the window; it eluded me every time I attempted to swat it. The warm, humid weather made my knee hurt. I was frustrated and bored, so I decided to take a second swim.

I changed in my bedroom, put on my bathing robe and crossed the cobbled street to Sambaqui's small beach. I hung my robe over the slanted trunk of the solitary palm tree and leant my walking stick against it. I paused for a moment to observe the walking stick that the hospital had returned to me via Linda Pereira. What if that fateful day hadn't been humid, if my athritic knee hadn't ached, if I had left the stick at home? What if I had told Pietro that I still had that piece of amber in a little box? Would things have turned out differently? But it is easy to get lost in a world of 'ifs'.

I waded out into the water of the bay. It had rained during the night and the water was a little turbid. In the distance a bank of cloud was amassing. It would probably rain again during the night.

I began to swim south, towards Florianópolis. The water was warm and there was no swell. I swam for ten, for fifteen, for twenty minutes. Usually, after twenty minutes, I feel at peace. My mind is emptied of thoughts. The regularity of my breathing encourages a meditative calm. But not this time. The truth is, I feel guilty about what happened at the interview.

I read in the newspaper that the interview was screened as part of Raposo's show. In fact, the newspaper said some very unflattering things about me. That is upsetting, but more upsetting is my sense that I have failed Pietro. I never intended to deceive him about the amber, but it is too late to explain that now.

The thoughts keep intruding. Maybe I am not pushing myself hard enough? I start to strike out more vigorously. Usually I breathe every other stroke. Now I decide to challenge myself, or possibly to punish myself. I breathe every third stroke. It is years since I have swum like this. But it feels good. There is no discomfort in my hip. When I look to the coast on my left, I am astonished by the speed of my progress.

I push myself harder still. This is not how people my age

are supposed to swim; this is not the tentative breaststroke that resembles the stately progress of a U-boat with its periscope raised. No, I am swimming like a young man, like a racer. As a boy I was able to swim comfortably only breathing every fifth stroke. I try it now. After a minute or two my lungs crave oxygen; I want to gasp while my head is still underwater. But I wait for the fifth stroke until I allow myself a breath. It is like a slow, controlled asphyxiation. But there is also a feeling of pleasure beginning to flood through my limbs. The feeling reminds me of the morphine in the hospital. I force myself to maintain this rhythm and I lose all sense of time. When I take a breath on the left I cast a quick glance towards the coast. The waterfront bars and restaurants are switching their lights on one by one.

My calf suddenly cramps up – a tight tugging pain. I turn onto my back and try to extend my toes. I lean forward to touch them with my fingers but when I do my body sinks. The cramp passes. I float on my back, resting. After the intensity of my exertions, my mind also feels like it is floating. The sky above me is already dark. I realise that the storm clouds have rolled in fast. Tonight there was no twilight. I turn onto my front and swivel until I am pointing back the way I came, towards Sambaqui. I take a few tentative strokes but they are sufficient to cause a warning twinge in my calf. I realise that for now my leg is useless. It will take me a very long time to swim back using just my arms, and I do not wish to get caught in a storm. Safer to wade back in towards the beach and then walk along the coastal road.

The water in the bay is shallow a long way out and I only need to take a few strokes before I am able to touch the bottom. I make my way towards the lights whose reflection is now dancing off the dark water. I am tired, my calf is sensitive and my knee is sore. Ironically, it is only my hip that causes me no trouble at all.

By the time I finally make it onto the beach, it has started to spit with rain. I climb up the low sea wall that separates the sand from the raised road. Again I feel a warning twinge. I begin to hobble tentatively along the road. I wish I had something else to wear. The rain intensifies and for the first time I feel the cold. I try to stay warm by walking faster, but the uneven road surface is painful on my bare feet. I see the headlights of a car in the distance. It gets closer and I wave but the car doesn't stop. Its tires hiss on the wet tarmac as it ghosts past me.

Sambaqui is three kilometers away. I am astonished at how, once again, the past appears to be repeating itself. Just one month ago, I was struggling back across the windswept beach of Joaquina on my crutches. Now I am hobbling through the dark and the rain in nothing but my swimming trunks. Am I incapable of learning from my mistakes? Does this only happen to me, or do patterns repeat themselves in everyone's lives? The absurdity of it forces me to smile. I try to relax the smile but my muscles are so cold that nothing happens – they are frozen in that position. I am wearing a fixed grimace and there is nothing I can do about it.

In the middle distance there is a building with two flaming torches in front of it. It must be one of the new waterside discotheques; the inhabitants of Sambaqui are constantly inviting me to sign a petition to have them closed down on grounds of noise pollution. Since I never hear them at night I cannot, in good faith, append my signature to the list. As I approach the discotheque, I read a sign informing me of a party in honour of the Praia Mole surf competition. The name of the discotheque is picked out in bright lights on top of the building – 'Inferno'.

To the left of the road is a narrow strip of grass, a few trees and a low wall that drops down to the beach. Between the trees there are a number of benches designed so that you can choose to sit either facing inland or out to sea. On the right of the road is the discotheque. It appears to be a popular place: the queue to get in is at least a hundred metres long. The girls are dressed for the most part in small, clingy dresses; they try to protect their hair from getting wet by sheltering behind towering boyfriends whose muscles bulge through tight t-shirts. The air is sickly with cheap cologne. Really, this place has been well named. As I walk past the queue I feel their stares, and I hear the sound of ill-suppressed giggles in my wake. Under my breath I whisper: *'Lasciate ogne speranza, voi ch'intrate!'*

I am cold and tired and decide to take a rest on one of the benches on the other side of the street. Maybe I can ask the managers of the discotheque to call me a taxi? Anna-Maria should be home; she will be able to let me in and pay for the taxi. But will the taxi driver trust me? I can see that the burly doormen are already eyeing me suspiciously. They are standing either side of the flaming torches by the entrance, controlling the entry of the patrons. Both doormen are bald and their wet scalps glisten beneath the flickering light. The smaller of the two is speaking into a telephone. He glances at me from time to time. The way he looks at me does not embolden me to request his assistance. I suspect he thinks I am an exhibitionist intent on exposing myself.

I sit on the bench and start to rub my shivering wet limbs. When I look up I see that a third doorman has joined the other two. Now all three of them are looking at me. Behind them, the discotheque is made entirely of glass. I can see right in, like a fish bowl. For the most part I only see people's backs – they are pressed up against the glass. However, further back there is a raised platform. A spotlight is trained on the platform. The individual standing on the platform, bent over his musical equipment, is wearing a red pompom hat. The red pompom hat is familiar but I cannot remember where I have seen it before.

As I stare at the glass wall, I become aware that people inside are turning around to stare out. They appear to be staring at me. Then I notice that red and blue flashing lights are being reflected in the glass. Looking away from the glass, I see that a police car has pulled over to the side of the road just a few metres from where I am sitting. There is no siren but the headlights are pointing directly at me and I am forced to shade my eyes from their glare. Then the headlights are switched off and two police officers step out of the vehicle. Both are holding torches. The red and blue lights on top of the vehicle are still flashing; their reflection dances on the wet tarmac.

The officers look perplexed.

'What are you doing here?' asks the first.

'You can't stay here. It's indecent,' adds the second.

I try to reply but my face is so cold that the muscles refuse to form the words. I try to warm them by tensing my cheeks but the effect is not what I had intended.

'He's drunk,' says the first officer.

'Or crazy,' adds the second.

I want to tell them that I live in Sambaqui, that I am just trying to get home, but when I try to speak the sound is incoherent.

'We'd better take him to the hospital,' says the first officer. 'He might have escaped.'

Both officers take a step towards me and place a hand under my armpits.

'At least he doesn't appear to have pissed himself yet,' says the second. 'Please don't piss yourself,' he says to me. 'We've got another eight hours of this.'

I try to explain but the sounds are still incoherent. The officers ignore me and their strong arms jerk me off the bench. I want to resist but my limbs are too weak. But at that moment I catch sight of the figure in the pompom hat running out of the building. He rushes past the three burly doormen and removes the pompom hat as he runs. Now even I think I may be going crazy.

'Seu Otto!' shouts Pietro. For it is Pietro.

'Leave him alone!' he shouts at the officers. They turn towards him, astonished. 'Don't you know who this is? This is Otto Eisinger, the hero of Sambaqui, the man who was in the news for fighting the gunmen who held up the store!'

Both officers look at me again, then they look at each other.

'We had a picture of him in the station,' says the first officer. 'The commissioner put it there. But isn't he a Nazi?'

'No, he's not a Nazi. That was a mistake,' says Pietro.

'Huh,' says the first officer. 'Well, he doesn't look very dangerous now. But what is he doing here half-naked?'

'Got cramp,' I whisper under my breath, just as I had done when I walked past the queue to the discotheque. 'Walking home. Cold.' Pietro and the two officers incline their heads towards me. I whisper again. This time they appear to understand.

'Seu Otto,' says Pietro, 'is Anna-Maria at home?'

I nod.

'Then will you let the officers drive you home? Or would you like me to drive you? I have to work but if you would prefer me to drive you then I will.'

'Officers are fine,' I whisper. I am very grateful to Pietro for his help, but I already feel guilty enough without imposing upon him any further.

Pietro speaks briefly to the officers, then he supports me gently as I hobble towards the police car.

'Are you sure you'll be alright? I won't let you go by yourself unless you are absolutely sure.'

'Absolutely sure,' I whisper.

Pietro helps me onto the back seat. 'Seu Otto, maybe this is not the right time, but I have been meaning to apologise for everything that happened with the interview and with Dr. Raposo. I forced you into a horrible situation, and I did it for selfish reasons. I'm sorry.'

When I hear Pietro's apology, all the difficult emotions melt away. I am touched by his words. After all, it is really me who should be apologising to him. I would like to embrace him but I am already on the back seat, strapped in by a seatbelt. So I take his hand in mine and squeeze it. Perhaps it is a relief that I am unable to speak. There are so many things I would like to say, but I would not know how to say them.

'Seu Otto, I was wondering,' says Pietro, 'next weekend I am driving up to Blumenau with Anna-Maria. We're going to meet with Jorge – my grandfather Horst's best friend – and then we're going to visit Horst's grave in the cemetery in Pomerode. I know it doesn't sound like fun, but if you would like to join us, I would be very happy if you came. Just think about it.'

'I would love to come,' I whisper. And I squeeze Pietro's hand again.

*

The officers put the heating on full in the car. Nevertheless, I am still shivering when we pull up in front of my house. The front door opens and Anna-Maria rushes out with a blanket. She drapes it around my shoulders and shepherds me indoors. Apparently Pietro had already phoned to let her know that I was on my way. She wants to help me up the stairs but I send her back down to offer the officers some coffee.

I open the door to my bathroom and see that my bath is already run. I test the temperature. A normal bath would be too hot for my cold limbs but this is perfect. I lower myself in and think to myself that Anna-Maria is truly a remarkable woman. Then I lean back and listen as the drumming of the rain on the roof becomes fainter and fainter and then stops altogether.

It takes half an hour until I am fully warm again. I get out of the bath and dry myself. I intend to retire to bed as soon as I have eaten. It seems pointless to dress in my usual clothes. Instead, I put on my pyjamas and wrap myself in the matching dressing gown with the sumptuous green piping. I slip my feet into the sheepskin *pantoffeln* which Anna-Maria gave me for Christmas. She will be happy to see me wearing them.

I enter the kitchen where Anna-Maria is preparing my dinner. I expect her to respond with surprise to my unusual dress but she appears not to notice. Or, if she does notice, she disguises it well. I also half-expect her to launch into a speech about my evening's misadventure, but even that is not forthcoming.

'Seu Otto, would you like to eat right away?' she asks.

'Not right away, thank you Anna-Maria. I was wondering, perhaps you will join me for a drink in the garden? It has stopped raining and I would enjoy the company.'

Anna-Maria looks at me with some surprise. In all the years that she has worked for me, I have never invited her to join me for an evening drink. I have always considered it a bad precedent. But tonight things seem different. I would like a drink, and I would like company.

'I feel that tonight is a special night,' I say.

'Well, if you insist,' she says, a little sceptically. 'But I have not put the tray out.' At 7 o'clock, Anna-Maria usually puts my scotch on a tray with a bottle of soda water and a small ice-bucket.

'Please, I will arrange the drinks,' I say. I think back to our lunch at Bar do Arante, when Pietro drove us to look at houses in Pantano do Sul. We were served caiprinihas which Anna-Maria declined. I remember her requesting a gin and tonic, upon my insistence.

'A gin and tonic for you, yes?'

Anna-Maria's eyes open wide. It is a pleasant feeling to have surprised her with my knowledge of what she likes.

'Yes, thank you,' she says.

I fill the ice bucket then repair to the library to fix the drinks there. I switch on the record player which hasn't been used for years, then I put on one of Tom Jobim's records. I open the double doors that lead across the patio and into the garden. Now that the storm has passed, the night is sultry once more.

Anna-Maria and I sip our drinks in companionable silence. Occasionally a drop of water falls from the vine that casts its pleasant shadow over the patio by day. The drop lands with a little splash. One by one the insects of the night add their song to Jobim's plaintive bossa nova.

'Seu Otto,' Anna-Maria begins tentatively. I fear that she is going to interrogate me about my evening's swim and my return in the police car.

'Seu Otto, I think I can smell the honeysuckle.'

The honeysuckle has been growing vigorously since I bought the house. It has even put out abundant flowers, but they all appear to be scentless. I sniff the air and it seems that Anna-Maria may be right, there is a faint honeyed fragrance.

We lever ourselves out of our chairs and approach the lawn.

'The grass is still wet. Your *chinelas* will soak up the moisture,' saya Anna-Maria.

Of course she is right, but I do not wish to get my shoes. I remove the sheepskin *pantoffeln* and step barefoot onto the lawn. The grass is cold and soft and springy beneath my naked feet. The little shoots tickle my toes. It is a pleasant sensation. I make up my mind to walk barefoot on my lawn more often. I may cut a ridiculous figure, but does that matter?

We cross the lawn to the corner where the honeysuckle grows. The smell is stronger here. I take one of the fine white flowers and hold it close to my nose. The smell transports me back to a sunny afternoon in our *Heim* in Bochum. There had been honeysuckle climbing up the window frame; the scent used to waft into the small wooden hut on hot summer afternoons. I close my eyes.

'Seu Otto, are you alright?'

'Yes, yes, I am just enjoying the smell.'

'It is a wonderful smell,' says Anna-Maria. 'It reminds me of when I was a young girl, back in Blumenau. We had honeysuckle in our garden. It seems such a long time ago.'

'Yes,' I say, 'sometimes childhood can seem so long ago. At other times it seems so recent.'

'I was very pretty when I was a little girl. Everyone used to say so. That seems a very long time ago.'

I can just make out the last chords of Jobim's *Desafinado: No peito dos desafinados também bate um coração*. I close my eyes again and concentrate on the feeling that is rising in my chest. It is quiet like the music, but when I concentrate on it I feel it grow. I don't remember when I last felt like this. Perhaps when I last smelled honeysuckle.

*

When I have fixed us both another drink and we are once again sitting in the garden chairs, I broach a topic that has been weighing on my mind for many years.

'Anna-Maria, there is something that I have been meaning to say to you for a long time: I was very sorry when your husband died. I only knew him a little, but he was a very fine man.'

Anna-Maria looks surprised, then she smiles.

'Thank you Seu Otto. He was a good man, but it is a long time ago.'

We sit in silence. After a while I say, 'There is something else that has been on my mind. I know that Horst's mother died in childbirth, but do you know anything else about her?'

'Well, she was sent to Brazil from Germany because she got pregnant during the war. She was very young. Her name was Freya.'

Freya – the blond girl at the end of the jetty.

Siggi and Freya.

'But why do you ask?'

'No reason,' I say. I have to look away so as not to betray my excitement.

There is one other little thing I have been intending to take care of since I left the hospital. I ask Anna-Maria if she knows a reputable lawyer on Santa Catarina. She replies that her daughter Lua is bound to know one. Then she asks, 'What kind of lawyer?'

'I don't know,' I say. 'Any kind.'

I intend to make a will. I shall leave my house to Anna-Maria and everything else to Pietro. But I'm not going to tell them.

Chapter 30

I T IS shortly after midday and the sun hangs over the tropic of Capricorn. The air above Brazil's Atlantic coast is unusually bright and clear. A flock of scarlet tanagers is circling; they are waiting to gather sufficient numbers to embark upon the long migration north. If the scarlet tanagers were to desist from their manoeuvres for a moment and look down, they would see a VW camper van turning off the main road, away from Blumenau and towards Pomerode. The van is easy to spot: it is decorated with bright, swirling images of flowers. The van's movement is irregular – it is forced to zigzag left and right in order to avoid the many potholes.

The van is being driven by a tanned young man with sun-bleached blond hair. He is wearing a freshly pressed white shirt. Occasionally the young man tugs at the shirt in a way that suggests that he is unaccustomed to wearing a collar.

A much older gentleman is reclining in the passenger seat. He is wearing a dark suit. His eyes are closed and his head is inclined towards the window. When the air is channelled through the open window and onto his forehead, a half smile creeps across the old man's face. It appears that he is content.

There are three people sitting on the bench behind the

two front seats, two women and one man. The women are seated beside the windows. They are dwarfed by the man sitting between them. One of the women is young and pretty. The other woman wears the black clothing of a widow. She is not young but her bright eyes give her face a certain charm. The large man between them is holding forth in a deep, resonant voice. He does not appear to be speaking to anyone in particular.

'Pomerode was founded by Pomeranian Germans in 1861. Most German-Brazilians speak Hunsrückisch, but in Pomerode they speak Pommersch. It is one of the few places where German is still the first language.'

The large gentleman leans back and folds his arms, but only for a second. His attention is caught by a sign beside the road. He immediately leans towards the window and points at the sign.

'There, look!'

The women follow the direction of his arm. The sign is painted a cheerful green; it is decorated with carved wooden flowers and ladybirds. The writing on the sign reads: *Seien Sie herzlich willkommen.*

The older lady says: 'Jorge, please. You are going to crush Marina.'

'It's ok,' says Marina.

'It's only another five minutes from here,' replies Jorge.

The camper van bounces over yet another pothole.

'Pietro!' says Marina.

'Sorry,' mutters Pietro. He looks over at the older gentleman, who has his eyes closed and is still wearing a contented smile. It is unclear whether he is sleeping or just resting.

The road snakes between the houses of Pomerode. For the most part, the houses are built of red brick and dark-stained wood. The roofs are also red and their gables are narrow and pointed. The surrounding countryside is green and gently undulating. This could be northern Germany, though only the elderly gentleman whose eyes are closed would be able to recognise the similarity.

The camper van passes a house with a porch. A boy with pale blue eyes is sitting on the porch. The corners of his mouth are stained red from the rich tomato sauce with which his lunchtime spaghetti was generously garnished. He is wearing the bright yellow football strip of the national team, and on his lap he is holding an accordion. The camper van slows as it passes by.

'Look,' says Jorge, 'I told you that they preserved the old traditions here. That boy is playing a German accordion.'

'What a trip,' says Marina.

'*Nossa,* that could be a postcard sent from Germany,' says Pietro. He turns to the passenger seat and sees that the elderly gentleman has opened his eyes.

'Look Seu Otto, a boy with a German accordion.'

Seu Otto does not respond but the smile does not leave his face.

*

The camper van passes the last house and continues along the potholed road, which now begins to switch back and forth as it climbs the slope rising from the meandering Itajaí-Açu river. When the river is a little way below, the camper van turns off the road and into a gravel parking area. Pietro climbs out of the driver's seat and opens the twin side doors. Anna-Maria emerges first, gingerly placing her foot on the grey pebbles. She is followed by Jorge, who gallantly offers his hand to Marina. There is a sudden gust of wind and Marina attempts to smooth down her summery white skirt. Her movement brings to mind the image of Marilyn Monroe standing on the subway air vent.

Pietro helps Seu Otto descend from the passenger seat. Jorge reaches into the back of the van and passes Seu Otto his walking stick. Then he pulls out a large plastic bag and passes around an assortment of flowers until everyone has a few to hold. Everyone apart from Anna-Maria; she has brought her own flowers.

'I picked these this morning,' says Jorge, almost apologetically. 'They are nothing special, just a few wild flowers from around my house.'

Then Jorge turns and leads the way through the gate at the entrance to the cemetery. The gravel crunches underfoot as the small party make their way up the footpath and towards the gravestones. Pietro and Marina walk behind Jorge. Pietro's free hand seeks out Marina's. Seu Otto and Anna-Maria are walking side by side behind the young couple, but their progress is slower and they soon fall back a small distance.

The gravel path has been well maintained, but the grass grows high around the gravestones themselves. The path winds around the cemetery. Occasionally the visitors pass through an area of dappled shade cast by one of the cypress trees next to the path.

Jorge turns to see Pietro staring up at the branches overhead. '*Cupressus sempervirens*,' says Jorge. 'The cypress was used extensively in Ancient Roman funerary rites. The bodies of the dead were laid upon cypress branches prior to interment. The cypress is the principal cemetery tree in both the Western and Muslim worlds, but it is not native to these shores. The early German immigrants planted these trees.'

'What is so special about the cypress?' asks Marina.

'Well, Ovid tells the story of Cyparissus,' says Jorge. 'Cyparissus was a beautiful boy and a favourite of Apollo. Apollo gave him the gift of a tame deer. Cyparissus loved the deer above all else until, in a terrible accident, he killed the deer with his javelin while it was asleep in the undergrowth. Cyparissus was heartbroken; he asked Apollo to punish him with everlasting gloom and to let his tears fall forever. Apollo turned the sad boy into a cypress tree. According to Ovid, the droplets of sap on the trunk of the cypress are like tears. That is why the cypress is the tree of mourning.'

'Poor Cyparissus, what a sad story,' Marina says.

Pietro squeezes Marina's hand and then releases it. He walks up to a bench in the shade of the cypress tree. He kneels on the bench and inspects the bark of the tree, then he picks off a small droplet of golden sap and holds it beneath his nose.

'It smells like pine,' he says.

'Same family,' says Jorge.

'So, over tens of thousands of years, this sap would also harden into amber?'

'Yes, I don't see why not.'

Pietro rolls the sap between his fingers before pressing it against the back of the bench as if it were a piece of chewing gum.

Once Seu Otto and Anna-Maria have caught up, Jorge

leads the party towards a small group of tombstones at the very top of the cemetery, just a few metres from where the forest begins.

'I love this place,' says Jorge. 'The carved tombstones, this gravel path and the cypress trees are like a European cemetery. But the forest which begins here stretches northwest for thousands of kilometers. You could walk from here and not see a road or another town until you reached the Caribbean coast of Venezuela. You would pass through the heart of the Amazon, through the thickest and wildest and most unexplored jungle on earth. You might meet tribes who have not had any contact with the Western world, tribes whose way of life has not changed for thousands of years.'

'You really think there are still tribes like that out there?' asks Pietro.

'Of course. There are sixty uncontacted tribes in the Amazon that we know about. There must be more that we don't know about. But the tribes are small, rarely more than a few hundred people.'

'But how do they live?' asks Marina.

'They live as we all used to live, in harmony with nature. The jungle provides for their needs. Ritual and tradition connect them to the past. They believe that the ancestors live through them, that no one ever truly dies. But what would it be like to see the world through their eyes? I would love to know.'

*

Jorge has led the group to a grave. At the head of the large stone slab stands a plinth and on this plinth is a sandstone sculpture of an angel. The angel's wings are folded in repose and the stone is weathered, but the pensive, childlike quality of the angel's face is still evident. The angel's head is bowed and he appears to be holding an object close to his breast. Is it a dove? Or the Holy Book? Impossible to tell. The wind and winter rain have eroded the soft Brazilian sandstone beyond recognition.

The grass around the stone is knee high. It is healthy grass, shiny like newly washed hair. When the breeze blows, the grass whispers. Occasionally some of the longer blades are blown in front of the plinth, and then the letters that are engraved on the stone are obscured. Jorge bends down and strokes back the blades; he does it gently, as if they were a girl's fringe. The letters can be deciphered but the dates have fared no better than the object in the angel's hands. Jorge reads out the name: *Horst Teichmannn*.

Anna-Maria places her bouquet of flowers on the flat surface of the stone slab. Pietro follows her and places his bouquet next to hers. Then he puts his arm around his grandmother's shoulders. Seu Otto, Marina and finally Jorge add their flowers to the growing pile. The bouquets are not tied and the breeze scatters the flowers over the stone.

After a while, Anna-Maria says to Pietro: 'It's sad that your mother couldn't come today.'

'Yes,' replies Pietro. 'But she doesn't like graveyards. They upset her.' After a pause he adds, 'I suppose that's why she never brought me here.'

'She should have brought you here,' says Jorge. 'He was your grandfather, after all. And a wonderful man.'

Seu Otto is standing behind the others. He shifts his weight from left to right in a manner that suggests that he is anxious to keep moving. After a couple of minutes, he turns away from the group and continues to walk along the gravel path. A few metres further on, he stops and gingerly leans forward to clear the grass from a much smaller grave in the lee of an old tree stump. The headstone is very simple – just a rectangular slab set directly into the earth. The inscription has seen more winters, but the tree must once have protected the stone since the indentations are less weathered. Seu Otto bends down and stares at the weathered indentations. He deciphers the letters one by one:

Freya Teichmann, geb. 2 Oktober 1929, gest. 5 März 1946

Seu Otto mouths the name over and over to himself. Freya. Freya. Freya. His finger traces the inscription. When he comes to the '6', he traces it again and again.

Anna-Maria and Jorge are still paying their respects beside Horst's grave. Pietro takes Marina's hand and together they approach Seu Otto.

Pietro looks at the headstone. 'This must be my great grandmother's grave,' he says. 'I didn't know she was buried here. Jorge told me about her; she had a hard life. Look, she was only 16 when she died.'

Marina notices that Seu Otto's walking stick has started to shake. He appears pale. 'Seu Otto, are you feeling alright?' she asks.

Seu Otto does not reply immediately. 'I think I'd like to sit down,' he says.

Marina and Pietro help the old gentleman to walk back to the bench in the shade of the cypress tree.

'There's a bottle of water in the car. Shall I get it?' asks Marina.

'Yes, please,' replies Seu Otto. Once Marina is out of earshot, Seu Otto addresses Pietro.

'Pietro, there's something else I didn't tell you in the hospital. When Siggi and I swam across the lake it wasn't just to talk to the girls.'

Pietro smiles. 'I thought that something else might have happened,' he says.

Seu Otto appears not to have heard. 'That was the first time I slept with a girl,' he says. 'And also the first time Siggi slept with a girl. And her name was Freya.'

After a few moments, Pietro says: 'You think that the Freya buried here is the same one that Siggi slept with?'

Seu Otto does not reply. Incredulous, Pietro continues: 'But there must have been thousands of girls in Germany called Freya. Tens of thousands.'

Seu Otto looks at Pietro. He says, 'When I was in the hospital, I started to think that you might be related to Siggi. It explained so much. I knew that Horst's mother had been sent here from Germany because she was pregnant. Then, the other night in the garden, Anna-Maria told me that her name was Freya.'

'Yes,' says Pietro excitedly. 'And she died in childbirth.'

'But she died in childbirth in 1946,' says Seu Otto. 'That's the wrong year. Siggi and I visited the girls' camp just once, and that was in June 1944. Siggi died 3 months later, in September 1944. But your grandfather wasn't born until 1946. Siggi can't have been Horst's father.'

Seu Otto is beginning to tremble again. 'I hoped so much that, that...' but he doesn't finish the sentence. He leans forward and hides his face in his hands. Pietro moves closer to the old man. As he does so, his hand catches on the small, sticky ball of resin that is still stuck to the back of the bench. He brushes it away, then he places his hand tentatively on the old man's shoulder.

'But Seu Otto, does it matter? Would it change anything? *Somos quem somos.*'

After a while, Seu Otto raises his head. 'Yes... You are right, Pietro. We are who we are. That is what matters.'

*

The scarlet tanagers circle high above. They fly playfully now, enjoying the freedom of the open sky and the energy that courses through their young bodies. They are waiting for others to join them; soon they shall depart for warmer climes. But if they were to look down, they would see a young girl with a kind heart striding purposefully up a gravel path, water bottle in hand. They would see a large man and a widow dressed in black, their heads bowed, standing either side of a flower-strewn grave. And they would see a tearful old man embracing the young friend who will always remind him of the dearest companion of his youth.